STABBED IN THE RACK

WITH BONUS: ROUGH HEM JUSTICE

BONNIE & CLYDE MYSTERIES

JULIE ANNE LINDSEY

STABBED IN THE RACK

JULIE HATCHER

Copyright © 2025 by Julie Anne Hatcher

All rights reserved.

No part of this book may be reproduced in any form or by any electronic or mechanical means, including information storage and retrieval systems, without written permission from the author, except for the use of brief quotations in a book review.

The characters and events portrayed in this book are fictitious or are used fictitiously. Any similarities to persons, living or dead, is purely coincidental and not intended by the author.

Published by Cozy Queen Publishing LLC

To my Cozy Queens

A NOTE FROM THE AUTHOR

Hello Lovely Reader,

Thank you so much for joining me on Bonnie & Clyde's newest adventure! I hope you're having as much fun in Bliss as I am.

You can keep in touch between the books via my Cozy Queens & Author Dreams Newsletter.

Now, let's go check in with your favorite furry little outlaw!
 -Julie Anne Lindsey

CHAPTER ONE

The hot August sun shone brightly overhead, warming my skin from the outside while a rush of adrenaline did the same from within. Strands of my wild red hair lifted on a faint morning breeze off Cromwell Lake, and my boyfriend, Sheriff Mason Wright, balanced on one knee before me.

A lot of unexpected things had happened to me in the past year or so since leaving my awful husband and fancy life in Atlanta. For starters, I'd returned to Bliss, the small farming community in southern Georgia where I'd grown up. I never thought I'd be back to stay, but being here as an adult was wonderful. My parents and grandma, Gigi, were nearby. I'd rescued a cat I adored and made my passion for turning trash into treasure a thriving business. Then I'd accidentally, unintentionally, wholly, and irrevocably fallen in love.

Additionally, I, Bonnie Balfour, became the first woman in my lineage to buy herself a home. No man, husband, or male co-signer involved.

I'd faced off with a number of killers this year, too, and I'd helped Mason solve a lot of crimes. The town's good sheriff had become my best friend. Our energies matched and just being in his presence made me feel whole. Even when he was occasionally making me nuts.

My life was full and adventurous. There was rarely a dull moment.

Like this one, for example.

I'd barely been up for an hour, and already, seated at the patio table, enjoying the morning breeze, I got to look into the soulful blue eyes of my supremely gorgeous boyfriend.

The sincerity in his expression and the deep, gravelly tone of his voice as he'd said, "I have something to ask you," sent a cascade of goosebumps over my skin despite the late summer heat.

I shivered, then held my breath, absorbing every precious detail of this perfect moment.

It'd only been ten days since my most recent run-in with a killer, and I'd barely begun feeling calm again. Now my heart was sprinting with nowhere to go and no exact reason to run. Because Mason hadn't asked his question.

His phone, lying face up on the table beside us, began to ring.

My gaze snapped to the cursed device, then back to him.

His eyelids drifted shut, and he cussed before releasing a small, humorless laugh. He raised a finger, stretched onto his feet, and kissed my forehead. Then he took the call.

The number was private.

Who accepts a call from a private number? Especially at a time like this?

Had I mistaken what was happening here?

Was I right, and he'd planned on proposing marriage, but he changed his mind?

Was my proposal thwarted by someone trying to reach him about his car insurance?

Had he only gotten on one knee to tie his shoes?

If that was true, then what was his question?

I gripped the arms of my chair, mentally rocked by the whole, incredibly brief, extremely strange set of events.

Mason muttered and grunted into his cell phone between long bouts of silence. He paced my patio on long jean-clad legs and cowboy boots. Then he turned away and scraped a hand through wind-mussed brown hair before glancing over his shoulder in my direction.

The sound of a car door pulled me from my internal struggle and set Mason in motion.

He ended his call, put the phone in his pocket, and strode purposefully toward the corner of my home with one hand on his holstered sidearm before I managed to get to my feet.

The familiar voices of my mama and Gigi carried on the breeze. Then, my doorbell rang.

"We're out back," I hollered, projecting my voice into the sky.

Mason eased his hand from his holster.

"Everything okay?" I asked Mason.

He blinked, then nodded. "Yeah."

I went to him. "Who was on the phone?"

Mason pulled me close and kissed my head. "Sorry. I'm needed at the station."

"But—" I began and faltered, unsure what else to say. How did I ask him if he'd been about to ask for my hand in marriage, but chose to take a phone call instead?

Mason waited. His navy blue Bliss Sheriff's Department t-shirt clung to his broad shoulders and lean frame, pasted on by the heat.

"Bonnie!" Mama called, appearing on my side lawn with open arms. "You'll never believe who's getting married!"

I slid my eyes to Mason, and he shifted uncomfortably.

"Hello, Mason," Mama said, hugging me quickly, before turning her attention to him.

He greeted her and Gigi quickly, then made his excuses about work and lit out.

Gigi took a seat at my patio table and helped herself to coffee from the carafe. She added one of the pastries I'd baked for relaxation the night before. "Where's the fire?" she asked, tossing a look in Mason's direction.

If I only knew.

Mama sat beside Gigi and folded her hands on the table.

I returned to my seat.

"Did you put honey in these?" Gigi asked.

"Yeah." I sipped my coffee, mind reeling.

The older women smiled back at me.

I looked like Mama and Gigi, which was to say we all bore the red hair, hazel eyes, fair skin and freckles of our Irish ancestors. Side by side, we were three versions of the same woman in one of those age progression videos. It was nice knowing I'd be so beautiful when I got older.

"Well," Mama said. The expectant look in her eyes suggested I'd missed something. "Aren't you going to ask?"

I searched my rattled mind. I had missed something. "Ask what?"

"Who's getting married," Gigi said. "More importantly, ask who the mother of the bride wants to bake the wedding cake, provide the flowers, and outfit the wedding party."

Considering Gigi owned a bakery, my parents owned a flower farm, and I recently opened a fabulous resale shop, where I turned donated items into adorably updated designs, I had a solid idea.

"Us?" I guessed.

Mama patted a rhythm on the table with her fingers. "Correct," she sang. "Isn't it exciting? Who doesn't love a wedding?"

"That's not necessary," I promised. "I'm sorry I'm so distracted, but I'm coming."

"Good, because Sadie Clarke, Farmer Clarke's only daughter, is marrying her high school sweetheart next weekend, and I promised her mama a beautiful event. That includes dresses for the entire wedding party."

"Next weekend?" I asked. A bolt of alarm shot through me as the words registered. "Is that even possible? How big is the wedding party? And who plans a wedding in a week? What's the rush?"

"We can do it," Mama said. "We'll work together, and it'll be fabulous. We're meeting the bridal party in a couple of hours. Then, we'll know what we're dealing with in better detail."

I looked at Gigi, attempting to absorb some of her confidence. "We've probably done harder things, right?"

"Darn skippy," Gigi said. "And the rush is that her fiancé's about to become a country music sensation!"

I screwed my expression into a knot. "What?"

Mama sighed. "You really aren't feeling well, are you?"

Clearly, I'd missed more than I thought. I pressed my lips together. "Just a quick reminder."

"George Banks—that's the groom-to-be—took Sadie on a weekend trip to Atlanta. They were at a bar doing karaoke, and a talent scout grabbed him up! It's so exciting to see someone from a little town like ours catch a big break. You know?"

I thought of our little community, the generations of farmers, the financial struggles and losses. Bliss was widely composed of hardworking people who rarely caught any size break, let alone a big one. Our low socioeconomic reality was the main reason I'd learned to breathe new life into old things. Growing up, we couldn't afford more than the necessities, so I made the best with what I had. Mama and Gigi

I pressed my lips together. Who indeed?

After spending my entire adulthood married to a man who didn't love me, and quite possibly never really liked me, I'd become adamant I'd never fall in love again. And I'd never *ever* consider another marriage.

Then I met Mason, and the disappointment I'd felt watching him rise from his knee to answer the phone was monumental and crushing.

Seriously, who had called him? Did he know who was on the other line before he answered? Even though the number was private? Was he expecting the call?

Why begin a proposal while expecting a call?

"Grab Clyde," Gigi said. "We'd better hit the road."

I frowned, unsure what she meant. "Where are we going?"

Mama's expression of delight became one of concern. "You don't seem like yourself this morning. Maybe you should get out of the sun."

I shook my head. "I'm fine."

"Then," Gigi said, rising and waving a hand. "Grab your cat. Let's go!"

I followed her as far as my back door. "I'll meet you there," I said. "Remind me where we're going." Sitting home alone to stew over what Mason was up to would only make me batty. I had two women asking for my help and a shop to open.

The women in question exchanged a look.

"We're going to your shop," Mama said. "To prepare for the bride and her mama."

I nodded, but none of that sounded familiar. How lor had I been daydreaming?

Mama set her hands on her hips and narrowed her e "I'm serious, Bonnie. Maybe you should lie down for an } or so, then meet us in a bit."

taught me that. These days, I continued the tradition and sold the rejuvenated pieces at prices everyone could afford.

Seeing someone from Bliss become a music star, or just get his record on the radio, would carry our town on a collective high for decades.

"Wait." My frown and confusion returned as a new question came to mind. "Why does this mean they have to rush their wedding?" Why not wait until he got a recording contract, then have a huge party?

Gigi's expression turned mischievous, and I had a feeling there was a juicy story to come. "Because George's new talent manager wants to move him to Nashville where all the big deals are made, but George doesn't want to leave Bliss without Sadie. And Farmer Clarke doesn't want his little girl moving to another state with a man who isn't her husband, so George proposed, and now they're getting married. Fast."

Oh, that was juicy.

"Let me get my cat," I said.

Mama and Gigi smiled and took off around the side of my house, toward their car. "See you at the shop!" Mama called.

I hurried through the back door of my home and locked up behind me. How had a normal, relaxing morning taken a series of such unexpected turns? If mental whiplash was a condition, I was afflicted. And I had no idea what to do about it. So, I rushed forward on autopilot and prepared myself for the day.

Twenty minutes later, I'd chosen a teal and navy maxi dress with no sleeves and lots of room to breathe. My hair was pulled up in a messy bun, and I'd shoved bare feet into nude espadrille sandals.

Clyde, my furry little sidekick, former alley cat, and recovering thief, curled on my bed, watching me hunt for my favorite earrings.

"I know that look," I said, finally, recognizing the laissez-faire expression on my sleek black feline's face. "You stole my hoops. Didn't you?"

We locked eyes as I approached, then hoisted him off my comforter to reveal the missing jewelry.

"Busted," I said, nabbing the stolen goods and returning him to the bed. "We talked about this, Clyde. You can't take things that don't belong to you."

He seemed to roll his eyes, then he ran a paw over his head, cleaning his face in a move that resembled giving me the bird.

"All right," I said. "You have to choose your bowtie." I slid my hoops into place, then examined the rack of collars, each with a small bowtie, Clyde's favorite. "What do you think?" I asked, selecting a brightly colored, slightly funky number. "Feeling like summertime? Maybe something hot pink with little lemon slices?"

Clyde continued grooming, wholly uninterested.

"Okay." I put the collar back and selected another. "If you like what I'm wearing, we can match." I held a teal collar in one hand, a navy one in the other.

Clyde cast a glance in my direction but didn't commit.

"I don't suppose you heard there's a wedding coming," I said. "The bride and her mama will be at Bless Her Heart soon. Perhaps you want to go full-out fancy with a white satin bowtie against that sleek black coat?" I asked. "Embrace the whole tuxedo look. James Bond in kitty couture."

Clyde stood, arched like a Halloween cat, then moved to the edge of my bed and waited while I fastened the final option into place.

"You look like a million bucks," I said. "And I hope you're in the mood for gossip, because I have a lot on my mind."

CHAPTER TWO

I drove to work in my little white convertible, top down and Clyde crated at my side. The route from my home by the lake to downtown Bliss was gorgeous any time of year, but I especially loved the views in summer. Curving rural roads, shaded by majestic, moss-covered oaks, slowly gave way to fields of green in every direction.

Farmhouses and barns peppered the landscape, distant at first, then growing into small communities. My mind raced with thoughts of Mason and his earlier intention. I pressed them repeatedly aside and cranked up my radio to drown out the mental noise. Thanks to Mama and Gigi, I had something to keep me busy. I hadn't planned a proper wedding since my own, and that was likely around the time this bride was born. Still, I didn't imagine much had changed, and I'd never been so glad for a spontaneous and time-sensitive crisis.

Eventually, the gridded streets of town carried me toward the square where I worked. The enormous grassy oval that had once been the high school football field was now lined in flagstone paths, dotted with giant, leafy trees and ringed in streetlamps carrying large baskets of flowers. A large white gazebo anchored one end of the space, and a dozen or so locally owned shops and cafés stood right across the street in all directions. My store, Bless Her Heart, and Gigi's bakery, Oh! My Goodies, included.

I slowed upon approach, forced to navigate a new traffic circle, initiated by the mayor and the town's Beautification Committee thanks to some excess funding. I wasn't a fan of the functionality. A traffic circle immediately before a giant oval seemed like overkill, but it was covered in gorgeous blooms that my parents helped maintain, so I couldn't be mad about it.

I parked along the curb and climbed out, then circled the hood to free Clyde and his carrier. A handsome man with dark, curly hair and bright blue eyes watched me from a bench on the square. Long shadows cast from a nearby oak gave him a distinctly mysterious vibe. He had a logoed coffee cup from a café several doors down and a copy of the local newspaper.

I forced my attention back to the matter at hand and hauled Clyde from the car, then closed the passenger door and turned away. I wasn't sure about the man's mama, but mine had taught me it was rude to stare.

I headed into my shop, unlocking the door and turning on the lights for business. Then I flipped the sign in the window from CLOSED to OPEN before setting Clyde free.

He lumbered forward, performed a deep, dramatic lunge, then took a seat and stared at me with luminous green eyes.

"No stealing," I told him. "We've got a wedding to plan."

Uninterested in anything that sounded like work, he went in search of mischief and let me be.

I tucked his crate under the counter with my purse and surveyed the scene.

The man on the bench caught my eye through the glass door. I couldn't tell from this distance if he was still watching, but on further inspection, I became certain he was not from around here. I was pretty sure his shirt and pants were both Burberry. Combined, the ensemble easily cost more than my first car. A pair of brown leather loafers completed the designer ensemble. He'd fit right in for a day at the country club. Except Bliss didn't have a country club.

I checked my watch and resolved to stay on track.

I'd recently changed my store displays to a traditional back-to-school motif. Backpacks and books, headbands and sneakers. My shelves were stuffed with reimagined jeans and lightweight sweaters, though we wouldn't need the latter for quite some time. I'd sewn pretty patterns around the pockets and seams of donated pieces to add creative appeal. Those were all much cuter now.

The big problem was that, at the moment, nothing about Bless Her Heart suggested it was the right place to outfit a wedding party.

I went to the glass door at the far side of my shop, past the free-standing dressing rooms, and unlocked the deadbolt. Gigi's new bakery filled the space beyond, and the door was a little something we'd added for ease of travel and frequent chitchat.

It wouldn't be long before she arrived with coffees and sweets, so I turned back to the situation at hand. I had just under three hours to make this place appear more inviting to a bride.

I glanced outside once more, checking on the mystery man before going in search of gowns. Tension eased in my shoulders when I found his bench empty and no signs of him in sight.

"I do not have a well-dressed, handsome stalker," I whispered. "Good to know."

Clyde darted past me at full speed when I grabbed my purse and carried it into the hallway on the far right of my sales floor. I left the handbag and cat in my office, then moved on to a large unfinished space where I kept donations, inventory, and off-season items until they were needed.

Formal wear, shoes, and accessories for bridal and prom season filled the far corner. I needed a whole lot of everything from back there, because I had no idea what sort of style the bride envisioned for her day. I grabbed the handle of a large canvas-sided wagon and got busy loading it.

When the wagon was no longer visible, completely drowned in lace and tulle, I piled heels, handbags, and boxed jewelry items on top.

Clyde appeared and climbed aboard.

"You're always around just in time for a free ride," I said.

He rolled into a loop and stretched one paw in my direction, as if to say, "Onward, peasant."

And I obeyed.

The little bell over my front door rang as we reached the sales floor.

My teenage shopkeep, Lexi, rounded the large circular desk at the center of the space and dropped her things beneath the register. Lexi was nineteen, smart as a whip, and cute as a button. She took notice of me and ran to great Clyde. "Morning, Bonnie. Hello, Mr. Handsome Face." She bent to stroke his shiny fur.

I paused the wagon so Clyde could greet another of his plentiful admirers.

"What's with the fancy wear?" she asked, straightening with a frown. "Didn't we just put most of that stuff away?"

"Yes," I said, grinning. "But we've got our work cut out for us before lunchtime rolls around."

"Okay," she said, drawing out the little word. "What's up?"

"Apparently, there's a wedding happening next weekend, and we're in charge of dressing the bridal party," I said, towing the cart toward the window.

"Whose wedding?"

"Sadie Clarke," I said. "She's the dairy farmer's daughter." Clarke Dairy was the largest, most successful dairy farm in the state and employed a good number of local workers. "Let's redress this window, so Sadie and her mama will see it and know they're in good hands before they ever step inside. They're coming in with the bridesmaids in a couple of hours."

Lexi pulled long, dark braids over her shoulders and pinched the ends with her fingertips. "Sadie and George are engaged?"

I couldn't remember the groom's name, so I wrinkled my nose and lifted my shoulders. "I think? Mama and Gigi ambushed me this morning at breakfast, told me there was a rush wedding going on, we're all playing our parts, and I needed to get ready. I missed a lot of the details." I kept the reason for my temporary discombobulation to myself.

Lexi released her braids and set her hands on her hips. She'd paired wide-legged jeans with layered tank tops, form-fitting peach against her skin and a wispy white number on top. Her leather sandals were perfect, and the massive backpack, still visible behind the counter, reminded me she was only here for a few hours. She took classes at the community college most afternoons all year round. "Wow. All right. I'm here until twelve-thirty. What should I do first?"

We climbed into the window display and got to work.

Lexi stripped the space of all back-to-school decor while I unbagged the gowns and redressed the mannequins. "She's got to be pregnant, right?" Lexi asked, putting the last of the fall clothing away.

"Lex!" I laughed. "Pregnancy is no reason to get married. Think about the poor child, for goodness' sakes."

She made a goofy face. "Well, it's got to be something, because those two have been dating for years. Why wait until now to get engaged, then suddenly be in a hurry for the ceremony?"

I told her what little I knew about the talent scout. "But that's third-hand information," I warned. "I heard it from Mama and Gigi, who talked to the bride's mama, who must've been informed by her daughter. A whole lot can get lost in translation. Like playing telephone."

"Hmm." Lexi's features bunched slowly as I spoke, moving from a look of interest to something along the lines of shock before becoming a full-on cringe. "His band members must be furious."

I puzzled while she removed garlands of little paper books, then hung strips of lace in its stead. I filled the empty floor space with mounds of white tulle and gratuitous amounts of silk flowers.

"Nice," she said.

I stood back to admire the work.

Clyde zoomed between us and pounced on the cloud of sheer fabric.

I turned away. The more I fussed at Clyde to leave something alone, the longer he'd be obsessed with it, and I was on a time clock. "Why will the groom's band be mad he got noticed?" I asked, refocusing on Lexi's strange comment. "Shouldn't they all be ecstatic?"

Lexi scoffed. "No." She shook her head and frowned, suggesting I was ridiculous for asking. "George has always been in a band," she said. "Always singing with someone or another. Always wanting to be a big star. Kids around here gave him a hard time, because it almost felt wrong of him to have dreams that big. Ya know? Like why did he think he was so special? It's dumb," she said, waving away the thought. "Anyway. George never sang alone. And as far as I can tell, this is the longest he's been with one group. They've probably learned and grown a lot together in the last couple of years. Now imagine, you're one of those other guys, and George takes his girl on a date, does a little karaoke, then calls you to say a talent scout found *him*. Now *he's* got a manager and *he's* moving to Nashville."

"They aren't happy for him because they're jealous," I surmised. I supposed I could see that, initially, but only for a moment. Then, sense should kick in, and they should know it wasn't as if he went renegade on them. He was living his life and something good happened. "What about the rising tide raising all ships?"

Lexi performed an exaggerated shrug. "I'm just speculating. I don't know these guys personally or anything. I didn't even know George finally proposed."

I looked at my wagon piled with gowns. "What do you know about the bride?"

"Not a lot. She was a typical popular high school girl."

I dragged the formal wear past the checkout counter to the dressing rooms on the other side, then cleared a clothing rack for their display. Lexi hung gowns while I arranged clutches and jewelry on a small stand between a pair of tufted armchairs. They were the best seats in the house to wait, then perform appropriate ooohs and ahhs when someone opened their curtain for a reveal.

We lined fancy shoes along the wall beside a standing mirror.

When Lexi didn't elaborate, I prepped my coffee maker on the refreshments stand and removed several lidded containers from the mini fridge, then set the baked goods on trays near the coffee. All I had to do was push the brew button when the group arrived.

"This legit looks like a bridal shop," Lex said, motioning to the area near the fitting rooms. "I'm impressed, and it barely took an hour."

I just hoped Mrs. Clarke and her daughter felt the same.

By lunchtime, Lexi and I had added fluff and frills to everything. The whole place was zhushed up by at least a dozen notches.

"Well, I'm starving," Lex said. "I'm going out for food before the bride gets here. Can I get you something?" She hoisted a large leather purse onto her shoulder and waited for my answer.

"Where are you going?" I asked.

"Somewhere serving chicken tenders," she said. "And sweet tea."

I walked her to the door and looked into the sunny summer day.

The town had come alive with shoppers and folks enjoying the park-like atmosphere of the square. Couples spread blankets for picnics in the shade. Children played chase between the trees, while moms pushed little ones in strollers and sipped iced coffees from the café.

The coffees reminded me of the man I'd seen earlier, but he was still gone, as he should be.

"Grab me some chicken salad on a croissant?" I asked, reaching into my pocket for my business credit card. "Lunch is on me today. Consider it your delivery fee."

She accepted the card with a smile. "If you insist." She was out the door before I could thank her again.

Clyde barreled past my feet a moment later, nearly tripping a customer as she approached the register. The train of white tulle wrapped around his body and trailing behind him was at least six feet long.

Clearly, I had work to do before Lexi got back.

CHAPTER THREE

I handled customers, captured my furry little outlaw, and righted the window display before Lexi returned. We ate in companionable silence at the front counter, taking turns to ring up sales.

She got a whole lot chattier when the sugar from the sweet tea hit her system.

"I was thinking about high school," she said, taking another heavy pull on her straw. "George and Sadie were dating by the time I became a freshman. They were seniors who definitely didn't know I existed, but everyone knew them, because they were at the center of everything."

"Go on," I said, nodding at the image she painted. "This is great. Anything you know will help me prepare for her arrival and guess where her head might be in regards to this ceremony."

Lexi chewed thoughtfully. "She was super smart, pretty, a cheerleader, homecoming queen, involved in student council. All of that." Lexi circled her chicken tender in the air. "An it girl." She attempted air quotes and nearly dropped her tender. "Sadie seemed to have everything. The right clothes and shoes. Perfect skin. She even drove her own truck. George's family had a single mom and a ton of kids, like mine, with just as little money." She rolled her eyes. "My younger sister went to school with one of his kid brothers."

I related lightly to Sadie. I'd had a cushy adult life in Atlanta, if I didn't count my unbearable husband. But I'd grown up struggling financially like George's family. Spending my teenage years on a fledgling flower farm had taught me some important life skills, like how to find the beauty in everything and to be thrifty in the extreme. I applied both with a double dash of creativity when I opened Bless Her Heart, because everyone deserved to feel like a princess, regardless of their income.

I glanced at the assortment of gowns near the fitting rooms. Quite a few would likely fit the bill for style and class, thanks to a wealthy debutante's donation. She'd been older than Gigi, but her family had the kind of money and style that didn't go out of fashion, and now I had the bulk of her formal wardrobe. "Do you think I should set out a few more options?"

Lexi looked past me to the rolling rack. "Not yet. They'll just get overwhelmed," she said. "I'm still stunned you have so many wedding gowns."

I smiled as I bit into my sandwich. "I hit the jackpot when Brenda's Bridal went out of business in Salem."

"I forgot about that!"

"I almost felt bad for the prices I paid, but she was just glad to unload the inventory," I said.

Lexi scrolled on her phone, lunch demolished and tea nearly gone. "Huh."

"What?"

She pulled her lips to the side. "You'd think Sadie

would've announced the engagement online. With a cutesy story, some cheesy photos of him on one knee or something."

I stilled mid-chew and Mason flashed back to mind. "I'll look for her mama's accounts," I said, glad for the distraction.

I typed *Evelyn Clarke* into my search bar and clicked on the top result. The account was set to private, but a handful of photos that had been her previous profile pictures made it clear I had the right account. I recognized the backgrounds in several images. "I can't see anything useful without being her friend."

"I found Sadie on Instagram," Lexi said. "She's posting stories, which I can't watch without her knowing I viewed them."

"I guess I have to be patient," I said. I took another bite from my sandwich and let the perfection of the crisp, buttery croissant wash over me. The cool, creamy chicken salad was the exact right balance of smooth and crunch. The café had added bits of green grapes and pecans to the blend.

Lexi gathered her lunch things quickly and shoved them into the trash beneath the counter. "Looks like your wait is already over."

I tracked her gaze through the shop window to a cluster of women headed our way. Then I chewed a little faster.

The group leader appeared roughly my age and looked strikingly similar to the younger blond with a friend hooked to each arm.

"Here we go," Lexi said, as they reached the door.

I smiled brightly, hoping not to have chicken salad stuck in my teeth, and hurried to greet them.

Lexi cleaned up after me as I bustled past.

"Welcome to Bless Her Heart," I said as the foursome entered. "I'm Bonnie Balfour. This is my shop."

The younger trio trilled and giggled.

The older woman folded her hands in front of her on a labored sigh. "I'm Evelyn Clarke. I believe I spoke with your mother and grandmother."

"You did," I said.

"Then you understand the rush."

"I do."

Evelyn sighed again. "I wish I did," she muttered, then waved to the younger women. "This is my daughter, Sadie, and her best friends, Ava and Gracie."

"Welcome," I said. "I've gathered a number of things for y'all to try on, and I've got more in the back if none of these will suit. I'm also handy with a sewing machine if any alterations are necessary." I extended an arm in the direction of the fitting rooms and assorted gowns.

Evelyn marched onward.

Sadie stopped in front of me. "Thank you so much for doing this," she said. "Your family has been a complete lifesaver. I cannot thank y'all enough."

"We're glad to help."

"I'm Ava," the taller, narrower friend said.

The more petite of the brunette friends gave a small, hip high wave. "I'm Gracie."

"Come along, girls," Evelyn called. "We have lots to do and very little time."

The group spent several minutes examining the options while I kept my distance so they wouldn't think I was hovering.

I hit the brew button on my coffee maker and moved a few bottles of water from the mini fridge to the table. Trying on clothes was exhausting under the best conditions. The time crunch and Evelyn's current mood were likely to increase the fatigue for the whole group at double speed.

When I returned to check on them a few minutes later, all four ladies were in the fitting rooms, and there was a remarkable amount of empty space on the rolling rack. A good sign they saw plenty of things to like!

Evelyn exited her fitting room and grabbed a pair of shoes. She stopped when she noticed me and rerouted.

"Everything okay?" I asked.

"I'm sorry for the rush my daughter has put on you." Her tone was clipped, her expression tight. "It's certainly not what my husband and I wanted for our little girl, but I suppose we make do with what we're given."

I opened my mouth to comfort her, but the harshness of her words silenced me.

"Mama," Sadie scolded from behind her curtain.

Evelyn rolled her eyes, turned on her heels, and went back to her fitting room. "Am I supposed to be happy about this? I don't want you to go," she complained, projecting her voice and continuing the awkward conversation publicly, but also out of sight. "I hate that Beau What's-his-name is making you do this his way. It's awful. Why is George going along with this? Why are you?"

I looked to Lexi at the mention of Beau What's his name, wondering if she knew who that was.

She shook her head, clearly as confused and uncomfortable as I felt.

I didn't know the details of this particular rushed wedding, but it seemed to me that the only people responsible for the timeline were the bride and groom. Obviously the strong opinions of the bride's mama didn't matter. So, who was Beau? The talent manager?

Evelyn reemerged in a floor-length black gown composed of a thousand sheer layers over satin. "Sadie asked George to stop by and give opinions on the dresses for the girls and the color scheme," she said. "I don't think men have any place in making these decisions, but I also didn't think they got to choose when to have the wedding either."

"Mama," Sadie hissed. She snatched back her fitting room curtain and walked out in a mermaid bridal gown with a slit up one side and a plunging V neckline. The look was dramatic, shimmery, and runway worthy. The style hugged every youthful, flawless curve. She gaped at her mother. "You cannot wear black to my wedding!"

"Oh, no you will not," her mother said, ignoring Sadie's comment and pointing at the mermaid dress instead. She set her hands on her hips and squared her shoulders. "You've forced me into a rush job of an event, made me cobble together the best day possible on zero notice, made it impossible for half our family to be present on such little notice, because not everyone can just call out of work to fly to a wedding with no time to save or prepare. You will absolutely not be immortalized in photographs wearing that."

I pressed my lips together, fighting the urge to tell Sadie she looked incredible, or remind Evelyn that, however hurried, this was her daughter's day. Not hers. Because none of this was any of my business, even if that business was being tossed around in front of me.

Lexi cleared her throat, and I dragged my eyes to her, hopeful for an escape. She waved her keys, backpack already in place. "I'm late for class, but I'll be back first thing tomorrow."

I nodded, and she bolted.

And I was alone. I needed to magically defuse this situation and turn things around. This should be a fun and memorable day. Not a battle.

Sadie thrashed back through the curtain. Her friends popped free from their rooms and followed close behind her. They'd stayed hidden during the heated exchange. I didn't blame them.

Evelyn growled and turned to me, eyes closed and one hand on her head. "I hate this," she said.

I grabbed a bottle of water from the refreshments table and offered it to her, then I motioned to the chairs. "We can sit," I suggested. "There's no rush on choosing a gown. You have me all day. I can hold anything you like for a second look later in the week."

She sat and rolled the cold bottle across her forehead. "I hate this whole situation. Especially George's new talent manager," she seethed. "He's the reason for all this. Taking George's hopes and dreams of being a star and using them to control him. Now that's bled over to my baby, and now me! I'd like a few minutes alone with that guy and my hogs."

I felt my eyebrows climb into my hairline. Everyone knew hogs could make short work of anything, including a human body, and do it better than just about anything else. Except maybe a woodchipper.

I grimaced. I never had thoughts like that before returning to Bliss.

My therapist would say it had something to do with my new knack for finding dead bodies, but I tried not to think about that. I supposed it was a good thing I was in therapy.

I dragged my attention back to the problem at hand.

Whatever else was happening, I had to give the groom credit for having enough interest to come and support his bride on her choices. My ex-husband, Grant wouldn't have done anything of the sort. Or anything else for me, as it turned out, for more than two decades. This couple was already doing better than I had, and that surely counted for something.

Sadie reappeared with her bridesmaids, this time wearing a more traditional, cupcake-shaped dress.

Evelyn set the water aside. "Better," she said.

The bridesmaids wore tea length dresses in different shades of pink. Together, they were sweet and would look incredible for photos in my parents' wildflower fields.

I gave the group some space and went in search of my mischievous cat, who hadn't made an appearance in far too long. I tried not to wonder if Mason would be involved in the details of his wedding day. As far as I knew, he wasn't getting married.

CHAPTER FOUR

Two hours later, the ladies had narrowed down their choices. Evelyn found two structured knee-length numbers, one in navy, the other in deep plum, after Sadie insisted black wasn't an option for the mother of the bride. Ava and Gracie chose a variety of styles in shades from rose to lavender. They each found several that fit their personalities and flattered their figures and heights.

Sadie stood before the large gilded mirror wearing the dress her mother preferred, a traditional gown with a beaded, heart-shaped neckline, fitted bodice and full skirt with a train. The sleeves were small and puffy. A large bow on the back rested just above her bottom.

The gown she wanted hung inside her fitting room. A simple, satin sheath with delicate, wispy straps, designed to fall over her shoulders, and a small loop of fabric hidden beneath the extra length, which could be worn around her wrist to keep the material off the ground while trailing behind her.

Evelyn asserted that the simplistic design was better suited to a formal dance than a wedding. Sadie argued that nothing about a wedding put together in a week was traditional, and therefore a traditional gown was inappropriate for the event. Possibly flat-out ridiculous.

For the most part, the bridesmaids stayed out of it. I tried my best to do the same.

Eventually, I approached the bride from behind, giving her time to notice my reflection in the mirror over her shoulder. "May I?"

She nodded, clearly fighting tears.

"If you decide to go with this one, I can remove these sleeves," I said, tugging on the poofy fabric. "We can take in the bodice and adjust this to be sleeveless, or I can make new sleeves. Maybe something more like the other gown, but in a style that coordinates with this one."

Sadie wet her lips. Her gaze moved to the little sleeves. "You can do all that?"

I smiled. "I can do almost anything with a needle and thread. Once I get my hands on a sewing machine— watch out."

Her cheeks twitched, the first hint of hope I'd seen on her in more than an hour.

"Everything will be perfect," I whispered. "It's your wedding day. You're marrying your best friend." I hoped.

She nodded, tears reappearing.

"All this stress will be forgotten, and all that will matter is that man waiting for you at the end of the aisle."

She released a small sound that crossed between a laugh and a sob, then wiped a falling tear from her cheek. "I know you're right," she said. "It's going to be great. And I think I'll love Nashville. I read all about it online, and I even got a job as a receptionist for a big architectural firm downtown."

"How amazing!"

Her smile widened. "I was worried about how we'd make it, financially, while George's career took off, so I started looking for work right away. I saw the ad, and I called the firm. I've worked in our farm's offices all my life. One of the partners grew up on a dairy farm, and he offered me the job right on the spot."

"That's incredible," I said, meaning it to my core. Her enthusiasm lifted my spirits. This really would be the adventure of a lifetime for them. "You're going to have the time of your life, making memories in a new place with your new husband."

She shimmied a little, eyes bright at my final word. Her gaze flickered over her shoulder in the direction of her mama. "I can't wait. I've never worked anywhere as nice as the photos I saw online. I don't even think I've ever seen a place that fancy."

I felt her words in my marrow. "I moved to Atlanta right out of high school," I said. "Moving to that big city for college, seeing so many things I never had outside of movies and social media was amazing. Thrilling even. I think you'll love it."

She stood a little taller, maybe refilled with hope and a little joy.

I cleared my throat so I didn't get misty too. Her good mood was contagious, and I wanted it to continue. "If the skirt is too full, I can remove some of the layers to minimize the poof. I can also reduce the length of the train, and I can definitely take off this bow." I wrinkled my nose, and she released a small laugh.

Evelyn moved into position beside me, behind Sadie. Our combined reflections gave a distinct angel-and-devil on her shoulders vibe. "If you're going to do all that," Evelyn said, "it won't be the same gown. You might as well get the plain one."

Sadie beamed, and her mama scowled.

When the fussing began anew, I went for snacks and drinks.

Thankfully, the effort was a welcomed distraction, and everyone took a seat to regroup.

Evelyn and Sadie sat in the chairs, clearly exhausted and barely making eye contact.

Ava and Gracie chose the floor. The frill and material of their gowns piled over their crisscrossed legs.

I evaluated the jewelry options on the little table while considering the dress styles the ladies had whittled down. Then I went to the back to grab a few more. I stacked an assortment of little boxes into a pile on my hands and headed for the front when I heard the door chime again.

"Welcome to Bless Her Heart," I called, reaching the sales floor a moment later.

A pair of men stood near the counter. One was broad-shouldered and showing off a full set of white teeth as he smiled, the other in his mid-thirties and sporting a frown.

The bride ran immediately to the better-looking, younger man, and his arms opened for her in a burst. *This must be George*.

The other man scanned the shop, a look of boredom and distaste on his clean-shaven face. His hair was dark, eyes blue. I tried to make him into the man I'd seen on the square earlier, but this man was slight in frame and dressed in a distinct western style. His jeans appeared new, and his black shirt had pearl buttons with white rope piping along the collar and pockets. His cowboy boots had likely never met a horse or seen a day of physical labor.

Was this supposed to help us remember he was from Nashville? I'd been to the city a number of times, and I recalled everyone looking far more understated.

Something told me the man I'd seen on the square wouldn't be caught dead in this ensemble.

Sadie squealed, pulling my attention back to her and

George. He enveloped her in an embrace and rocked her off her feet.

She buried her face in the curve of her neck, and the bridesmaids pressed hands to their hearts.

Ava and Gracie rose and moved a little closer, waiting for their turns to say hello, I presumed.

Evelyn crossed her legs and set her snack aside, but she didn't bother getting up.

I hurried to meet the new arrivals.

Sadie landed back on her feet as I approached. Her smile was bright and wide as she introduced us, never releasing her groom's hand as she spoke. "Bonnie, this is my fiancé, George," she said. "God, I don't think I'll ever get used to calling him that."

George gazed down at her from a significant height difference. "Good thing you don't have to worry about it for long."

Somewhere behind me, Evelyn scoffed.

"George," Sadie continued, either not hearing or not caring about her mama's continued protest. "This is Bonnie Balfour. She's helping us pull the dresses together. No bridal shop in the area could guarantee delivery of anything in our sizes so quickly, never mind making the necessary alterations. Her grandmama is handling the cakes and sweets. Her folks own Bud and Blossom's flower farm. They're making all the bouquets and arrangements. We have to visit there tonight. You can make it, right?"

"My folks want me to meet with our family members who are coming in from out of town," George said. "I'll try to do both. Let me know how else I can help. Is there anything I can work on today while y'all sort the dresses?" His eyes widened as he seemed to finally realize what she was wearing. He raised her hands at her sides, then released one to twirl her. "You look amazing. Is this the dress?"

"Not anymore," Evelyn complained.

Normally, I'd worry about bad luck from the groom seeing the dress before the wedding, but in this scenario, Sadie got a big dose of good luck. Now she could wear the dress she wanted without a fight from her mama.

Sadie clearly had a similar thought, because she beamed. "Nope."

George pulled her close, then looked at me. "I'm so sorry. Where are my manners?" He extended a hand. "It's nice to meet you. I appreciate your family helping us with all this. We know we're asking a lot, and I'd understand if no one wanted to take on a wedding with this timeframe, but we're really glad you did."

I balanced the jewelry boxes in one arm and accepted his shake, fully charmed by his kindness. "We're glad to help. Who are we to stand in the way of true love?"

Ava and Gracie made soft sounds of *aww*.

The man at George's side snorted.

George's smile fell by a fraction. He angled toward the other guy. "This is Beau Mercer, my new manager."

And the reason Evelyn isn't getting her daughter's dream wedding, I thought. He looked like the sort to ruin dreams, but hopefully he would help George reach his, on the career front anyway.

"Hello," I said. "Welcome to Bliss."

He tented his brows, expression bemused, as if the idea he'd find pleasure in being in our town was unlikely. "Thanks. I'm just here to move all this along." He motioned to the couple, then the bridesmaids, then the shop around us. "George has a real talent, and I think I can turn that into a lot of money. Unfortunately, I can't get started until we get back to civilization." He chuckled as if his rudeness was funny.

Sadie and her friends appeared shocked. George looked exhausted.

I didn't turn to see Evelyn.

Instead, I narrowed my eyes in warning and increased the saccharine in my smile. "I guess you should get going, then," I said. "Let us get back to it."

He chuckled again. This time he lifted his palms in mock innocence. "Don't get your ruffles twisted. I didn't mean any harm. I just think we all want George working on sponsorships and marketing as soon as possible. We still need to record his first hit single. And we can't do any of that here. I don't want George to fail." Heavy emphasis on *I*, as if the others in the room didn't mind if George's future was ruined.

My right eyelid twitched, and I realized I'd been holding my smile too long. I let my face relax before the expression turned maniacal.

"There's definitely no time for a honeymoon," he continued. "We can all agree on that, I hope."

Sadie bristled. "I don't care about a honeymoon, and I care very much about George's dreams."

Beau flattened his palms in the air and pumped them, as if telling her to calm down.

George turned away, placing himself between his obnoxious manager and his bride. "How about I get him out of here?" he asked, then pressed a kiss to her head.

"I want you to see the bridesmaids' dresses," she said.

Ava and Gracie moved closer.

I joined Evelyn so George and Sadie could admire the gowns.

"I hate that guy," Evelyn said, not bothering to whisper.

My gaze jerked to Beau, whose lips quirked on one side, indicating he'd likely heard her comment, and he didn't care. Why would he? He clearly thought this town was beneath him, and Evelyn was part of the reason his work making George a star was delayed.

"You know," George said, eyes brightening once more.

"We can make our own honeymoon in Nashville. We can get a room in one of those fancy hotels downtown. As long as we're together, I'm happy. You don't start your new career until the following week anyway. Let's steal the time in between just for us."

I felt my bottom lip push forward a little. How sweet was this kid?

Beau snorted again.

The group beside him turned and stared.

"What?" he asked, raising his hands again.

I looked at Evelyn, feeling more aligned with her than I had all day. Five minutes after meeting Beau, I hated him too.

"Answering phones for some downtown office is hardly a career," Beau said, finishing his obnoxious thought aloud.

George's boy-next-door demeanor evaporated. He released his hold on Sadie so quickly that I didn't register it'd happened until both his hands were on his manager. "Outside," he growled, spinning and shoving the other man in two swift moves.

Ava and Gracie bookended Sadie, twining their arms and closing ranks.

George hauled his new manager onto the sidewalk outside.

Evelyn jumped up and chased the girls to the door. I was hot on her heels.

Together, we watched through the glass as George informed Beau that he was no longer permitted to say Sadie's name or speak about her in any capacity, or those would be the last words he uttered. Furthermore, he demanded Beau apologize to all of us for his ugly display and to Sadie, specifically, for being rude. Then he was never to look at her again. If he did, he was to tell her she was beautiful, then leave the room.

I adored George all the more but wondered a bit at his temper.

A flash of sunlight off a passing car's windshield pulled my eyes to the road. When the vehicle vanished, a pair of figures in the distance caught my attention. Mason and a tall blonde stood between buildings across the square. I recognized the woman immediately.

Cat made regular appearances in town, though she worked for the Cleveland, Ohio FBI. She first met Mason when he was an undercover detective in the city, involved in a joint task force. Mason had lost everything during that initiative, and he wound up on a hit list for The Investors, the same pocket of organized crime the FBI had tried to capture and arrest.

The last time Cat appeared, it was for Cami's surprise engagement to Dale, a remotely employed colleague of hers.

Was she here now because Mason planned to propose?

Or were The Investors finally getting close enough to finding Mason that the FBI had sent a messenger to warn him?

The women scattered, and I realized Beau and George were on their ways inside.

I hurried behind my counter.

Beau apologized as he was told.

I did my best to seem present.

But my thoughts were across the square, in an alley, with Cat and Mason.

CHAPTER FIVE

Mason showed up at Bless Her Heart a few minutes after I flipped the sign from OPEN to CLOSED. I'd never been so happy to see seven o'clock roll around. I let him in with a kiss and melted against his chest, thankful for a safe place to land.

The hours I'd spent with Evelyn, Sadie, and the bridesmaids, surrounded by low simmering tension, were exhausting.

"Sorry I had to run off this morning," he said. "That was not how I planned things to go." He pulled a small bouquet of wildflowers from behind his back when I released him.

My cheeks and neck were warm, and I'd felt a little icky since Sadie and her group left. I accepted the flowers, thankful for his apology and thoughtfulness.

"Are you okay?" he asked.

"I'm emotionally depleted," I said. "I either need to eat or sleep for about twelve hours."

Plus, anytime Cat appeared, I feared for Mason's safety.

And I was still confused about his breakfast behavior. "You said this morning didn't go as planned. What did you mean by that?" I asked, hoping he might clarify his one-kneed position.

He grinned. "Let me take you to dinner," he said, in lieu of an answer. "I made reservations at the little Italian place you like."

My stomach gurgled in celebration.

"Come on." He tipped his head toward the door and smiled. "I'll drive. Do you want to leave Clyde here and pick him up after? Or run him home first?"

"Can we take him to my parents' place?" I asked. "I think he'd like the extra time with Bessie."

Clyde appeared from beneath a nearby rack. "Meow."

Mason laughed. "Heard your girlfriend's name and came running, huh?"

"Meow."

Mason bobbed his head.

Bessie was a four-year-old barn cat that lived at the flower farm. My parents found her as a kitten and tried to make her an indoor cat, as I had with Clyde. Bessie wasn't interested, so after a long battle of wills, they made her a place in the barn for rest and warmth. They also kept a litter box, plus food and water bowls in the house for the days she blessed them with an extended indoor presence, but those rarely lasted more than a few hours. Bessie's name came from her black and white markings, which made her resemble a little cow.

She and Clyde had recently become inseparable on the days he visited to avoid a long day inside the shop. Their kitty relationship was beyond adorable, and everyone encouraged it to the max. Lately, I had more pictures of the cat couple on my phone than Mason and me, and that was really saying something.

"Let me get these flowers in some water and reset the shop for tomorrow morning first," I said. "It won't take long."

Mason helped, and the process was finished in half my usual time.

"All right," I said, a short while later. "Are you ready, Clyde?" I shouldered my bag and set the cat carrier on the countertop. "Your chariot awaits."

I didn't have to ask twice.

Clyde leapt gracefully up, then slipped into his crate. He turned to watch me fasten the little gate, a small red length of ribbon caught in his mouth.

"Bringing Bessie a gift? Or is this your kleptomania in action?"

He set the ribbon down inside the carrier. "Meow."

"I think he told you to mind your business," Mason said, hefting the carrier with one hand. He moved to the door and held it for me.

I locked up, then scanned the square on my way to Mason's Jeep. I wasn't sure what I was looking for, but I felt better when I didn't find it.

The drive to my folks' place was peaceful. I told Mason about my day, and he told me about his. He did not, however, mention Cat. And neither did I.

He parked in the gravel lot outside the big flower barn closest to the main road.

I peered through the window, feeling slightly more unhappy at the sight of a familiar vehicle. "I think that's Evelyn Clarke's ride," I said. I'd watched the group climb into the giant SUV after leaving my shop. "I'd hoped they'd be gone by now."

Mason patted my hand, then gave my fingers a squeeze. "Should we stay or go?"

"Stay." I sighed, resigned to wear my forced smile another minute or two. "I'll be quick. Drop off Clyde, hug my folks, and put this day behind me."

Then bury my troubles in a vat of fettuccine alfredo.

Mason met me at the front of his truck carrying Clyde's crate. He took my hand as we went in search of my folks. "What all are they doing here?" he asked. "Picking out the bridal bouquet?"

"That," I agreed. "And flowers for the bridesmaids, the boutonnieres for the groomsmen and fathers of the bride and groom, corsages for the moms and grandmas. The maid of honor and best man usually have something slightly different, but I'm not sure if Sadie has a maid of honor." I'd only met two bridesmaids, and she hadn't mentioned another member of the bridal party. "They'll also choose flowers for centerpieces at the reception and for the arch Sadie mentioned getting married under. They might want flowers for either side of the aisle as well." I rocked my head over each shoulder. "There are a lot of flowers involved in a wedding."

A few steps later, a shiny red sports car came into view, previously hidden by the large SUV.

Mason whistled. "Who belongs to that beauty?"

I scowled. I could only think of one person who'd drive a car with a six-figure price tag in Bliss. "I'm going to guess Beau Mercer, George's rude talent agent."

Mason tugged me close. "I've got you," he promised. "We'll be in and out in five minutes. Tonight is our night, and it's going to be perfect. I still have to make up for breakfast."

My intuition spiked, and images of him on one knee returned. If his plans to propose were interrupted earlier by a ringing phone, did he plan to finish the job over dinner at my favorite Italian restaurant?

That could explain why Cat was in town. No murderous criminals hunting the man I loved. Just a friend here to celebrate an engagement, as she had for Dale and Cami.

A thrill shot through me at the possibility.

We checked the fields for my parents and peeked into the big flower barn. Then we moved toward their home.

The waning sun cast an eerie orange glow across the flagstone path at our feet.

A group of people came into view before we reached our next destination.

Mama, Evelyn, and Sadie meandered in our direction, each carrying a few select blooms. They all wore smiles, and I relaxed a little at the sight. Mama waved when she took notice of our approach, and the other women followed suit.

"I hate all this rush," Evelyn said as they continued in our direction.

"It's no problem," Mama said. Her usual denim overalls hung on her petite, youthful frame. "I enjoy a challenge."

Sadie's smile widened.

"Weddings aren't supposed to be rushed, that's all," Evelyn pushed. "It's just bad luck."

The group stopped in their tracks. I did as well.

On a whole, Blissers were a happy, hardworking, carefree bunch. But we had a major hangup when it came to luck, specifically of the not-good variety. We were superstitious to a fault, and we never said things like Evelyn had aloud for fear of bringing them to fruition.

"Mama," Sadie scolded. Her whisper cut through the thick evening air.

Mason bent to set the cat carrier on the ground and open the door.

Clyde bolted free, in search of Bessie no doubt, red ribbon trailing from his little mouth.

"Bonnie, Mason," Mama said, shaking off the momentary shock of Evelyn's words. "I wasn't expecting you." She offered us each a hug. "You know Evelyn and Sadie Clarke," she said to me. Then she introduced Mason to the ladies.

I scanned the dimming farm as they exchanged greetings.

My dad wasn't anywhere in sight. And where was Beau Mercer? Hopefully not somewhere ruining Dad's night. "We saw a red sports car in the lot," I said when the conversation around me quieted.

"Beau," Evelyn groaned. "He followed us here."

"I thought he might've brought George," Sadie said, looking wholly disappointed.

"He just wanted to catch Sadie alone and persuade her to get married some other time," Evelyn groused. "So he can get George back to Nashville a week sooner." She crossed her arms in a huff. "Finally, we agreed on something. Weddings shouldn't be rushed!"

Sadie deflated at her mother's side. "She and Beau agreed on something," she repeated. "But they argued anyway."

Evelyn shrugged, unbothered.

"He was rude as usual," Sadie said. "George wasn't around to stop him, so your dad cut in, then escorted him out."

Go, Dad! I thought.

Mama frowned. "That was a while ago. I wonder why Bud hasn't come back?"

I glanced in Mason's direction, wondering if he'd volunteer to track down my dad, but his eyes were on his phone screen.

"Everything okay?" I asked him.

He grunted and pocketed the device.

Mama sneezed, and I started. "Sorry," she said. "I've had a little tickle in my throat today. Changing seasons and all that."

I frowned. I hadn't felt great today either, but I'd chalked it up to stress.

Mama coughed into a closed fist and shook her head. "I am so sorry."

"There's a bug going around," Evelyn said. "A few

farmhands had time off for it last week. With a little luck, the wedding party won't catch it."

I definitely didn't want it. "I hate to rush off," I said, taking the announcement of illness as my cue. "But we're on our way to dinner."

Sadie waved a hand. "Enjoy yourself."

"I think we have everything settled here," Mama said. "They're meeting with Sutton in the morning to talk about adding succulents to the centerpieces."

"You'll love her," I said, shifting my gaze to Sadie. "Sutton's Gigi's best friend."

Sutton had grown up with Gigi, and they were thick as thieves to this day. She had her quirks, but didn't we all?

We turned, and the trio followed us toward the parking lot.

"I'll be back for Clyde tonight," I told Mama.

"No rush," she said. "He's never any trouble, and Bessie enjoys him so much."

"I'm going to see if I can find Bud," Mama added, splitting off from our group. "Let me know if you think of anything you'd like to add or change," she told Evelyn and Sadie.

"Will do," Evelyn said.

The sun had dropped behind a nearby hillside, sending shadows over the path. I took each step carefully and held fast to Mason's arm.

When we reached the lot, the sports car hadn't moved. Gooseflesh crawled over my skin at the sight of it.

I followed Mason to his Jeep and waited as he unlocked the door.

"I can see why you're exhausted," Mason whispered as I climbed inside.

I glanced at the Clarkes, already seated in their SUV. "You have no idea."

Mason straightened to close my door then froze at the sound of my mama's scream.

His face whipped in the direction of the noise originated, and I jumped back into the lot. We made eye contact for the space of a heartbeat, then we were in motion, racing toward the sound.

I stopped short at the sight of my parents in a wildflower field, the happy blooms stretching up my mama's body to her hips. She covered her face with trembling hands while Dad pressed her to his chest. Too many recent and terrible experiences barreled through my mind, unsettling my stomach once more.

Mason swung one arm wide, silently, unnecessarily, telling me to stay back.

Heart pounding. Head swimming. Fear rooted my feet into the soil.

My parents were safe. But something was horribly wrong. I felt it in the air.

Mason finished the trek to my parents' side. The flashlight app on his cell phone ignited, and he searched the area at their feet.

Mama sobbed, and I was in motion once more, closing the final distance between us.

Dad opened his arms and pulled me into their hug as Mason crouched before the lifeless body of Beau Mercer.

A bloodied pair of gardening shears lay on the ground at Dad's feet.

CHAPTER SIX

An hour later, the flower farm was lit up like a circus and just as busy.

Spotlights had been erected in the crime scene periphery. Most pointed at Beau Mercer's body. A handful of deputies scoured the nearby fields, kicking their ways through an abundance of wildflowers and tall, decorative grasses in search of additional evidence. An ambulance, the coroner's van, a fire truck, and two patrol cars lined the edge of the field. Their emergency lights scored the night sky, drawing in people like moths to flames.

A growing crowd of locals, neighbors, and lookie lous gathered shamelessly at the yellow crime scene tape now stretched along the edge of the gravel lot.

News of the murder spread through Bliss at double speed, thanks to our local crime reporter, her police scanner, and new livestream feed from her phone.

My stomach coiled and rolled with upset and hunger.

Mama clung to Dad, as if he might be arrested and taken away from her at any moment. She shook with sniffles and silent tears. Her every whimper broke my heart further.

Gigi, on the other hand, had sprung into action doing what she did best: mingling, feeding folks, and collecting gossip. She'd arrived with a picnic basket full of baked goods and was making good time through the crowd while doling them out. "Can you believe it?" I heard her ask. The stage whisper stretched across the crowd. "Just awful. Unbelievable. I mean, who in this town even knew this man?"

When life threw lemons, Gigi served them as tartlets in trade for information.

A few yards to my left, inside the yellow tape with me, Evelyn and Sadie waited impatiently to leave.

"This is plain bad luck," Evelyn complained. "It's bad enough we were here when it happened, and planning your wedding, no less. To be seen so close to the body by half the town? We'll never scrub this from our reputations. Who will want to come to the ceremony now?"

"Shh!" Sadie scolded. "You shouldn't be thinking about that right now. It's rude and self-obsessed. Besides, people will hear you."

She was right about that. If I heard her, so did everyone in the lot. Blissers could sense the mention of bad luck from six counties away. And none of them wanted any part of it.

My head lightened as I dragged my gaze to the evidence collection before me. The coroner scraped under Beau Mercer's fingernails and put the findings into a little tube. Mason bagged the gardening shears as evidence. Paramedics prepared the gurney and body bag to take Beau away.

Whispers mixed with Mama's soft cries in an otherwise quiet field.

And my stomach churned with every ragged heave of her chest.

The local reporter's voice rose above the other sounds a moment later as she formally interviewed folks in the crowd. Maribelle was in her eighties. Mr. Dinky, a morbidly obese Pekingese, was at least twice her age in dog years, and he wore a bright yellow collar to match her velour track suit.

I was confident they'd stolen the "matching ensembles" idea from Clyde and me. But we hadn't exactly trademarked the concept, or even started it, so I let that go.

These days, Maribelle streamed everything live to a YouTube channel owned by the local news station . Some kid from the local community college set her up with the app as part of his required service hours for graduation. Now she never put down her cell phone, and everyone thought it was fantastic. Except local law enforcement and anyone overheard behaving badly.

Between the teens with their TikTok and Maribelle with her livestream, nothing was sacred anymore.

I pressed a palm to my forehead. When did I get to be so crotchety? I blamed the heat and hunger.

"Croissant?" Gigi asked.

I nearly leaped into the atmosphere.

She stood three feet away with her basket of baked goodies and a smile.

"Whoa," she said. "What's gotten into you?"

"Are you kidding?" I whisper. "You snuck up on me."

"I called your name," she said.

I pressed the back of one hand to my cheek, seeking coolness and finding none. "Sorry. I'm on edge. This is awful."

Gigi pursed her lips. "It is," she agreed. "Since we need a silver lining tonight, I remind myself that our new sheriff is excellent at what he does. He'll figure it out," she said, tipping her head in Mason's direction. "There will be justice for this poor soul. I'm not worried."

"I'm worried," I squeaked, unable to match her calm. "This looks bad, and Dad wouldn't last five minutes in prison. He's a marshmallow. And look at Mama!" She might commit a crime just to be locked up with him until he was moved to the county jail.

Gigi handed me a croissant. "Here. Have something to eat."

I took a bite, trying not to panic more than necessary at a crime scene. The soft, buttery layers immediately improved my mood.

Gigi patted my shoulder. "There you are. Here's another." She placed a second croissant into my free hand. "I'll be back to check on you in a bit."

"Wait. Heard anything useful?" I asked, around a mouthful of heaven.

Her eyes flashed with mischief. "Apparently, Patsy Humbert fills a metal tub with ice water every morning and sneaks out back in her swimsuit to dunk in it before the sunrise. I knew that woman had a health and beauty secret she was keeping from us. She's never sick, and she looks ten years younger than me."

"She is ten years younger than you," I said. "If I dunked in ice water, I'd have a heart attack, so I think the result probably varies."

Gigi thought it over. "I'm going to see if Sutton wants to try it with me tomorrow."

A smile crossed my lips as I thought of the neighbors spying on Gigi and Sutton in bathing suits before dawn. "You ought to charge for that show," I said, feeling more like myself with every delicious bite of baked goods.

She cocked a hip and worked her brows. "Don't I know it!"

Somewhere nearby, Evelyn complained again, and I cringed.

Gigi's shoulders climbed to her ears. Clearly, she'd heard that too. "She needs to stop saying those two words before she brings bad luck on the whole town." Like a proper local,

Gigi mouthed the words "bad luck" without giving them voice.

I leaned slightly to the right for a peek around my grandma and spotted Evelyn and Sadie. The crowd had thickened several feet away from the Clarkes, allowing plenty of space for the unwanted and negative energy.

"Folks don't want that bad juju sticking on them," Gigi said.

I wasn't superstitious, but I absolutely felt the same way.

Mason broke away from the other deputies and moved in our direction. Tension marred his handsome face, and exhaustion seemed to cling to his limbs. "Maybe she should say that loud enough to send the crowd home for the night," he suggested.

I smiled. Apparently, Gigi and I weren't as quiet as we thought, either.

"Impressive hearing," Gigi said.

Mason grinned. "It's a gift. Comes in mighty handy."

I ran a palm down his arm. "You look as if you're ready to collapse."

"Have a croissant," Gigi offered.

"Thanks. We were on our way to dinner." His expression pinched, but he accepted, then made short work of her offering.

She passed him another, and it met the same fate. "Quite alright," she said. "I've got you both covered."

My gaze traveled to Mama and Dad, huddled together nearby. "How's it looking over there?" I asked. I wasn't sure which of my folks was more distraught.

"Not great," Mason admitted. He set big tan hands on trim hips and released a puff of air. "Coroner agrees the murder weapon is likely the shears. And your folks verified they belong to the farm."

I wrinkled my nose. "But—"

"Your dad saw them on the ground before he noticed the body, and he picked them up."

I groaned.

"Yeah," Mason agreed. "It's not looking great for him right now."

"But the manager was struck from behind," I say. "Anyone could've done that."

Mason nodded. "That's right, and we'll know more once the body can be moved."

Gigi perked up. "On my crime shows, the lab people can tell by the angle of the stabbing how tall the attacker was. That should help clear Bud."

"It could," Mason said. "The coroner will perform a full autopsy soon. Right now, we're trying to preserve evidence, but it's about time to go."

"Sheriff?" A deputy called.

Mason lifted a hand in acknowledgement, then looked into my eyes. "I'm sorry about this."

"I know," I said. "Go ahead, I'll be right here."

He strode away, and I took another croissant from Gigi's picnic basket.

"He'll figure it out," she said. "Everything will be fine."

I wished I had her optimism. "I'm going to see what I can learn too," I said. "I know this farm and the suspect better than anyone, except Mama." She was too shaken to think of anything other than losing Dad. But I could be useful, so I would.

Mason returned a moment later and kissed my forehead. "I'm going with the coroner. Are you okay to stay here? You probably want to be with your folks?"

I nodded. "I do."

A beam of light cut through the night, and we turned in the direction of Maribelle and her camera.

"Ms. Maribelle," Mason says. "Please turn that thing off.

This is a crime scene and an open investigation. Livestreaming anything right now will do more harm than good."

She shrugged and cut the camera.

"How long have you been filming us?" I asked, hyperaware of the private declaration I'd just made to Gigi about inserting myself into this investigation.

"Long enough to know where the story is," she said. Her drawn-on eyebrows lifted high on her forehead, creating a mass of wrinkles just below her white beehive hair. "Or where it will be."

"I'm going to have to ask you to get behind the line with everyone else," Mason said. "I'm happy to provide an interview in the morning."

"Come along, Mr. Dinky," she said, spinning away on orthopedic sneakers. "We've got everything we need anyway."

Mason ran a heavy hand down his face in her absence. "I hate when she gets that cat-that-ate-the-canary look," he said. "Whatever she's up to usually makes me mad."

I smiled as innocently as possible and took another bite of my croissant.

The crowd and most of the first responders left with the coroner and Mason. Gigi and I went inside with Mama and Dad.

I made a pot of tea, and Gigi arranged the rest of her snacks on the kitchen table. We all took seats and sipped our drinks in companionable silence for a long while. Then it was as if the floodgates opened.

"I can't believe this happened," Mama said.

Dad rubbed her hand where it rested on the table. "I

thought the shears were muddy. In the grass, with the sun set like it was, I couldn't tell it was blood."

"Why would you think it was?" Mama asked. "Why would that possibility even cross your mind?"

"I wouldn't have picked them up if I'd known," he said, turning his gaze to me.

"I believe you," I said. "We all do."

Mama's brow pinched, and she fixed her mother with a peculiar stare. "How'd you know to bring the snacks?" she asked. "You were one of the first to arrive after the ambulance, and you brought food. How'd you know one of us wasn't injured or sick or something?"

That was an excellent question. I looked to Gigi as well.

"I had a feeling," she said. "I saw Mason's SUV, so I knew you were safe. He'd have called me otherwise."

"You can see the lot clearly from your place?" I asked.

Gigi's home was positioned at the edge of the flower farm, but my parents' property was huge. They'd bought the piece of land when Grandpapa and Gigi built the cottage, no longer interested in caring for so many acres. I'd spent plenty of time at Gigi's, even lived there for a short time, but I couldn't recall if I'd ever tried to see the lot from the window.

"Sure," she said.

"Even after dark?" I asked.

"I mostly see headlights at night," she said. "There were plenty of those. Cutting across my window all the time. I looked almost every time, because I wanted to visit after Evelyn and Sadie left. I thought we could talk a little more about the wedding cake and the flowers they chose. I wasn't in a hurry to see them again today, because they fought at my shop, and I'm fresh out of patience for the nonsense." She shook her head and heaved a sigh. "Evelyn is normally a lovely person, but right now, she is exhausting. I felt terrible for Sadie, just wanting to marry the man she loves, but her mama seems bound and determined to ruin it. Sticking her hands in the mix everywhere she can."

"Evelyn was being a pill," Mama agreed. "Weddings bring up a lot of emotions. I guess putting one together in such a hurry exaggerates that side effect."

Gigi nodded. "I suppose that's right. Anyway, I saw their SUV, so I waited. Then there were more headlights. But the SUV remained. Then I saw Mason and Bonnie arrive. I was sure the next set of headlights had to be Evelyn and Sadie leaving, but their ride never moved. I was starting to think they took y'all hostage."

Mama laughed softly.

I was thankful for the first smile I'd seen on her in hours.

I was also curious about a detail or two in Gigi's story. "How many sets of headlights did you see tonight?"

Gigi wrinkled her nose. "I don't know. A bunch, why?"

I turned on my seat to face her. "You saw our headlights," I said.

"Yeah."

"When we arrived, only Evelyn's SUV and the manager's car were in the lot," I told her. Whoever killed Beau must've been here and gone before Mason and I arrived. "Do you remember the car that was here, then gone, right before ours?"

Gigi's gaze climbed to the ceiling as she thought. "I remember seeing the headlights, but I was baking and having a little dinner, so—" She sighed. "No, but now that you mention it, I remember wondering if I was mistaken about seeing more headlights. Someone had either arrived or left, but the cars in the lot hadn't changed."

I got my phone. "I'm going to let Mason know someone else was here tonight."

My phone dinged with his response a moment later.

"That was fast," Mama said. "What did he say?"

I scanned the message. "He's going to look into it in the morning. He's talking to the coroner about the murder weapon right now."

Dad set his elbows on the table and dropped his face into waiting palms. "I've never found a dead body like that," he said. "It was awful."

"It's not great," I agreed.

Dad lifted his face to look at me. "I've always hated that this kind of thing happens to you. Now I'm sick just thinking that you've felt like this so many times. It's horrendous. How are you okay?"

In general, I was the official pilot of the Hot Mess Express, but more specifically, I was made from different stuff than my dad. I was emotionally resilient and internally driven to overcome. In fact, I was pretty sure I could get through anything if I could find something better to focus on. So, yes, finding murder victims was traumatic, and I'd found more than my share in the past year or so. But whenever that happened, I just shifted my thoughts away from those feelings of panic and focused on finding justice for the poor victim instead.

Dad was the sort of person to feel his feelings and process them to a point of healthy resolution rather than distract himself with crime solving. His way was probably better.

CHAPTER SEVEN

I stayed at my parents' house until I was sure they'd be able to sleep. Gigi stuck around a little longer to care for her daughter, which I appreciated deeply. I was sincerely worried about Mama.

I called Cami when I got home and filled her in on the news while I fed Clyde his dinner. Then I changed into my pajamas. Unlike most of the town, Cami and Dale were having a movie night and hadn't heard about the murder.

After I filled them in, I let them get back to their movie. Then I dove into an online rabbit hole. I wanted to know anything and everything I could about Beau Mercer. And who might want to kill him. I read and researched until fatigue won out.

Mason crept in a little after two A.M., told me he had to threaten the local news media with a cease and desist on Mirabelle's livestream, then went right to sleep.

Our current living arrangement was thanks in part to the fact I'd accidentally been involved in sinking his houseboat. Now he was building a lake house nearby and homeless until the project was completed. Regardless, living with Mason wasn't a hardship. Except when it was late, and I knew he wasn't home, so I worried.

He still hadn't mentioned that Cat was in town, which made me wonder if he was busy with Beau Mercer's murder until two A.M., or if he had another secret meeting with his former colleague. And if so, why?

It didn't make sense for him to keep her presence a secret from me. Unless he planned to surprise me with an engagement, like Dale had done for Cami.

Either that, or trouble was afoot.

I hated the second option, because it meant Mason was in danger.

I woke to an empty bed just after dawn, so my plans for a breakfast interrogation went out the window.

"Dang it." I pushed up to sit and scanned the room for signs he might still be home. Maybe making coffee or taking a shower.

I found none.

Clyde stood at the end of my bed and performed a deep lunge stretch. His mouth opened wide enough to swallow a volleyball, then snapped shut like jaws. He leaped onto the floor and sauntered through the open bedroom door, presumably to wait for me near his food dish.

I grabbed a robe and followed. One look through the front window confirmed what I'd expected.

Mason and his Jeep were gone.

I took my time getting ready for work, then donned an emerald green wrap dress with a floral print and put a matching bowtie on Clyde.

The morning was beautiful. The sun was shining. Birds were chirping, and I was trying to think of only happy things as I parked outside Bless Her Heart.

I spotted clusters of new faces on the square and seated at outdoor cafés. Sadie's and George's wedding guests were likely arriving soon, hoping to spend time with their families before the big day.

A familiar dark-haired man smiled when he caught my attention. Seated on the same bench where I'd seen him yesterday, the stranger raised his logoed coffee cup and winked one clear blue eye.

I freed Clyde's carrier from the passenger-side seatbelt and hauled him quickly indoors.

When I checked the square again for signs of the watching man, he was gone.

Perfect, because he gave me the willies, and it was time for a sidewalk sale. The area was crowded, and I was in the market for information. I didn't have croissants like Gigi, but I had cute clothes, shoes, and trinkets. Also, a nice selection of handbags and potted plants from the flower farm.

I redressed the shop window with adorable items for fall, then dragged two folding chairs outside. I arranged a rolling rack of clothing on one side and a table with some of my newest, most pick-upable things in between the seats. Satisfied with the setup, I got comfortable and started saying hello.

My best friend, Cami, appeared behind a trio of locals, carrying two cups of iced coffee.

I smiled at the sight of her.

Cami wore a sleeveless white dress with orange threading along the neckline and hem. Her gold hoop earrings and matching necklace accentuated her flawless brown skin. Her hair was twisted neatly into a tight chignon.

I whistled when the group ahead of her passed me. "Look at you," I said, rising to greet her with a hug. "You look incredible, as always."

She handed me a cup when we broke apart, then took the empty seat beside mine. "Thank you. You do as well."

I sat and sipped, savoring the rush of caffeine and sugar

into my blood stream. "Hazelnut vanilla cream is my favorite," I said. "I needed this today."

"I thought you might," she said. "You were all worked up when we spoke on the phone last night. I figured you probably didn't sleep well."

"Correct." I took another, longer drink and melted a little against my chair. "Delicious."

"How'd the research go?"

I grinned.

"That good, huh?"

I nodded and checked the immediate area before unloading my findings.

I'd hit the jackpot for information on Beau Mercer. "Apparently he was kind of a big deal as a new music agent," I said. "His career has been humdrum the last few years, but when I went back a little further, I found a completely different story."

Cami crossed her legs and got comfy. "Go on."

"Beau used to keep a roster of some pretty impressive clients. He was old friends with someone who hit it big and let him manage his career. That led him to meeting other artists who also signed with him, and he became a rising star of his own kind for a while."

"Ooo," Cami cooed. "I'm sensing a but."

"But," I said, "his biggest client, Ruby Maxwell, overdosed in her hotel room while on tour, and it was later revealed that Ruby was only there because of Beau. She'd been in rehab for several months when he convinced her to leave and go back on tour. He told her that her career wouldn't survive if she stayed out of the spotlight any longer. So, she went, despite her doctor and therapist's advice against it, and she didn't make it past the third stop."

Cami pressed a palm to her chest. "Goodness, that's awful."

"She wasn't ready, and she knew it. But he didn't care."

Cami's expression mirrored my feelings. It was the most heartbreaking of stories.

"Instead of repenting, Beau doubled down on his decision during interviews, insisting his advice was solid. Then he went viral in a clip where he claimed that Ruby would've met the same fate if she hadn't toured and lost her career because of it."

"But she'd still be alive to rebuild." nodded. "Yeah, no one agreed with him, and his clients all left. He's been trying to climb back out of the hole he dug since then. He's actively scouting new talent, trying to get back on top."

Cami sipped her coffee, clearly contemplating. "Seems reasonable that Beau Mercer might've had a number of enemies," she said. "People who didn't want to see him succeed after what he did to that poor girl."

"That's what I told Mason," I said. "I texted him as soon as I found the story."

"What'd he say?"

"That it was after midnight, and I should get some rest. Then he said to leave his investigation alone."

Cami laughed. "It's as if he doesn't know you at all."

"I can't walk away from this one," I said. "Not until he finds another prime suspect. My dad is innocent."

"How's your mama holding up?" Cami asked. "My mama said they spoke at length last night, and Blossom barely stopped crying."

Our mothers had been best friends all our lives. I'd met Cami while we were still in diapers. "She's taking it harder than Dad," I said.

Cami tilted her head over one shoulder and narrowed her gaze. "How are you doing? You look paler than usual, if that's possible."

"Mama's sick, and she might've gotten me sick," I admitted. "But I honestly feel better today than I did yesterday."

"That's good. How are the wedding plans coming along?"

I made a sad face. "This wedding is pure madness."

A couple tugged on the door to Gigi's bakery a few yards away, then shielded their faces with their hands and pressed their foreheads to the glass.

"Where's your grandmama?" Cami asked.

"She's opening late— officially. She was up all night baking sample cakes for Evelyn and Sadie to taste test. She's probably in there now setting up for their return. I guess they stopped at her shop yesterday and Evelyn made a bunch of special requests. Then she started arguments with Sadie, which ticked off Gigi."

Cami nodded. "I can see that. Why can't she let the girl enjoy herself? It's her wedding for goodness sakes."

"Agreed," I said. "Evelyn really should be kind to her daughter and make as many good memories as possible before she moves to Nashville."

Cami froze, and I stared.

"Wait. Do you think they're still moving to Nashville?" I asked. "Or did Beau's death put an end to that?"

Cami hiked one perfectly sculpted brow. "Wouldn't that be nice? Any chance Evelyn wasn't accounted for at some point last night? Maybe right before your dad found Beau's body?"

I bit my lip. "I don't know, and I don't think anyone asked."

Lexi's little blue pickup truck rounded the corner and parked a few spots away. She hopped out with wide eyes and an open mouth.

"Looks like she heard the news," Cami said, rising onto her feet. "I'll let you get back to work. I'm headed over to City Hall to discuss our next beautification project."

"Okay," I said. "If you must." I hugged her, then stepped back as Lexi approached.

"Hey, Lex," Cami said. "The tea is piping hot this morning."

"Just the way I like it," she said. "I came early to get a double serving."

Cami laughed. "Bonnie, let me know if you think of anything my mama or I can do to help your folks through this."

"I appreciate that," I said. "Thank you, and thanks again for the coffee."

Lexi took the newly vacant seat and dropped her bag at her feet. "Tell me everything. People are saying Maribelle livestreamed a ton of folks talking and speculating. Then, apparently, she got you saying you're getting involved again to clear your dad's name. People are getting behind that. Your adventures in sleuthing have people thinking they can do anything they set their minds to, even pick up a new sport or hobby after forty."

My smile fell as her comment went from something like *you're an inspiration* to something more like *you are old*.

I opened my mouth to tell her sleuthing wasn't a hobby or a sport. It wasn't as if I'd taken up needle point or pickle ball. But it wasn't a job or a lifestyle either, so—

An arriving group of women engaged Lexi in conversation about items in the window display, and she showed them inside. The look she gave me as she passed said we weren't even close to finished with the chat we'd barely started.

I went back to my coffee until Evelyn and Sadie appeared. I inhaled a calming breath, then forced a smile. Today would be rough for all of us, but these two had answers to at least two of my questions. Was the wedding still on? Even if there wasn't a reason to rush anymore? And was the happy couple still moving to Tennessee?

Also, what would happen to George's music career if his manager was gone?

The thought barely registered before I wondered if one of his bandmates could've been jealous enough to kill if it would keep George from moving on without them.

"Good morning," Sadie said, reaching me a few steps before her mother. "We're meeting Gigi at the bakery, but she told us to come in through the side door so folks don't think she's open for business just yet."

"Say no more," I said, rising to hold the door to Bless Her Heart. I followed them to the etched glass door separating my shop from Gigi's bakery and knocked. "Lexi has things covered here," I said, as my grandma unlocked the deadbolt on her side. "I think I'm going to tag along and join you."

Maybe I'd get an answer or two to my questions, and some cake samples for breakfast.

CHAPTER EIGHT

*G*igi ushered us inside with a welcoming smile. "Good morning," she said. "It's lovely to see you."

Her eyes were bright and her expression warm, despite the awful events of the previous night.

Evelyn, Sadie, and I each greeted her as we passed into the dining area.

She'd paired hot pink capri pants with a white t-shirt and matching sneakers. Her top carried the Oh! My Goodies logo, as did the apron lying across her counter.

The mother-daughter duo took a moment to look around, and I pulled Gigi into a hug.

She raised her brows as she released me, and I interpreted the move as a silent question. *Have you heard anything new about the murder?* Or, maybe, *has Mason found another suspect?*

I shook my head and forced a tight smile. Her shoulders dropped a little, as did her smile, and she nodded.

Evelyn and Sadie perused the perimeter, chatting softly to themselves.

Gigi's shop opened for business several months ago, but getting inside wasn't easy. Folks had to be early and willing to wait in a queue. The line often stretched around the block before I got to work. As a result, she frequently sold out early and knocked off to enjoy her day. She was a one-woman show, in no hurry to expand or hire help. She baked what she wanted, which meant the menu often changed according to her mood and ingredient availability. Whenever possible, she bought from local farms and suppliers, doing her part to support the Bliss economy and community.

I smiled as I watched the bride and her mother discussing the bakery's design and décor. Evidence of my grandma's big, loving heart was everywhere.

Oh! My Goodies was arguably too extravagant to fit into our laid-back little town, where we prided ourselves on the simplistic, easy pleasures of life. But Gigi thought everyone deserved to feel fancy from time to time, and she designed the bakery's atmosphere with that in mind.

Miles of gleaming white covered the floors and counters. Soft crème-colored walls featured framed photos taken around our town, often in dramatic black and white. Accents in soft shades of pink and teal adorned shelving with pre-packaged items, like Gigi's bagged cookie and cake mixes, or locally farmed honey and jams, for purchase. Oh! My Goodies was both welcoming and indulgent, brimming with Southern Georgia charm.

Sadie turned an apologetic expression in our direction. "Thank you so much for meeting with us again. After last night—"

Gigi lifted a palm. "That has nothing to do with your wedding. We're going to let the sheriff handle that. You and I are going to choose the perfect cake to cut with your new husband next weekend."

The younger woman visibly relaxed.

Her mother rolled her eyes. "I don't see why we have to continue on this bullet train path. Without Beau to rip you from your home on a moment's notice, it seems to me you can stay and take your time with things."

I shot Gigi a pointed look, and she widened her eyes.

"Go ahead and have a seat when you're ready," Gigi told her guests. "There's no rush needed in here. Bonnie and I will get the cakes and be right back."

I spun and beetled along behind her as she grabbed her apron off the countertop and headed into the kitchen.

"Well?" Gigi whispered the moment we slipped out of view. "Do you think she could've done it?"

I selected an apron from a set of nearby hooks and dropped one over my head. I didn't have to ask for clarification. I'd had a similar thought about Evelyn, based on her complete disdain for Beau Mercer.

I fastened the apron's ties at my waist while I considered my answer. "I don't know," I said finally. It was a complicated question. Did Evelyn want to kill him? Maybe. But would she do it? I didn't know her well enough to guess. And I liked to think most people wouldn't go through with something so awful.

Then again, since my return to Bliss, I'd learned that anyone was capable of lashing out in a moment of anger. Anyone could change their future and someone else's irrevocably and regret it forever.

"Who are our other suspects?" she asked. "I mean besides —" She tipped her head in the direction of the dining area and raised her brows.

I pressed one finger to my lips.

"I didn't say it," she whispered.

My eyes stretched wide, and I did the finger thing again.

Gigi pulled a silver tray from a cupboard and set it on the counter, then retrieved a rolling cart and several plated mini-cakes from her walk-in pantry. The designs were simplistic. Six perfectly round, smoothly iced replicas, though the shades of icing varied slightly. A pristine cardstock triangle stood before each cake, the flavor combination neatly scripted in black ink.

> White Chocolate with Raspberry Filling
> Lemon with Elderflower
> Salted Caramel and Dark Chocolate
> Almond
> Champagne and Strawberry
> Coconut

My stomach growled, and Gigi beamed.

"That's the response I'm looking for," she said. "So, no suspects?"

"A million suspects," I whispered. "Roughly, everyone who met him."

She wrinkled her nose. "Yeesh. Grab the plates and settings, would you?"

I followed her gaze to a stack of white, floral-printed plates and linen napkins with silver forks. "These are beautiful."

Gigi's expression turned wistful as she admired the stack. "They're from my wedding."

Gigi and my grandpa had met as children in Bliss, fostering a friendship in young adulthood that turned to love by high school graduation. His death took her from us, too, for a while. She'd lost the love of her life, her best friend, the father of her child. I wasn't sure anyone ever really recovered from that, but Gigi tried.

I stroked a palm down her arm from shoulder to elbow and offered a little squeeze.

She added a crystal bud vase with a single white daisy to her cart and smiled. "Ready?"

"Ready."

Gigi got behind her cart to push, then shot me a wicked grin over her shoulder. "Let's go see what the bride knows about Beau and his enemies."

It wasn't very nice, or appropriate, to shake down a customer for information on a recent murder, but at least the cakes were a sweet trade. And maybe Sadie and Evelyn wouldn't mind talking about something so relevant to them.

Plus, it was Gigi's business, and who was I to stop her?

The bride and her mother were seated when we reached the dining area. They'd chosen a small round table near the window overlooking the square. Gigi's white eyelet lace curtains were drawn for privacy.

I set a plate, napkin, and fork before each guest. Gigi parked her fancy white cart at an angle a few steps away, letting Evelyn and Sadie get a good look at the pretty display.

Sadie raised neatly manicured fingernails to petal pink lips. "Those are so pretty."

"Thank you," Gigi said graciously. "Let's hope we find a flavor that suits. I'll coordinate the tablecloths and accessories to your theme on the dessert and cake table at the reception. Blossom will add her floral touches to the cakes, and Bonnie will find the perfect accents to enhance the whole display. Have you decided on a theme?"

"Bliss," Sadie said. "The town and the emotion." She folded her hands on her lap and smiled. "George and I really want to honor the place where we grew up, where we met, where our families have lived for generations. It's defined who we are, and it breaks our hearts to leave, but we're starting our own adventure now, and we're really excited about that too."

I felt my bottom lip jut a little. "You can have roots and wings," I said. "You don't have to let go of one to embrace the other."

Gigi nodded. "Tell us more about your vision for the overall look and feel of your day."

"Farm girl chic," Evelyn said, answering for her daughter. "We're paying homage to the farm that makes this all possible."

I slid my gaze from the bride's mama to the bride and bit my lip against an internal wince. Evelyn managed to make Sadie's lovely concept sound like it wasn't about her at all.

Sadie scowled. "You can say it my way, or you can say it like Mama," she groused. "And make my wedding sound like a backyard barbecue."

Gigi's waning smile bottomed out, and she cleared her throat. "I could still use a little more detail."

Evelyn sat taller, apparently holding onto the reins. "Burlap bows, red and white checked table coverings, candles, little hay bales. Lots of natural-looking floral displays. Mason jar glasses, sweet tea and lemonade. Wildflowers and daisies, things seen abundantly on the farm and around town."

Sadie wet her lips, resigned. "Chic, not elegant, is what I'm aiming for," she said. "A day to honor and celebrate all the other days. I want it to be special without looking as if I'm taking a day off to step into someone else's life. I don't need a Cinderella wedding. This— marrying George in front of everyone we love— that's my fairytale."

I pressed both palms to my heart.

Gigi cut and served the first cake while I pulled my emotions into check. "Lemon cake," she said. "This one has a sweet glaze icing and a back story."

The ladies lifted their forks and sampled dainty bites. Gigi plated one more slice and passed it to me.

"This recipe is centuries old and came from distant relatives in North Carolina. I've never met them, but my grandmama swore this cake would protect a husband's heart. I like to suggest it as a groom cake."

I sank the tines of my fork into the soft yellow dessert and slipped the sample into my mouth. The fresh lemony taste drew a smile over my lips, and the delicate glaze felt like magic on my tongue. A tiny shiver wiggled through me as a little voice said this would be my wedding cake.

I told the voice to pipe down, because no one was getting married.

—Besides Sadie and George.

"Next," Gigi moved on to the coconut.

Sadie caught my eye as the slices were served. "Do you think the wedding theme is silly?"

"Not at all," I told her. "I think it's meaningful and precious. Besides, weddings are about the bride and groom. No one else's opinion matters. It should be the story the two of you want to remember and tell your grandkids."

Evelyn snorted. "Thankfully your groom's awful manager won't be around to ruin it."

"Mama!"

"Well?" She shrugged and took another bite of the lemon cake. "He hated everything about this place and our people." She turned her eyes on me, then Gigi. "He thought we were all beneath him and he didn't bother trying to hide it. If you ask me, I think he was trying to ruin the whole wedding by being as difficult as possible. Look at how that turned out for him."

Sadie groaned.

Gigi gave me a hearty dose of side-eye. "We're terribly sorry about George's loss, and that y'all had to be around for such a terrible thing last night."

Sadie looked away, cheeks pink, then fixed a withering stare on her mother. "We talked about this," she said. "Not during cake testing. You can complain all the other hours of the day, but please, let this be about me."

"I'm talking about your wedding," Evelyn said. "That is about you." She turned back to Gigi and me. "I heard he had a problem with marriages in general, because he was in the middle of a divorce. Not a surprise since he was the absolute worst. And Beau was fighting with a much nicer colleague of his over managing George's career, so his desperation to get out of Bliss made every little thing we did a huge problem for him. Which is ridiculous, because he was the whole reason we had to rush our only daughter's wedding." She huffed. "Personally, I think George lucked out by going with the other guy. My husband was so insulted by Beau's treatment of Sadie he insisted he not be allowed to attend the wedding at all."

I turned to Gigi, mouth agape.

I wasn't a mind reader, but I was pretty sure the shocked expression on her face echoed my thoughts.

Evelyn had just delivered a whole new host of suspects.

CHAPTER NINE

I took a pastry box with lemon cake back to my shop. I couldn't wait for Mason to try it. Assuming it lasted until I saw him again. The stress of the last two days had my sweet tooth in an uproar, and I couldn't seem to get enough sugar or comfort food. At this rate, if Mason proposed, I'd have to order a dress made of elastic to accommodate my expanding waistline.

I dragged a pair of dress forms into the space behind my service counter and arranged one bridesmaid dress onto each. Business was slow, which meant I had time to start on the alterations. Now that I'd gotten details about the wedding theme, I was excited to see Sadie's vision take shape.

Leaning heavily into bliss as a verb instead of the town name as my inspiration seemed the obvious choice. The town would always be here, but Sadie and George would only share this special day once.

Ava and Gracie had decided on sundresses in muted shades of rose and periwinkle. Each design was classic and understated, but both dresses were longer than the ladies preferred, and Sadie asked me to coordinate the pair through subtle embellishments.

I turned the forms one way, then the other, envisioning my plan. Then, I searched through my drawer of lace and ribbon spools, hunting for trim in the right width and shade of cream to go nicely with both dresses. When I found what I wanted, I measured twice, then cut.

I pinned the lace to the shoulder straps, hem, and neckline of each dress, preparing it for the sewing machine.

The thrill of making something old new again brought me immense joy, and I was soon lost in the creation. I'd made similar changes so many times in my life that my hands shifted quickly to autopilot.

My mind, however, returned to the conversation with Sadie and Evelyn. I mentally replayed everything said about Beau Mercer. Then I started pulling the proverbial threads.

For starters, it was ironic that my dad, who hadn't met Beau until that night, was a murder suspect, while Sadie's father, who apparently hated the guy, wasn't even on my suspect list until now. He didn't go to my parents' place with his wife and daughter last night, but that didn't guarantee he never showed up. It seemed possible that Mr. Clarke could've popped over to the flower farm, confronted, then stabbed Beau, and headed home without anyone seeing him. Gigi had seen an extra set of headlights that night.

Evelyn's utter disdain for the man kept her on my list, but I wasn't sure how high to place her. People from Beau's past didn't like him. People from his present didn't like him. After meeting him briefly, I was certain people from his future would not have liked him either.

And he had an ex-wife! That hadn't shown up in my online search. Spouses and love interests are always prime suspects, so I figured her into the mix, too. The reason she'd married him was another mystery altogether.

The crowd of suspects pulled numbers from a ticket machine in my mind, then began to form a queue.

One more reason to be a nice person with a kind heart. Should I ever be murdered, it shouldn't be hard to find the one person angry enough to harm me.

The collection of bells over my shop's door jangled, and I exhaled, thankful for the change of subject. "Welcome to Bless Her Heart," I called.

A flash of black fur darted out from behind a nearby box, and Clyde stole a length of ribbon before my slow limbs could react. "Thief!" I yelled, but he was already gone.

Gigi's best friend, Sutton, chuckled as she headed toward the counter. Her long, shapeless muumuu was printed with large blue and green flowers to complement her Birkenstocks. Her pink socks matched nothing as far as I could see, but they were a fun pop of color. "He's been waiting for that opportunity," she said.

"I saved him from life on the streets, but he refuses to give up his life of crime."

Sutton smiled. She claimed the ability to talk to plants and animals, and she frequently delivered one of the former to me for completely random reasons. Home protection. Peace in the garden. Removal of trespassers. I hadn't been a believer in any of it until a succulent named Judy saved my life, then a cactus named Peanut helped capture a killer. Now, I put my opinions aside and tried to be useful.

"Can you believe it?" she asked. Her shoulder-length gray hair floated on the breeze from the closing door. "Another murder? There's some seriously bad juju going on in this town. I'm not sure there's enough sage in the county to cleanse it. We'd need a bonfire on the square."

I pressed my lips together and glanced around, thankful for an empty shop and no listening ears. "Ix-nay on the ad-bay uck-lay."

"What?"

I let my eyes close briefly, then decided to move on. I wasn't going to say the thing we didn't speak of. Anything that went wrong after that would be my fault, and I had enough on my mind.

"It could be the star alignment," she said, moving on. She glanced at my shop ceiling as if the universe was visible there. Sutton believed in all things unseen and every manner of what had once amounted to nuts and bananas in my mind. But the world was far more complex than I liked to think about, so I tried to focus on the little I understood.

"Does that make sense?" Sutton asked.

I tried to recall what she'd said, but I missed it. Something about the stars aligning? Misaligning? Asparagus in Gatorade, or some such. "I think so," I lied.

She nodded, pleased, and I relaxed.

"Sometimes there's a harbinger," she went on. "From what I gather, the murder streak started right before Gigi returned from the commune."

I didn't like the term *murder streak*, but what I read between the lines was even worse.

"That was right after I came home," I said. And I'd found nearly every body since then.

"Hmm." Sutton frowned. "That was when the HANS arrived as well, wasn't it?"

I smiled despite myself. Ladies around town had given Mason the nickname, HANS, as a way to talk about him without him knowing. The acronym stood for Handsome New Sheriff. I didn't disagree with the thinking.

"Yeah," I said. "But neither of us is a harbinger."

Sutton shrugged. "We're all here for different reasons." She placed a small potted succulent on the countertop and patted the top of its shiny leaves. "Judy had a baby," Sutton said, nudging the little plant in my direction. "She's exhausted and in need of time to replenish. This little one is leeching all the good nutrients, so I thought I'd separate them for a bit. The others can hardly stand Judy's attitude, and it's making for a hostile work environment. I hoped you could help."

Judy was a potted succulent. The "others" were a variety of plants sold at Sutton's shop across the square.

"This is Judy's baby?" I asked.

"Edith," she said. "I figured Judy could use some time alone in the pot with hyper-fertilized soil. Would you mind doing a little babysitting?"

"Not at all." I carried Edith to a stand holding used books and silk scarves near the window then set her in a shaft of sunlight.

Sutton had another plant in her hand when I returned. Did muumuus have pockets?

"This one's for you," she said. "She's a Pink Princess."

"Thank you." I smiled. "Any special reason?"

"Yes."

I waited, but she didn't elaborate. "Should I guess?"

"You know," she said.

I forced a smile, confused as I often was when speaking with Sutton. "Thank you."

Sutton nodded

"Are you on your way to Gigi's?"

She glanced in the direction of the etched glass door between shops. "We're testing a few organic flavors for the bliss-themed reception sweets. Lavender is always an underrated addition, as are fresh mint and rose."

I walked her to the bakery door and stopped short when my phone rang. I pulled it from my pocket and spotted Mason's name and number on the screen.

Gigi ushered Sutton inside as I answered the call.

"Hey, hon," I said. "What's up?"

"Nothing good," he said.

The long pause that followed told me I needed to take a seat before he continued.

I headed for the nearest chair. "Go on."

"The coroner confirmed your parents' shears as the murder weapon, and your dad's prints are the only ones on them."

Heat rose over my chest and neck.

That lemon cake was definitely not making it home to Mason.

CHAPTER TEN

Mason arrived ten minutes later. His concerned expression melted my already breaking heart.

I completed the sale I was ringing and wished my customer a good day, then went straight to my best friend's arms.

He planted a kiss on the top of my head. "You're not mad?"

"No." I pulled back to look into his kind eyes. "I get it." I would've been upset a year ago, when I knew less about the processes involved in a murder investigation, and I didn't know the man before me as well as I did today. Unfortunately, I'd had a wildly unnecessary amount of experience in these matters since then. "I just hate it," I admitted. "And my parents are going to lose their stuffins. Especially my mama."

Mason gave me one more squeeze before releasing me. "I know." He ran a hand through already mussed hair, making me suspect this wasn't the first time today he'd done exactly that. "I'm stumped on this one. Mercer wasn't from around here, so few people knew the guy, but everyone who met him openly admits to hating him. I can't decide if someone followed him into town, bumped him off, then went home, which would mean I'm chasing my tail talking to folks in Bliss," Mason said. "Or if the culprit is someone he upset after his arrival, and I might have a fighting chance of getting justice for the guy."

"Good luck," I said, turning toward the business side of my desk. "Hungry?"

His brows lifted with interest. "Why? Whatcha got back there?"

I hadn't had a chance to eat the lemon cake Gigi sent with me, thanks to the timing of my most recent customer. "Dessert," I said, pulling the cake from behind my counter. "Apparently this recipe is from a distant relative in the Carolinas, and it's meant to protect our heroes or something like that."

Mason strode forward, eagerly surveying the slice. "So I'm still your hero? Even after the news I delivered?"

I rolled my eyes and opened the small white pastry box, revealing the cake.

His gaze jumped from me to the box, and his smug expression morphed instantly to awestruck. "That smells incredible."

I leaned forward for a better whiff. The scents of lemons and sugar weren't just pleasant, but somewhat short of incredible. "I had a piece earlier when I joined Gigi, Sadie, and Evelyn for cake tasting." I passed him a fork. "Oh! Did you know Beau was getting divorced?"

"Yeah." Mason took a bite of cake, and his lids fluttered on a long hum. "This is amazing."

I gave the slice another look. It was good cake, but I wasn't quite as taken as Mason. Maybe he needed the pick-me-up more than I did. I waved the fork away when he tried to pass it back to me. "You eat it. I've had plenty already."

When the cake was gone, Mason settled a soothing palm

over my slightly shaking hand. "I'm not arresting your dad," he said. "There isn't any motive, but—"

"But what?"

Mason wrinkled his nose. "I have to bring him in for questioning."

I closed my eyes and felt my jaw lock.

"It's procedure."

My eyes opened, then narrowed. "Good luck explaining that to my mama."

Mason's unusually impish grin gave me pause. He took a tiny backwards step toward the door. "That's one of the reasons I wanted to stop by —"

I frowned, belatedly seeing his little visit for what it truly was.

An ambush.

"I can't do the interview, because there's a huge conflict of interest, but my deputy will stop by later and invite your dad to the station. I thought they might benefit from some advanced notice and time to process," he said. "And the best way they could receive this news is coming from you."

"Mason!"

"What?" he squeaked, then cleared his throat. "She likes me," he said, eyes pleading. "I want her to keep liking me. But I have a job to do, and they won't be as upset if the information comes from you."

I pressed my palms against the countertop. "Shame on you!"

My phone rang, and Mama's number appeared on screen. "Jeez. That's her calling now!"

"Love you!"

The bells above my door jangled as I jerked my gaze back to Mason, but the coward was already waving from the sidewalk. He mouthed the words "I am sorry," then sprinted to his waiting Jeep.

I chucked the empty cake box into the trash before answering the call, avoiding the inevitable for a few more seconds.

"Hello, Mama," I said.

"Oh! Good!" she sang. "I got her," she said softly. "Bonnie, your dad and I are on our way to visit an attorney. Don't worry! It's just precautionary, but after what happened—"

"About that," I said.

"We made bouquets for Sadie and Evelyn," she continued, whispering directions to Dad as they drove. "After what happened," she said again, apparently having decided this phrase was better than *murder*, "we wanted to be an encouragement. But we left them on the cutting table in the greenhouse. Oof." She sighed. "This whole thing just has us so rattled."

"You mean the thing that happened," I said, allowing my misplaced irritation to enter the conversation. Luckily, she was too distracted and polite to take offense.

"Yes, exactly," she said. "You understand. Well, anyway, we're late and can't turn around to get the flowers or we'll miss our appointment. Would you mind picking them up and getting them to the ladies? Oh, dear, you missed the turn," she told dad.

His muffled curse carried across the line, and I smiled.

"No, I don't mind," I said. "I'll head over to your place when Lexi gets here. She's working the afternoon shift and shouldn't be long."

"We appreciate it so much," Mama said. "I hate to rush off, but I should say goodbye and help your dad get where we're going. He's— Now you've missed it again."

"Mama," I said flatly. "Can you put me on speaker for a sec? Maybe ask Dad to pull over if he can."

I waited while they complied.

"All righty," Mama said a few minutes later. "Honey, is everything okay?"

"You pulled over?" I asked.

"We're at the bank," Dad called. "Parked in the lot. Probably looks like we're staking out the place."

"Oh, Bud," Mama cooed.

"What?" Dad groused. "If anyone in this town can truly believe I killed a stranger—fifty yards from my front door, no less, why wouldn't they think I'd rob a bank? I'll probably need to rob a bank to pay the lawyer."

"Stop saying 'rob a bank,'" Mama said. "Someone will call the police."

I dragged a palm down my face. My parents weren't like this. My parents were endlessly patient, highly organized, and unflappably kind. Most of all, they were happy in the face of every storm. They didn't forget flowers for customers or fuss at one another in parking lots. Though, I supposed their location was partially my fault.

"Mama," I tried again. "Dad. Please listen."

Their voices quieted, and someone turned off the softly playing radio.

"Thank you," I said. "Mason was just here, and he wanted me to pass on what he learned about the shears Dad found near Beau Mercer."

Mama made a little sound of excitement. "News! Bud, she has news!"

"I hope there were fingerprints," Dad said. "I never should've picked up those shears. I just saw them laying there, and I thought it was dangerous to leave them where someone could get hurt."

"No one blames you for that," I said. "The problem is that there were only one set of fingerprints."

I waited while they processed that.

"But I picked them up," Dad said.

Mama whimpered.

"We know," I said.

"I didn't kill that man," Dad announced, a bit more loudly than desirable in a bank parking lot.

"Oh, dear." Mama's shaky breaths puffed across the receiver, and I imagined her pulling the device closer to herself as her muscles tensed.

I inhaled slowly to steady myself, then pressed onward. "A deputy will stop by your place and ask you to visit the sheriff's department for an official interview," I said. "You aren't being arrested. This is just the next step in the process."

"The process of arresting me," Dad said.

"Bud!" Mama wailed.

I dropped my head against one waiting hand and listened as Dad attempted to soothe my mama. And I fought tears as she cried.

"It's going to be okay," he told her. "Mason's an excellent investigator. We trust him with our lives. More than that," he said. "We trust him with our little girl."

My heart clenched and fresh tears fell. Something about being called their little girl, despite being forty, and knowing my parents loved and trusted Mason as much as I did, had me pressing tissues to both eyes.

"Bonnie?" Mama asked.

"Yeah?" I croaked.

"What happens if Mason can't find the person who did this?"

"What do you mean?"

"Well, Mr. Mercer was from Nashville. What if the real killer is long gone, and Bud is the only suspect?"

I considered her words a moment, in search of the thing she wasn't saying outright. "He won't be arrested as a scapegoat," I said. "Is that what you're asking? If someone has to pay, and they can't find a better match, is Dad close enough to take the punishment?"

"Well," she said thoughtfully, "his fingerprints were on the weapon."

"The shears belong to him," I said. "Of course his prints are on them. That's circumstantial," I said. "Dad was right. Mason is an excellent detective, and Dad has no motive to hurt Beau Mercer. Just hang in there, okay? And figure out where you're going before you get back on the road. Distracted driving causes too many accidents."

Dad made a low, throaty sound. "I told the guy to take a hike that night, after he upset Sadie and her mom. If they mention that in their statements, it could go on record as evidence of a fight that got out of hand."

I sighed. He wasn't wrong, but he was overthinking. "Mason knows you didn't do this," I said. "Just hold on to that knowledge for now and see what your lawyer says."

At least hiring legal representation would give them something else to concentrate on, and provide added protection, just in case.

We disconnected the call a few moments later, and I tidied the shelves until Lexi arrived.

Then I was on my way to the farm, thankful for the opportunity to be useful to my parents, who did so much for me and everyone else who crossed their paths.

I brought Clyde along so he could visit Bessie.

She trotted along the path between the barn and my childhood home as I parked my car. Wind blew across the land, and she lifted her nose then flattened her ears.

"It's just us," I called.

She crouched and watched as I climbed out, rounded the hood to my passenger door, and set Clyde free.

He shot in her direction the moment I unlatched his carrier door.

It was nice to see their feline love in bloom. All my best memories were once made on this farm, and I hated that something so awful and ugly had happened here. I hoped Beau's murder wouldn't linger in my parents' hearts forever and ruin any part of the beauty they planted and grew here.

The thought turned my head in the direction of the recent crime scene, and my feet followed, pulling me along until I arrived at the spot in question. Swaths of wildflowers lay smashed and dying around me. Memories of Beau's body, the emergency responders, the crowd, and the lights flashed back to mind. The white noise of two dozen voices. Mama's cries.

I crept over the toppled flowers, searching the ground for signs of anything the police might've missed that night. Some little clue swallowed by shadows and the night. Something that might reveal itself today, give Mason some direction and my parents some relief.

I toed the ground with the tip of my shoe, gently moving the wilted buds and blooms.

Something rustled in the field of flowers, and I stilled.

Goosebumps pebbled my skin, and a chill raced down my back. "Clyde?"

I scanned the flowers, which moved gently with the breeze. Maybe I'd only heard the wind.

Or maybe it was the cats.

Maybe it's time to get the heck out of here.

I spun on my toes and hastened toward the green house.

Clyde and Bessie met me outside the open door. I supposed that meant it hadn't been them in the wildflowers a moment before. They hadn't crossed my path, and there wasn't another way to get here without me seeing them.

All the more reason to get those bouquets and get off the farm.

"Meow," Clyde said. He followed on my heels as I darted inside and headed for the cutting table.

Two bundles, neatly wrapped in lavender paper and tied in white gossamer ribbon, came into view. I picked up the pace. "Time to go," I told Clyde. "Tell Bessie we'll be back to visit when my parents are home."

A flash of black fur temporarily disrupted my view as Clyde leapt onto the table and released a low growl. Bessie curled around my calves, stopping me short of my destination.

"What are you two—"

A pile of roughly removed flower heads lay in a pile between Clyde and the neatly tied lavender paper, which now contained only stems.

Two small white cards, meant for the bride and her mother, were sliced cleanly in half. The papers lay at my feet beside a pair of Mama's pink-handled garden shears, their blades jammed firmly into the earth.

CHAPTER ELEVEN

Mama, Gigi, and I met at Bless Her Heart early the next morning, ready to try on dresses for the wedding and talk about the recent chaos. Evelyn had invited the three of us, and a plus-one each, to stay for dinner and enjoy the reception. Mama and Gigi only planned to stick around until the cake was cut and served. I wanted to stay and watch my suspects in action, but after last night, I was no longer allowed to do anything alone.

With a little luck, Mason would agree that being a fly on the proverbial wall had its benefits, especially after the bar opened. "Who knows," I said. "Maybe Mason will have this whole thing wrapped up by then."

Gigi exited her changing room in a red A-line number that fit like a flapper's dress without all the heavy beads and sequins. "Could be," she said. "I wouldn't mind sticking around if the killer's been caught. Otherwise, a big, loud event like a wedding reception seems like the kind of place a ne'er-do-well would like to wreak havoc." She twisted at the waist, admiring her reflection in the nearby mirror. The gauzy, accordion-folded material danced around her knees as she moved. "Speaking of havoc, how's Bud doing?"

Mama opened the curtain to her little room and emerged in a simple navy skirt and sleeveless cream blouse. "He was glad to be at an attorney's office when Bonnie called yesterday," she said. "The lawyer went home with us, then drove him to the sheriff's department for the interview. As if he might've left a threat behind for his own daughter." She rolled her eyes and pressed her hands against her hips. "The concept is madness. Why not assume the threat was meant for us, or for Sadie and Evelyn?"

I agreed, and from what Mason had told me, Dad's attorney was top-tier.

I counted the blessings wherever I could find them.

"I like your dress," Mama told Gigi. "It looks great with your new hair color."

As suspected, Gigi had dyed her fading locks a deep, fiery red.

Gigi curtseyed, then laughed. "Thank you, kindly. Sutton's getting really good at it. You should call her if you ever want to change your color."

"I'll keep that in mind," Mama said. "What do you think of this for the wedding?" She motioned to the skirt and blouse.

"You look like a librarian," Gigi said. "It's a wedding. Don't you want to take advantage of the chance to dress up?"

Mama's shoulders slumped. "I don't feel like celebrating. I'll be there as long as necessary to make sure things go smoothly during the ceremony and help set up the flowers at the reception, but then I'm headed home to Bud. I hate that I have to leave him at all, but he doesn't have any interest in going out. He still thinks people believe he might've killed that man." Her gaze flicked to me. "Unless Mason arrests someone else before the wedding, we're going to lay low."

I moved to the nearby rack and pulled out a sky-blue

sundress with an empire waist and a scoop neckline. "Try this."

"I'm too old for that," Mama said.

Her mother's expression hardened and she pointed to the fitting room. "We can wear whatever we want to wear."

Mama went to change.

I gave Gigi a high five. "What do you think of this?" I asked, pulling the hem of my skirt wide. The dress I'd chosen was knee length with a fitted bodice and full skirt. I'd added layers of crinoline and let them peek out from the hem. The garment originated around the time Mama was born, and I was thrilled to see it come in as a donation. I loved a good vintage number, and this one had sunflowers in the print. "It goes well with the wedding theme. I just wish it didn't pinch."

Gigi frowned. "Can you let it out a little?"

I inhaled to allow myself more room. "It's fine as long as I don't sit down."

She shot me a concerned look, but didn't comment. Instead, she asked, "Do you have something I can wear in my hair with this?"

I passed her a black feather on a clip from the table of accessories at my side. Then, I rolled my shoulders back and tugged the hem of my dress, searching for an extra inch of room. "Ugh. All the stress eating is killing me."

"Hey!" Mama called through her curtain. "Why are you stressed? You told me I had nothing to worry about."

I scratched my head and wrinkled my nose.

Gigi grinned as she worked the clip into her hair. "She's got ya there."

Mama reappeared in the blue dress, and I pressed a hand to my heart.

Gigi performed a wolf whistle.

"You look amazing," I said.

"Really?" She turned to face the full-length mirror on the wall and smiled. "It is very cute."

"We love it," Gigi said. "This is definitely the one for you."

Mama twirled, letting the skirt of the dress fly out around her. "I'll take it." Her smile fell by a fraction when she turned appraising eyes on me. "Are you that uncomfortable?"

I dropped my hands to my sides, attempting not to fuss.

Mama moved closer and tugged at the band of unforgiving fabric around my ribcage. "You look marvelous in this. You're absolutely glowing. Don't you think so, Mama?"

"You betcha," Gigi said. "It's a good one. Definitely worth the time to get the fit right. You want to be comfortable at a wedding."

"Thanks," I told them.

Mama took a seat in the chair across from the fitting rooms and adjusted the material of the skirt over her knees. "I wish I knew how to cheer up your father. It was bad enough when our biggest problem was him being a murder suspect. Now someone has been on our farm while we were away. They went into our greenhouse and left a threat behind. What was the point of that? Bud's already the main suspect."

Gigi tipped her head in my direction. "I'm installing one of those doorbell cameras, and you should too," she told Mama. "I can only see so much from my front window. A camera will be a nice addition."

Mama nodded. "I hate that it's come to this. We've been thankful never to need surveillance. Who would cause a problems on a flower farm?" She waved her hands. "I know. I know."

I rubbed a comforting hand down her arm from shoulder to elbow. "Sorry, Mama. I know Dad didn't leave the message, but I'm afraid that threat really was meant for me," I said. My parents and their lawyer had left with Mason almost immediately last night. So, they'd missed me giving my statement.

Mama's eyes widened. "What?"

I wet my lips and sighed. "Before I found the flowers, I felt as if someone was watching me. I think they saw me searching the crime scene for missed evidence."

She knitted her brows. "How did they know you were there?"

"It's possible that they followed me," I said. "Or they might've been there for the same reason. I've already told Mason, so you don't need to worry about that. He's aware." *And heavily freaking out.* "I won't go anywhere alone for a while, just in case."

Mama's eyes brimmed with unshed tears.

Gigi passed her a handkerchief.

"I'm sorry," I told her. "I didn't mean to make things worse for you."

"It's okay," she said, her voice high and squeaky. "It's just that there's so much going on and none of it is good. People aren't coming to buy plants and flowers anymore. After what happened, this town is treating Bud's and Blossom's as if it was renamed to the Felony Farm."

Gigi snorted.

I winced. "Well, don't call it that. Jeez."

Mama shrugged. "It's true. Isn't it? Everyone saw the emergency crews and the coroner driving away with a body. Now this."

I went to the chair beside her and sat to offer comfort.

The sudden, earth-quaking *rip* of my too-tight dress interrupted my thought.

"Shoot!" I jumped up, but it was too late, the seam split completely down one side of my bodice.

"Oh!" Mama cried.

I ran for the dressing room and changed into my work clothes, fighting a nonsensical wave of humiliating tears.

Mama and Gigi hugged me when I stepped out again, and I bawled.

"I'm sorry. My emotions are everywhere," I cried. "And Mason hasn't told me why Cat's in town."

"Cat's in town?" Mama asked.

Gigi retrieved a bottle of water from the mini fridge at my refreshments stand. "The FBI agent?"

I wiped my nose on a tissue, then took a long sip from the bottle. "Yeah, and—" My bottom lip quivered.

"What is it, sweetie?" Mama asked.

I couldn't hold in the other news any longer. I told them about Mason's one-kneed question that was never asked.

They goggled at me a long moment, then exchanged equally crazed looks.

"Right?" I asked. "That's exactly how I felt. Then Beau Mercer was murdered, and Dad picked up those shears, and someone is probably following me, and now it feels as if I'll never know if Mason was going to propose."

The women came at me with another group hug.

"I'm so stressed out. One day I can't eat or sleep, and the next day I can't stay awake or eat enough."

They released me, and Gigi's feather floated to the ground.

"I've got it," Mama said. But before her fingers reached the floor, Clyde swept out from beneath my chair and stole the little clip.

"Clyde!"

Gigi shook her head. "He's gone."

I let my head drop back. "Furry little outlaw."

The bells above my shop door jangled, and Lexi strode inside. She waved, then flipped the sign from CLOSED to OPEN and dropped her things behind the counter.

"Morning, Lexi," I called.

She headed in our direction. "Don't you all look nice."

"We're choosing dresses for Sadie's wedding," Mama said.

Lexi's appreciative gaze slid from Gigi and Mama to me. "You're not dressing up?"

"I have to make some alterations," I said.

The door's bells sounded again, and Sadie appeared with her bridesmaids.

"We couldn't wait," the young bride said. "We're dying to see what you've done with the dresses."

I could thank my sleepless night for the progress I'd made on those. "Of course."

"Do you want me to get them?" Lexi asked.

"No, thank you." I raised a finger to Sadie, Ava, and Gracie, signaling I needed a minute. Then I carried the ripped dress to my office and tossed it on my desk. I grabbed the dresses I'd finished during the night and carried them back to the sales floor.

Lexi stood near the fitting rooms. Mama and Gigi were missing, presumably changing out of their wedding ensembles.

"Come on over," I told Sadie and her bridesmaids.

I removed Ava's and Gracie's dresses from their garment bags and fitted them over dress forms for display. "What do you think?'

"These are magnificent," Sadie said. "Total country chic."

"I'm glad you like them," I said. "Do you want to see yours?"

"No," she gasped. "You couldn't have finished my wedding gown already."

"But I did," I said, turning my back to them as I pulled the ultra-feminine, light-as-air white gown over the last available form. The overall look was nothing short of ethereal, with delicate looped sleeves meant to fall over her shoulders and piles of sheer silky layers over a cotton slip and lace-trimmed bodice. Nothing overtly fancy, no beads or sequins or nonsense, just cotton, lace, and gossamer with endless paper-thin layers and intricate details. She'd be an absolute angel in white.

I beamed, and Sadie's eyes misted. "Oh, no! What's wrong?" I glanced back at the dresses. "There's plenty of time to adjust whatever you'd like."

Sadie shook her head and laughed through the tears. "It's just that your family has been such an incredible blessing to me. Y'all didn't only agree to help me sling together this last-minute wedding, you put up with me and Mama fussing, and you did it all with grace and class. Even after what happened to Mr. Mercer, you let this be about me, and it's all very overwhelming at times."

"Oh, hon," I said, opening my arms.

Sadie stepped forward and allowed me to comfort her a moment, before returning to Ava and Gracie for additional hugs. "Mama still thinks we should wait to get married, because there's no reason to rush things now. But we're so close, and I want to marry George. I don't understand why we'd wait. So my folks can spend more money and do all this again later? So our friends and family members can go home, then come back in a few months?"

Gracie rubbed Sadie's back. "It's not as if y'all aren't still leaving. Your mama knows that, right?"

Sadie bobbed her head noncommittally. "We've told her, but she thinks George should take his time choosing a new agent."

"New agent?" I asked, feeling the tickle of curiosity climb my spine. "George has another offer already?"

She nodded. "Mike, this guy in Beau's agency, came in for the wedding. He wanted to partner with Beau on George's representation, but Beau shut that down. Mike's willing to handle the whole thing now."

Gracie turned her eyes to me. "Which means they're still leaving as soon as possible, even if her mama doesn't want to hear it."

I bit my lip against a frown.

"Yup," Ava said. "Exactly."

Mama and Gigi appeared, carrying their chosen dresses, and greeted the bridal party.

I mulled over the possibility that Beau's colleague, Mike, might've killed him to get control of George's future. "Do you ladies want to try on the dresses?" I suggested, not quite ready for them to leave. "You should make sure everything's fitting okay."

They eagerly agreed, and I removed the garments from the forms so they could give them a try.

Mama caught my wrist after the trio beetled away. "What are you thinking?" she asked. "You've got that look in your eye."

"What look?"

"Trouble," Gigi said.

I pulled Mama and Gigi back toward the dressing rooms. "Sadie?" I called through the curtain. "Any chance the new agent is tall, dark, and handsome with black curly hair, mid-forties, blue eyes?"

"Uhm." She giggled. "I'm not sure, but that is very specific. I've only met him once, and his hair was slicked back when I saw it, still wet from a shower, I guess. You'll meet him at the wedding, though. Why? Are you in the market?"

"She dates the sheriff," Gracie chided from her fitting room next door. "Remember?"

"The HANS," Ava stage-whispered, as if the acronym was still a secret code.

I smiled. "I'm not in the market," I said. "I just saw

someone I didn't recognize around town a couple of times, and he seemed to know me."

I frowned at my own words. Was that true? Had the man watched me so closely because he knew me somehow?

The shop door opened again, and Lexi called out to the newcomer. "Welcome to Bless Her Heart."

"Whoa," Mama whispered.

"Get a load of him," Gigi added quietly.

My gaze jumped to the six-foot cowboy casting a long shadow in our direction. He tipped his hat at Lexi and strolled confidently in her direction. He wore dark blue jeans and a nicely fitting shirt. Gigi would've called him a tall drink of water if she wasn't completely speechless.

He winked, and Lexi made a strangled sound.

"Hello," I called. "How can I help you?"

He turned toward us and tipped two fingers against the brim of his Stetson. "Ma'am," he said. "I saw a group of ladies come in here while I was finishing my coffee across the way. Any chance you saw which way they went?"

I considered my answer, forcing my eyes away from the closed curtains at our side. "Friends of yours?"

"I'm the best man in the blond one's wedding. The other two like to fight over me when they can." His grin spread slowly, and his attention flickered to the fitting rooms.

"James!" Gracie yanked her curtain open and glared. "You are so full of yourself."

Ava stepped into view next, and the pair greeted him with a hug.

In a show of impressive strength and epic flirtation, he raised them off the ground several inches, one in each arm.

"Okay," Sadie called, still hiding in her little room. "State your business, then go away. I'm in my wedding gown, and I don't want you to see it."

James moved in the direction of her curtain. "I just need your eyes for a second," he drawled.

Sadie poked her head out and cinched the curtain at her neck. "Oh! The hat bands are finished!"

"Yes, ma'am," James said, tipping his head forward to give her a better view of his Stetson. "George's band is white to coordinate with your dress. Mine's black, and the other groomsmen match the dads in ivory."

Mama nodded appreciatively, either at the cowboy or the news, I wasn't sure. "How clever," she said. "A little something to set the men apart. Isn't that nice, Mama?"

Gigi's eyes were still glazed over. She didn't respond.

"The hat band looks great," Sadie said. "Thank you for showing me. Now, please go away, so I can properly admire this amazing creation. Girls only."

James shook his head and chuckled. "Yes, ma'am." He tipped his head at Ava and Gracie, then shot the group of us a wink on his way out.

"It's nice he and George made up," Gracie said, moving to the mirror to admire her dress. "I hated all that animosity between bandmates. It's good the negativity won't be around to ruin your wedding day."

"True," Sadie said, leaving the fitting room in a flourish.

Gracie rushed to her side.

My expression must've matched my thoughts, because Ava stopped in front of me, nodding.

"Those two were at each other's throats for a hot minute. James thought George owed him an introduction to Beau, and George thought it was too soon to ask his new manager to audition a friend. None of that matters now, because the new guy is giving James a chance to impress him when he sings at the reception."

She joined her friends at the big mirror, and I turned to Mama and Gigi.

Just like that, we had two more local suspects. A new manager and a jealous best man.

CHAPTER TWELVE

I met Mason at the construction site of our future home after work. I loved the location: waterfront, like my current home, but with a dock and a bit of beach. The lake was deeper here, and a pontoon boat bobbed on the water where his sunken houseboat once lived.

I still felt a little guilty about the way that, quite literally, went down. But as with most things, something better came from the problem.

The property was technically in the next town, which was the only real downside. Cromwell and Bliss had been at odds since the towns were founded. Generations later, citizens on both sides lived in gently simmering hostility where the other was concerned.

I'd gotten over my lifelong aversion to a place and people group I'd never known after meeting Thelma and Louisa, a lovely Cromwell resident and her prized hen. As it turned out, Louisa also had a bit of a nosy streak where murders were involved, and we get along just fine. Clyde adores visiting her little farm community, where everyone lives off the grid, in tune with nature, raising gardens and animals. He especially loves her miniature donkey couple, Jack and Jill.

I made a mental note to stop by again soon and tell her all about the recent chaos surrounding George and Sadie's wedding.

Mason stood near the garage, his long, lean frame silhouetted by a setting sun.

Our general contractor, Leo, flipped through a stack of pages on a clipboard. Leo was a big, no-nonsense guy. His husky voice and clipped tone always made me feel as if I was being scolded, but he moved mountains when it came to getting things done on the new build.

He was the same height as Mason but wider and doubly as thick. He wore a tool belt around his blue jeans, which were both held up by faith, as far as I could see, and his yellow logoed t-shirt matched his hard hat. Neither Mason nor I had ever seen Leo without the latter, and we often played Guess What's Under the Hat. I thought he was bald and hiding it. Mason thought Leo's hair was a shaggy mullet. Probably also hiding it.

We might never know.

"Hey," Mason said, moving immediately in my direction. "How was work?"

"Busy," I said. "It felt nice to drive away."

He grinned and pulled me into a hug. "I'm glad you're here."

I sighed and relaxed against him. "I'm glad to be here."

"Where's Clyde?"

"I dropped him off at home," I said. "How's the house coming along?"

Leo stepped closer. "I was just telling your...Mason," he amended, "that we're right on schedule. Now that the place is under a roof, the rest will go fast. A temporary electric pole has already been installed, and we had two crews here today for a solid six-hour stretch."

I felt my brows raise. "Wow."

He nodded. "Yup. Why don't y'all follow me and we'll go have a look at the progress?"

The short gravel driveway led to a two-car garage beside a wide porch with a big black front door to match the newly installed roof. One day soon there would be white vinyl siding, handrails up the front steps, and a swing outside the bay window, but that would all come later with the details and trim.

From the front, the home was a single story. The walkout lower level made the home a two-story from the back. A large cobblestone patio and walkway to the lake would soon finish the overall outdoor appeal.

Mason and I followed Leo inside and received a rundown on plumbing and electrical.

I marveled at the progress since my last visit. Future walls framed in lumber outlined a small foyer beyond the front door. A future formal dining room stretched to the right. Floor to ceiling shelves of books would complete a library on the left. Ahead of me, the open concept living room and kitchen would soon be filled with family and friends. Each of those rooms featured an abundance of windows that overlooked a deck and the lake beyond.

A staircase at the edge of the future powder room led to the lower level. Three bedrooms, two additional bathrooms, a laundry room, and a living room would complete the floor below.

We walked the space with the contractor, signed off on supply sheets and work orders, then ventured onto the rear deck when Leo left.

I inhaled the cool breeze off the water.

"Penny for your thoughts?" Mason asked.

I shoved a mass of wild curls away from my face and decided it was time to be brave. "The other morning, you said you had something to ask me."

His jaw locked.

I waited, but he didn't speak. I supposed I hadn't asked a question.

"Your phone rang," I continued. "You took the call, then left without asking whatever was on your mind."

"Cat's in town," he said.

"I saw her," I admitted. "Is that who called?"

"Yeah." Mason turned his face to the lake. "She's chasing a lead on one of her cases."

"Which one?"

He slid his eyes briefly in my direction, then back to the water. "I'm sure it's classified. She's still FBI, and I'm a local sheriff."

I narrowed my eyes. "So a Cleveland, Ohio FBI agent followed a lead on one of her cases to Bliss, Georgia," I said. "Any chance this has anything to do with you?"

Mason barely moved, but I felt the tension in his frame, the bunching of his muscles and tightening of his jaw. "Unlikely."

I certainly hoped not.

"It's odd, though," I said. "Half the people in this state don't know this place exists, but someone from Ohio made it all the way here. Just like you." The last time Cat had come to town about a case, she'd been following a lead on the group who wanted Mason dead for his part in breaking up their crime ring.

Mason hung his head for one quick beat, then raised a mischievous smile and pulled me close. He sighed as he hugged me, sinking into my returned embrace. "I haven't gotten the chance to tell you how beautiful you look today, or how lucky I am to get to hold you like this so often."

I groaned. This was a top-tier distraction technique, and we both knew it. My love language was human touch, closely followed by words of affirmation, and Mason delivered both by the boatload.

Still, I didn't like the possibility Cat was here because Mason was in danger.

Nonsensically, I didn't want to let him out of my sight. I couldn't protect him from the kinds of people who wished him harm, but somehow, as long as I could see him, it seemed reasonable that he would be okay.

"Mason?" I asked, tipping back my head until I could look into his cautious eyes. "Do you want to come to Sadie and George's wedding with me?"

"I'd love to."

"Really?"

He grinned. "Of course. I like going anywhere with you."

I narrowed my eyes. "How about the rehearsal dinner tomorrow night?"

He pursed his lips.

"Problem?" I asked.

"I'll try," he said. "I have some appointments set for tomorrow. I'm really trying to get your dad off the hook as soon as possible."

"Hard to argue with that," I said.

Mason kissed my head. "You ready to go home?" he asked. "You had a long day. You're probably getting hungry. I know I am. And Clyde's waiting."

I turned to stare out at the lake and sighed. "Just a few more minutes."

Mason tucked me against him, and we watched the fiery glow of a setting sun slip into the water. "Take as long as you want."

. . .

I called my therapist in the morning and set up an appointment. My anxiety was through the roof. I'd had too many run-ins with too many killers, and the recent murder, among other things, had me all out of sorts. She fit me in on the Monday following Sadie and George's wedding, and she was sure to get an earful by then.

I was a mess. I couldn't differentiate between good and bad excitement anymore. Rushing to get to the rehearsal dinner on time felt exactly like being chased by a killer. Anything and everything that made my heart race turned to fear in my mind, as if my next breath could be my last.

I'd have insisted on seeing her sooner if I could've found a whole hour when I was available between now and then.

Meanwhile, I dressed for the wedding rehearsal in a flowy, one-piece romper with cap sleeves and long wide legs. The taupe color was neutral enough to coordinate and blend with the wedding theme. The white stretchy belt, rolled scarf I'd fashioned as a headband, and strappy sandals added a dash of personal style.

Mama and Gigi were already at the Clarkes' farm when I arrived. The rehearsal and dinner were being held a day earlier than was traditional, leaving a day between this event and the wedding due to scheduling conflicts. Making all this happen on such short notice was one thing; rearranging the calendar of a large dairy farm was another.

In truth, having the extra time between events was nice, especially for Gigi, Mama, and me. Everyone could take tomorrow to reassess and make any last-minute tweaks, have one last dress fitting, and finalize those beautiful desserts and bouquets. All those small details would add up to a big day of perfection.

I spotted the Bud's and Blossom's Flower Farm truck and pulled into the space beside them.

I followed the sound of instrumental music toward a

huge white event tent and welcome sign. A massive pergola fashioned before the entrance had been draped in white satin sashes and flanked by an array of large planters and floral displays. Grand, beautiful evidence my mama had been hard at work already today.

Inside the cavernous structure, round tables covered in linen cloths fanned out in a circle. Matching white bows were tied around the chair backs and sunflowers in mason jars acted as centerpieces. Miles of round bistro lights bobbed from metal supports overhead and hung in wide swoops near the head table and exits. A giant chandelier was suspended from the central peak. Its dangling crystals cast rainbows of sunlight over everything beneath.

Men and women in various levels of dress chatted and laughed as they sipped from sweaty glasses and cleaned their fancy plates.

I gave a soft wolf whistle as I took it all in.

Anyone who thought having a rehearsal dinner on a farm was boring or bland had clearly never been to a Clarke family wedding.

I spotted Mama and Gigi putting final touches on the desserts table, then headed in their direction.

"Hello, sweetie," Mama said, pulling me into a hug. She sniffled and coughed lightly.

I offered a small wave. "Still fighting that cold?"

She nodded. "All this stress isn't helping."

I took a step back, not wanting to catch whatever she had. My stress was also off the charts. "Am I late?"

"No," Gigi said. "Apparently some bickering started during the rehearsal, so they cut it short and brought everyone in here." She spoke softly, then turned her back to the room and rolled her eyes. "A little food, and some time out of the sun seemed to help them regroup."

I lifted my brows. "Yeah?"

Mama ran a tissue under her nose and nodded. "I heard the minister say they'll run through it all again when the sun goes down and it gets a little cooler."

I scanned the tables of men and women. Some in lovely dresses and heels, others in blue jeans and cowboy boots. "Who was bickering?"

"We didn't hear that part," Mama said. "Everyone has been fine since they came inside."

Gigi went back to her work on the dessert table and placed the final tray of cutout cookies shaped like sunflowers on display. "Let's eat."

Ninety minutes later, we'd enjoyed the lovely catered meal with everyone else, and it was time to move the festivities back outside.

I helped Mama and Gigi relocate a selection of desserts to a designated table, while the wedding party ran through tomorrow's ceremony once more.

Farmhands built a colossal bonfire in the field beyond the barn, and I watched in awe as it was lit. The whoosh of flames up the central column drew my hands together in a soft clap. The men smiled and tipped their hats in response.

The new, outdoor refreshments table held pitchers of lemonade and sweet tea along with a selection of wine and glasses. Mama and Gigi set out additional cookies as the wedding party made their ways to the fire.

Several groomsmen backed pickup trucks into a nearby row and let down their tailgates. Coolers of beer soon appeared, and country music lifted from speakers.

George took Sadie's hand and guided her into a spin while their friends hooted and applauded.

I scanned the onlookers as Gracie approached for a glass of lemonade.

"Aren't they the cutest?" she asked, nodding to the bride-and-groom-to-be.

"They are," I agreed.

"I hope you like a party," she said, eyes widening with pleasure. "It's going to get crowded soon. The Clarkes invited all the wedding guests to the bonfire."

As if on cue, folks soon appeared in droves, as if on cue. Smiling faces and merry voices heightened the already celebratory mood.

"I love this," I told her. "The night's shaping up to be a beautiful, blissful event."

Gracie grinned. "Exactly what Sadie wanted."

I scanned the growing crowd. "Which one is George's new talent manager?"

I thought again of the dark-haired man I'd seen twice on the square. I didn't see him in the mix.

"Apparently he's allergic to sunflowers." Gracie frowned. "Can you imagine?"

"No." I could not.

But if what Gracie said was true, and sunflowers were prevalent on the flower farm, especially in the field where Beau died, could he have been the killer? *Could he be somewhere else right now, healing from the exposure?*

Rising voices drew my attention to the groomsmen, now gathered near the tailgate of a large blue pickup truck.

"I can't believe you're getting married tomorrow," one man called to George as the song ended.

George dipped, then kissed Sadie before heading toward the other men.

"And leaving us," a second guy added. "Gone in forty-eight hours. How can it be?"

Gracie inched closer to my side. "Those are all his band members," she said. "Here comes James."

My gaze snapped to the man who'd recently visited my store, and I tracked him to the group.

"We were all supposed to go to Nashville together one

day," James called, jumping into the conversation as he closed the distance. "You take Sadie on one date for karaoke, and suddenly we're left in the dust." He smiled, but the congeniality didn't reach his eyes.

George shook his head. "It's not like that. You know it."

"Nah," the first man said again. "We know. We're happy for you, man." He clapped George on the shoulder, but his words didn't seem to resonate with the others. Especially James.

"That's Tom," Gracie said. "He looks nice, but he's mean as a snake."

"Do you think any of them are angry about George's stroke of luck?"

Gracie snorted. "Are you kidding? They all want to be him. If not for the chance at fame, then for his relationship with Sadie. Those two have been together since they were fourteen. No one else has ever had a chance, and they hate it. Can't blame them," she added. "Sadie's the best person I know, and I can't imagine not having the opportunity."

"You think Tom might be jealous for both reasons?"

As if somehow hearing me through the hubbub, Tom's sharp blue eyes jerked to mine, and I looked away.

"Busted," Gracie whispered, then turned with me to select two cookies. "I'd better get back to Sadie."

I nodded, unable to speak. Fresh panic welled in my chest. Surely Tom hadn't really heard us. It was impossible. Wasn't it?

"Sweetie?" Mama asked. She moved swiftly to my side and rubbed a palm against my back. "You feeling okay?"

"Mm hmm."

Gigi approached with a mason jar of iced water. "Here. Sip. Maybe sit."

The soft strumming of a guitar drew our attention.

Across the fire, George perched on a tailgate and looked

lovingly at his soon-to-be wife. "I wrote this song for you in ninth grade," he said. "And I knew I'd sing it on our wedding day."

Mama, Gigi, and I took seats and listened as he sang.

Tom fell into conversation with others in the crowd and, thankfully, didn't look my way again.

Night fell as the band joined George in several of their songs. When they took a break, someone turned up the radio, and guests began to dance.

"That's my cue," Gigi said. "I didn't mean to stay this long. Now I'll be baking until dawn if I want to open the shop tomorrow."

Mama rose and arched her back in a stretch. "It has gotten late. I hope Bud's okay." She turned to the dessert table and began to pack the extras into boxes, leaving the lids open for folks to continue sampling. The containers would make it easier for the Clarkes to transport the sweets inside later.

I dragged my gaze across the darkened field in search of Sadie, Evelyn, or George. "I'll say goodbye for us," I volunteered.

I moved slowly through the knots and clusters of people, listening to snippets of conversations as I passed. I wondered again about the jealousy of George's bandmates and the whereabouts of the new manager.

Evelyn had smiled more tonight than I'd seen before. The look on her face spoke of pride and reluctant joy. Even if she wasn't getting the wedding she'd had in mind for her daughter, Sadie's happiness seemed to make it difficult for her to stay angry.

Her dad, on the other hand, didn't speak or interact much at all. Aside from the occasional dip of his chin or lift of one hand in greeting, he was silent and stoic. Everyone gave him space. I couldn't tell if that was his general disposition or if something specific had upset him.

Currently, he, like the rest of his family, was nowhere to be found.

A flash of light in the distance drew my eyes, and everyone else's, to a scarecrow suddenly ablaze.

Time seemed to freeze before several of the men burst into action, racing first toward the barn, then into the field with buckets. Water sloshed over the edges of each pail as they raced into the stalks of corn.

I followed, unwilling to wait for a secondhand account.

Mama and Gigi watched, mouths agape as I hurried past them.

The flames were out when I arrived, easily squelched by fast, capable, cowboys.

But no one turned to leave.

Sadie and her bridesmaids stared, wide-eyed, at me as I approached.

Evelyn frowned from her position near the straw-stuffed scarecrow, now black from ash and dripping with water. Instead of the typical plaid shirt and denim overalls, this thing wore a dress. The face was blank, but its head was topped with a wig of ratty red hair— uncomfortably reminiscent of mine.

CHAPTER THIRTEEN

I was nauseous with fear all the way to work the next morning. I wasn't sure if Mason slept, but he'd checked on me frequently while I tried. As far as I could tell, he'd stayed awake on his phone or laptop long after we'd left the crime scene. His nerves were stretched thin, and he'd offered to drive me to Bless Her Heart after breakfast, but I'd hated the thought of being stranded without my car, so I declined.

My teeth chattered with excess adrenaline as I prepared the shop for the day and awaited my first customers. Lexi would be in for a while in the afternoon, and Sadie or Evelyn would be in to pick up their dresses, but until then I'd be alone with Clyde and Edith. I wasn't sure how much the cat or potted plant could do to protect me if needed.

The day was bright and sunny, but I'd chosen a long black skirt and matching sleeveless top with white piping along the hem and neckline. I wasn't one to wear black without reason; the color made my already alabaster skin impossibly fairer, like an ill Victorian-era child. But the ensemble felt right today.

I crossed my arms over a roiling stomach as I stood, anxiously behind my counter, working on a replica of the lake house to focus my restless energy. I'd found a little dollhouse at a thrift store last summer and brought it to the store, planning to sell it at Christmas. Then, I realized it was the perfect medium for testing possible design choices at Mason's new home. I used various small swatches of fabric as rugs and wallpaper, magazine cutouts for wall art, and occasionally actual dollhouse furniture as feng shui visuals.

I swallowed a yelp when my phone dinged with an incoming message.

Evelyn Clarke's name appeared onscreen. She'd be late picking up the dresses. Both she and Sadie were feeling ill.

I thought of Mama's recent cough and my increasing nausea. I'd passed my issues off as stress-induced, but perhaps everyone was getting sick. Was a bug going around?

A whole lot of people had gathered to celebrate last night. I hoped whatever affected Evelyn and Sadie this morning wouldn't spread. Something like that could ruin a wedding.

The bells over my door jangled, and I spun for a look at the newcomer.

My lifelong best friend, Cami, strode gracefully inside, a bright smile on her beautiful face. "Morning, gorgeous," she said. "How are you feeling today?"

I'd called her last night while Mason completed a report at the crime scene, and I'd filled her in on the scarecrow debacle. "Not great," I said.

She wrinkled her nose. "You look paler than usual."

"Black isn't my color."

She narrowed her eyes, assessing. Her warm brown skin was sun-kissed from a long morning outdoors. She'd probably finished a five-mile jog before I finished breakfast. The thought of running made me want to sit down.

I took a moment to admire her style, however. Today, she wore white capris with tan leather flats and a silk, navy blue tank top, all of which accentuated her lean and willowy figure. If Cami was elegant confidence, I was whimsical chaos. She was also the closest thing I'd ever had to a sister.

"Feeling any better about what happened last night?" she asked.

Memories of the charred scarecrow returned to mind, and I shivered. Images of the ratty red wig had haunted my night. "I just can't believe someone would do that," I whispered. "And at a wedding rehearsal."

Then again, someone had murdered Beau Mercer on a flower farm.

"Any ideas?" she asked.

My tired mental wheels creaked slowly into motion. "Anyone could've also gained access to the scarecrow," I said. "I have no idea how to narrow that down."

"Did any of the guests seem out of place?" she asked. "If Beau's wife killed him, then showed up to the rehearsal to threaten you, surely someone wouldn't noticed."

I shook my head. "I found her account on social media late last night. Apparently, she's an aspiring model, currently on a photoshoot in Fiji."

"Well, that's one person down, I guess," Cami said.

"It leaves George's jealous bandmates and Sadie's frustrated parents," I said. "Though I can't see Evelyn as a cold-blooded killer. She's more of an avid complainer."

"What about the new talent manager?"

"I didn't see him," I said. Then again, that didn't mean he wasn't there.

"The mystery continues," she said.

"Yeah," I agreed. And I had more than one big question left unanswered.

Her gaze wandered to a jewelry display on the counter, and she tried on a set of bangle bracelets before trading them for something more bohemian chic.

"Cami," I said, pulling her attention back to me. "Have you noticed a dark-haired man with very blue eyes around town? He's somewhere in the vicinity of our age and dresses a little too well to fit in quite right." I knew, even as I asked, that it was a thin description in a town full of wedding guests. But if anyone was out and about regularly, it was Cami. Her job as the head of our town beautification committee kept her on the move, overseeing anything and everything that might bring locals back downtown for shopping and increase tourism.

Her brow puckered. "I haven't, but I'll keep an eye out now. Why do you ask?"

"A hunch," I said. "I've seen the same man watching me from the square twice now, and I wonder if he's the new talent manager. Sadie said he wanted to help with George, but Beau wasn't interested. Then he swooped in and offered representation the minute Beau was out of the picture."

Her furrowed brow suddenly rose. "He certainly makes a solid suspect. Anything else?"

I inhaled slowly, then released the breath on a long sigh. "I can't believe I've forgotten to mention this, but Cat's back in town on a case. I want to be sure this mystery man isn't here looking for Mason and watching me as a means of finding him."

Cami's jaw dropped. "I'll ask Dale if he knows anything about Cat's presence. Meanwhile, be careful," she warned. "Mason's the sheriff. Anyone can find him. If they're after him but watching you— that is not good news."

I winced, hearing the implication loud and clear. If someone wanted to hurt Mason, getting their hands on me would do the trick. And I had too much on my plate at the moment to become some henchman's prey. "Point taken."

"How's Mason doing after the whole red-headed scarecrow thing?" she asked, voice softening as she returned the bracelet to the display.

"Not great," I said. "He was furious when he saw it, all business at the crime scene, then he barely spoke after we got home. He just held my hand and worked on his laptop until I went to bed."

I'd braced for his blame or a thorough scolding, but when I told him to get it over with, he'd looked stunned. "He was incredibly sweet," I said. "He assured me this wasn't my fault, and he barely let me out of his sight all night. When I didn't accept his offer to drive me to work, he followed me here and walked me to the door. I half-expected to find him waiting outside the bathroom while I showered this morning."

"He loves you," she said. "He's worried. And he knows how quickly bad people can take away the ones he loves."

I felt the air leave my lungs at Cami's reminder.

Several years ago, while undercover in Cleveland, as part of a joint task force with the FBI, Mason had fallen in love with a woman who was part of The Investors' crime ring. She was heartbroken when she figured out his secret, but she gave her life rather than admit his duplicity. Her death was an example for others, because The Investors had already known the truth. Her loyalty had shifted, and they couldn't—wouldn't allow it.

"I guess it's a good thing I packed my lunch," I said. "I'm suddenly certain I don't want to go anywhere else today."

"Excellent idea," she said. "Hey, what is that?" She pointed to my dollhouse.

"I'm planning the lake house color scheme and décor," I

said. "I thought it would be smart to mock up the interior design, before I start making and buying things."

Cami smiled, leaning forward for a better look at my work. "It's even got a little black cat."

"Of course."

Clyde darted onto the counter, and I swung a protective arm in front of my project.

"Do not," I said firmly. "This is mine."

He lowered onto his belly and watched as I moved tiny furniture from room to room.

"I can't decide where the couch should go, but I'm definitely making pillow covers in shades to reflect the natural elements and views beyond the windows," I told Cami. "I'm not sure about the overall style, though. Just the general palette."

"What about your house?" she asked. "Will you sell?"

I glanced away, then tucked the little replica behind the counter. "I don't want to," I admitted aloud for the first time. "And I hope he'll understand. I just can't imagine giving up my home to live with my boyfriend. I'm forty, not nineteen. I'm divorced. I know relationships fail. I'm not saying Mason and I will break up," I backpedaled. "I think what we have is different. It's mutual. Built on friendship and respect. I think we are highly likely to grow old together, if fate allows us both that opportunity, but —"

"You aren't interested in giving up your space and your security to live with him when you aren't married," she said. "It's a big risk that, heaven forbid something goes wrong, would leave you scrambling to reestablish yourself."

"Exactly."

"I get it," she said. "I'd feel the same way, and I know Mason will understand. Anyone would."

I hoped she was right.

Clyde flopped onto one side, looking listless, and drawing our attention.

"What's his problem?" Cami asked.

I rolled my eyes. "Speaking of relationships. I think he misses Bessie. We haven't been out to the flower farm in a couple of days."

Cami gave Clyde a pouty face, then stroked his sleek black fur. He purred in response to the attention.

"I plan to check on my folks soon," I said. I hadn't been there since I found the mauled bouquets. "I'll take him with me."

"How's your dad doing?"

"Okay, I guess," I said. "He and Mama say business is slow. They're worried people might think the place is bad l-u-c-k."

Cami grimaced. "Oof."

"I know," I agreed. "I need Sadie and George's wedding to go off without a hitch so I can spread word of my parents' beneficial involvement. Maybe even spin them as good luck charms."

"That would help. They could also offer up the farm for a special afterparty," she suggested. "The wedding's at eleven with a lunch reception. Everyone will already be dressed up and out of their houses. They might as well keep the fun going with a trip to Bud's and Blossom's that night."

I laughed. "Okay, but for what, if all the festivities are already over? The reception ends at four. Folks will be home in time for dinner."

Cami's gaze moved to the ceiling, and she bit her lip as she thought. "Oh!" She turned bright eyes back to me. "How about a paper lantern event at twilight? Guests can write prayers and well-wishes for the happy couple on those little floating lanterns, then release them onto Turtle Lake. Can you imagine how magical that will look? Surrounded by all those gorgeous flowers and the twinkle lights your parents have in the trees back there? It will be gorgeous!"

Turtle Lake was a large pond at the back of my family's farm. Gigi had named it while she was growing up on the land. Apparently, she saw a turtle on a rock in the water, and the rest is history. The name had stuck for seventy-or-so years so far, and it made me smile whenever I thought of Gigi as a rambunctious preschooler.

I felt a flutter of hope in my middle. A nice, positive experience like that would go a long way to assuage any lingering bad vibes with locals. "I'll call my parents and run it by them," I said. "Then I'll talk to Sadie and George. If everyone's on board, I'll get the lanterns and supplies."

The cost would be well worth it, if it helped ease my parents' minds about the future of their business and reputations.

Clyde stretched one long arm toward the little potted succulent, and I slid the plant a few inches away.

"Another gift from Sutton?" Cami asked.

"No." I grinned, realizing I'd forgotten all about the odd exchange with Sutton until now. "I'm babysitting."

Cami's lips curled into a smile. "Oh?"

"This is Edith, Judy's daughter," I explained. "Apparently she needed a break."

"Sutton?"

I shook my head. "Judy."

The small, indelicate snort that came from Cami's button nose made me laugh.

"Is this one special like her mama?" Cami asked. "If so, maybe she can lean fate in our favor. Help Cat with her mission. Protect you and Mason as needed. Find that music manager's killer and restore your parents' good names."

"That's a lot to ask of a little one," I said, lifting the little pot with my fingertips and affecting a silly voice. "Besides, she's just a baby."

"Her mama saved you from a murderer. Why can't little Edith carry on family traditions? Accomplish the impossible, bend Lady Luck to our will?"

I smiled at the small green lump in her terracotta home. "You heard her, Edith. We're all counting on you."

Cami pointed at the plant. "Get to work!"

CHAPTER FOURTEEN

*L*exi arrived in the afternoon, stunning as always in her wide-legged jeans and black tube top. She'd pulled her long dark hair into a low ponytail and tied it with a vintage satin scarf. The cherry-print pattern matched her red high top tennis shoes. Somehow Lexi managed to make every outfit seem chic, regardless of how casual the pieces were. She had an artist's heart and mind. If she had the desire, I was certain she'd be the next big name in design, fashion, interior, or otherwise.

We planned the new window display for about an hour, then split up when customers arrived. I liked to change the view of Bless Her Heart for passersby every ten days or so to remind folks my inventory was new all the time.

When Lexi went to help a group of ladies preparing for their high school reunion, I took the opportunity to clear my head of uglier things and returned my attention to the dollhouse. The pink and white exterior was a far cry from Mason's new build, but I had a good imagination, and inside, the space worked well— after I knocked out a couple of walls.

I'd started with online vision boards and color palettes but had since escalated to collecting fabric swatches and samples of anything that internet stores would send me. I was far too visual to take on such an enormous and important project without a plan I could see, touch, and manipulate to perfection.

Everything was going well until I took a break to look for information online but accidentally searched for The Investors instead.

There were a surprising amount of articles about the criminal organization without a whole lot of new information. I'd learned from Mason that The Investors were a group of shiny-looking crooks, each with a record a mile long. They appeared to be part of high society, when in truth, they were thieves. Safe crackers. Swindlers. Art burglars and frauds.

And on occasion, murderers.

I'd set up a Google alert last year to let me know when anything new was posted about them. All that had turned up lately was a single arrest. The write-up was thin on details, but I was happy nonetheless. The organization was small enough that every member behind bars made a significant impact on their ability to do harm. Hopefully the recent apprehension was the first of many to come. Maybe the affiliate Cat hat followed to Bliss was simply on the run and not looking for my boyfriend.

Or maybe she wasn't here on business at all. Maybe she was here for another engagement?

I bit my lip, fighting a smile, then panic swept in, and I began waffling.

Is Mason going to propose?
Is someone in town to kill him?
Are neither of these things true? Are both?

I wanted to puke again.

An eruption of laughter drew my attention to the front window and tensed my muscles to spring. I envied the group of passersby for their carefree expressions. I was in dire need of a few moments like those. My week had started with Mason's mysterious question, which looked suspiciously like a proposal, but was dropped and never mentioned again. Then the rushed wedding planning and Cat's appearance. A murder and threats. Mom's anguish. Dad as a suspect. Frankly, it was all just too much. My nerves were shot, and my stomach was wrecked.

My gaze shot across the street to the town square, making sure the handsome, dark-haired man wasn't there. Maybe he was just a tourist. A harmless wedding guest. A music talent agent. Regardless, he gave me the creeps.

I should've felt relief to find children on the bench instead of the stranger, but I only grew more anxious. If he was up to no good, where was he now?

I set my phone aside and practiced my breathing. Several deep inhales. Long, slow exhales. Then I shook my hands out at the wrists.

I wasn't sure the effort had helped, but that was all I could do at the moment. So, I returned my focus to the dollhouse. Specifically, the little pink nursery where I'd hung accordion-folded paper in the windows and did my best to cover the dancing circus animals on the walls. I arranged little bookshelves and a torch light, drawn onto cardstock and then cut out to create an office. But the space still looked as if a crib belonged in the corner.

I'd always wanted to be a mother. How could I not with a mother and grandmother like mine? Mama and Gigi had set the best examples and made their jobs look like blessings instead of work. They tackled parenthood with grace and joy, even when they were clearly exhausted or at their wits' end. They laughed when they wanted to cry. They declared things like, "One day I'll look back on this and see humor." Or "I know I'll miss this craziness one day. Today is not that day!" They said it was easy for them to see the positive and look beyond the troubles, because they knew they weren't alone. They had a community. A support system. A village.

I'd long yearned to follow their leads, but the Universe had other plans. My awful ex-husband and I tried for more than two decades. Pregnancy simply wasn't a possibility for me. I'd worried that might be a dealbreaker for Mason, because my ex never tired of telling me about his disappointment on the matter. He saw it as a personal flaw or failure. But Mason didn't see the problem.

In fact, he suggested we foster and adopt, if that was what I wanted. He said he didn't need to create biological offspring to be a father, and I didn't need to give birth to be a mother. He'd even planned a home far larger than necessary for the two of us, so we'd always have our options open. There was never any pressure with Mason, and there was always unconditional acceptance. I loved him more whenever I thought about that.

Lexi appeared in my peripheral vision, and I turned to watch as she approached with Clyde on her tail.

I hadn't even noticed him leave me.

"I have located the dragon's lair," she declared, opening her cupped hands to reveal a bounty of small shiny things. "Clyde made a new hiding place behind the stack of books on top of the shelving unit over there." She tipped her head in the direction of our floor-to-almost-ceiling unit. "I was dusting and costume jewelry kept falling off. I got a ladder to take a look and behold the bounty."

I laughed as Clyde leapt onto the counter, green eyes fixed on his stolen merchandise. "Well, he certainly has excellent taste," I said, stroking a hand down his sleek black coat while Lexi moved the items out of his reach. "Maybe he can help me decide between bronze and black stair railings at the new lake house."

"Meow," Clyde agreed. He dragged the sound out for several beats, and I laughed again.

"I think he prefers black," Lexi said.

"How could he not?" I agreed.

My phone rang, and Lexi walked away, likely to return the jewelry items to their proper locations. Clyde moved on to grooming his little black mittens and face.

I relaxed when I saw the builder's number on screen. "Hello?"

"Ms. Bonnie?" Leo asked.

"Yes."

He sighed. "Thank goodness. This is Leo, and I'm out here at your— Mason's build site. I tried calling him first, but he didn't answer. I don't want to worry you, but there's an issue, and a deputy is on the way to clear it up. I thought you could pass the information on to Mason for me. I left a message, but it seems like something he should hear from a person, not a recording."

I gathered my purse and keys. "Of course. I can be there in fifteen minutes. What sort of issue?" Anything that required a deputy was something I wanted to see for myself. Hopefully not a fire or vandalism. The home had only been under roof for a week. To have to replace anything so soon, especially now, would send me straight into the lake.

"Uhm," Leo said. "Actually, the deputy just arrived. I'm going to talk to him."

I covered the phone's speaker with one hand and caught Lexi's curious gaze. "Something's wrong at the new house, and I'm going to run out there for a few minutes."

She nodded.

"Was there a break-in?" I asked before Leo could disconnect our call.

"Yes, but there's no need to come all the way out here. I just wanted to be sure Mason got the message."

My muscles tensed, and I felt my shoulders climb to my ears. "On my way," I said. "Thank you, Leo."

I disconnected and dialed Mason as I walked to my car.

Clyde jumped into the window display and watched as I slid behind the wheel.

"Bonnie?" Mason answered as the call connected to the convertible's speakers. "Everything okay?"

"Nope," I said. "But I can handle it."

I started the engine and told him what I'd learned while he groaned.

"I didn't answer Leo's call because I'm in the middle of something," Mason said. "At least no one was hurt. You're okay?"

"I am."

"All right," he said. "I'll meet you there."

The drive to the lake was beautiful. The views, panoramic. Normally, heading this way was my favorite trip of the day. At the moment, however, my stomach was in knots. My chest, neck, and cheeks were unnaturally hot. And a dozen awful images played on a loop in my mind. Most featured the red-wigged scarecrow. As if the thing might've escaped its box in the evidence room at the sheriff's department and come to harass me at the new house instead.

My gaze trailed repeatedly to the rear-view mirror as homes became fewer and further between. When only trees and fields remained, I started worrying that this whole thing was a trap to draw me away from civilization. I feared the killer would appear in a car on my tail and crash into me, or wait for me to get out at the lake house, then pounce.

I turned up the radio to drown out my unhelpful thoughts and assured myself this wasn't a trick. I knew Leo's voice. He called me. This was real. A deputy was on the way, as was Mason. I was safe. Everything was fine. And whatever had happened at the house likely had nothing to do with me.

Still, my foot pressed the accelerator with renewed purpose. Better to rip off the bandage.

A gaggle of geese waddled onto the road when the lake came into view, and I stopped to wait while they passed at their leisure.

The silliness of it broke the spell of doom and dismay, and I smiled.

Get it together, Bonnie Balfour, I thought. *There's nothing to worry about until there is.*

Everything else was just a case of wild imagination with a heaping helping of catastrophizing.

When the geese finished the slow-mo parade, I motored onward with a clearer head and improved internal monologue. I relaxed when I rounded the final turn and saw Mason's Jeep already in the driveway.

I parked behind him and beside a deputy's cruiser. Leo's truck sat closest to the garage, tailgate down. A clipboard and toolbox lay on the little extended surface, as if the contractor had been ready to work until something stopped him.

It was time to find out what that had been.

I smiled at the layer of stone on the base of the home that hadn't been there on my last visit. A mason had started the process while I'd had breakfast and gone to work on the square. Painters had given the front door a heavy coat of black paint, making it appear regal and welcoming. I could easily imagine a white tulip wreath in the spring, a pine and holly berry version at the holidays, and two large potted topiaries on either side. A nice heavy rug topped by a welcome mat at the threshold.

Beyond the beveled glass side lights, several shadowy figures gathered inside.

I climbed the steps and hustled to join them.

Mason's eyes met mine the moment I entered the foyer, then he crossed the space to my side. An expression of concern marred his handsome face, and his dark brows drew into a V. "Two threats in two days doesn't bode well," he said. "I'm calling this escalation based on proximity."

My feet anchored in place as he took my hand. "What?"

"Coming to our home crosses that line."

I turned to face him as he spoke, keenly aware of the other two men quietly watching. "There was a break-in," I said.

Mason nodded.

Yet the front door and windows were in perfect condition.

"You think it was a threat?" I asked. He'd called it *an escalation.*

From what?

Mason raised our joined hands, lacing our fingers, then setting his free palm on top. His jaw locked as he stared into my eyes. Then he tucked me protectively against his side and turned us toward the vaulted space that would soon be our living room. "Let's take a look and see what you think."

I shuffled forward with him, nodding absently at the deputy and Leo as we crossed the heavy sheets of subfloor where a series of choppy letters were spray-painted in red.

You're out of time.

CHAPTER FIFTEEN

Mason and I rose before dawn the next morning, neither having slept much throughout the night. The message left at the new house had shaken us. Why would the killer go there and not to my place? Maybe the other location was an easier target? Or because there were few neighbors and less traffic out that way? Whatever the reason, the criminal had reached their goal. We were unnerved in the extreme and both lost sleep over it.

There was something especially sinister and invasive about coming into another person's home, even if the place wasn't quite finished. Leo promised to check all windows and door locks at the end of each day to prevent a reoccurrence, but that wasn't enough to put Mason's mind at ease. He researched home protection companies online and into the wee hours, then ordered a top-notch security system for installation as soon as possible.

I'd curled at his side, imagining a killer lurking just beyond our walls. I wasn't sure what I'd done to escalate things, but clearly someone thought I was too close for comfort. I took a small amount of misplaced satisfaction in that.

Mason and I moved slowly around the kitchen as the sun rose, making coffee and preparing breakfast. I'd assumed he would go to work, handle something or other there, then meet me at the wedding, but so far he was stuck to my side.

Another silver lining. I always had fun with Mason, and I loved weddings.

Sadie and George would marry in a few hours, and I dearly hoped the whole thing would go off without a hitch.

Meanwhile, there was peace in familiar processes as we moved through the kitchen, part of a well-choreographed dance. I mixed batter in a big bowl, and Mason scooped the finished product onto a little press, making golden brown waffles for us to enjoy.

I rinsed berries from the garden and piled them into a strainer for sweet toppings, then made a carafe of coffee.

We carried our meal onto the rear patio and enjoyed the final glow of sunrise over the water. I loved these moments, the cool breeze off the lake, this man, this house. And I knew in my heart I couldn't sell. Cami had understood. I couldn't leave myself with nowhere to go if something went wrong between Mason and me.

Maybe that was my trauma talking, but I had enough money to keep the property, and I would. Maybe I'd rent it as one of those Airbnbs.

I didn't have to ask to know Mason would understand. He never judged.

"You're awfully quiet," Mason said, finishing his waffles and kicking back a bit. He hooked one booted foot over the opposite knee as he appraised me.

"Just enjoying a lovely morning." I watched as the steam rose in curlicues from my cup and then lingered in the air.

I took another few bites of fruit and waffle, then set my fork aside when unease tightened my back and stomach.

"Feeling okay?"

My gaze flickered to Mason, then to the beautiful meal before us. "Just a little anxious, I think. It's been a doozy of a week."

He waited while I sipped from my mug, giving me time to say more if I wanted.

"Having much progress on the Beau Mercer case?" I asked.

Mason's lips quirked, as if he'd been waiting for a question like that. "Yep."

"Care to share?"

He tipped his head briefly, considering. "We were unable to determine the height of the attacker from the angle the shears entered his chest. More likely he was already down, or going down, when he received the blow."

I puffed out a breath. So much for that detail saving my dad's reputation. Or helping narrow the suspect list. "Do you think Evelyn could've been responsible for the scarecrow?"

Mason put his foot back on the ground and shifted forward into business mode. "It's possible."

I'd thought the same thing. "She was in and out of sight all night," I said, having given the idea a lot of thought. "Mingling with guests, coordinating details with the caterers and event staff."

Mason sipped his coffee. "I've already interviewed the key players from that night and read all the reports made by my deputies who talked to everyone else," he said. "And while I think it is possible for Evelyn to be behind the threat, I don't think it's likely."

I mulled that over and couldn't disagree. Evelyn wasn't thrilled about the wedding, but I didn't see her as a killer.

Still, she was more than just Evelyn Clarke. She was a dedicated mother and wife. "She might not have done it alone," I said.

"You think she partnered with her husband?" Mason asked, guessing exactly where my thoughts had gone.

I lifted and dropped my shoulders in a small shrug. "Sadie's dad wasn't a fan of Beau, and he didn't make a secret of it. He forbade Beau from attending the wedding based on the guy's poor treatment of his daughter. If Mr. Clarke lost his temper and killed Beau, Evelyn could be working to help him cover his tracks."

Mason sucked his teeth. "It's possible."

I slouched back into my chair. Apparently he wasn't as interested in this conversation as I was. So, I changed the subject. "Any more news from Cat about why she's in town?"

"No."

"Is she still here?" I hadn't seen her since getting that initial peek of her across the square.

Mason stared past me to the water. A moment later, his gaze fell to my plate. "Why aren't you eating? Are you sure you feel okay?"

"Just nerves," I assured. "I don't want anything to ruin Sadie and George's wedding, and I want to be comfortable in my dress all day. All my clothes have gotten tighter since you moved in with me. Why can't I be fat and happy without the first part?"

Mason's expression turned droll, and he reached for the arm of my chair. He pulled me across the cement until our seats touched. Then he released my chair, in favor of caressing my cheek and melting my soul.

"Show-off."

He grinned and winked. "You are perfect," he said. "In every possible way." He kissed the tip of my nose and set his hands on my shoulders before resting his forehead to mine. "It's a beautiful day for a wedding, and I'm honored to be your date."

"I'm glad you're coming with me."

"Me too." He pressed a gentle kiss to my lips, then rose with our plates. "I'm going to jump in the shower now, so you'll have plenty of time to do what you need to get ready. Holler if you need anything."

"Thanks."

It took a moment, after he'd walked away, for me to realize he'd dodged my question about Cat. *Darn his soulful eyes and his sweet words.*

I considered following him inside, then flipped my phone over and dialed the federal agent's number instead. She might not be able to tell me the details of an ongoing investigation, but I trusted her to tell me the truth. And all I wanted to know was if Mason was safe.

My knee bobbed as the call rang. Then the ringing stopped, something clicked, and my call went to voicemail.

"Dang it." I disconnected without leaving a message. Cat would see that I called, and that was enough.

The phone rang before I could set it down, and Cami's name appeared on screen.

I smiled. "Hello?"

"Hey!" She sang the word, obviously pleased with something. "Guess what is all worked out and ready to go?"

"Your wedding day ensemble?" I guessed.

"No. Well, yes, obviously, but also the lantern send-off at your family's farm!"

It took me longer than it should've to remember what she meant. The lake house threat had completely derailed my night. Then something else occurred. I'd spoken to my folks, updating them about the ugly message, but they weren't the only people I promised to contact. "I forgot to talk to Sadie and Evelyn!"

"Not a problem," Cami said. "I just saw them at the square while I was on my jog. They were going to Miss Priscilla's for hair and makeup, and we nearly smacked right into one another."

I hated that I'd dropped the ball on something so important, but I was immeasurably thankful for the perfect timing of Cami's jog. "I can't believe you went running already this morning. I'm still in my pajamas."

Cami made a deep, throaty sound. "If I didn't start my days with a run, I wouldn't have nearly as many friends," she said. "Everyone thinks I'm a health nut, but I'm just trying not to combust or get arrested."

I laughed. "Well then, on behalf of this sweet town and its people, thank you for running."

"You're welcome."

I smiled against my cell phone as I imagined Cami losing her temper on some unsuspecting councilmember or well-deserving creeper. "So everything is a go?" I asked.

"Yep. Morning wedding. Lunch reception. Afternoon break for photos and a change of clothes, then an evening lantern send-off on Turtle Lake."

"Thank you," I said. The words came a bit breathlessly. I appreciated her so much. "This was such a good idea, and I know it will help my folks to see people having fun at the farm again."

"Let's hope," she agreed.

My phone beeped, announcing an incoming call, and I peeked at the screen. "Speaking of my mama," I said. "She's calling. I should probably answer and then get ready for the wedding."

"Sounds good," Cami said. "Tell Blossom I said hello, and I'll be out to help with the lantern setup this afternoon."

"Will do!" I said my goodbyes and switched over to Mama's call.

"Bonnie!"

I started. "Mama? Are you okay?" The tone and decibel of her speech clearly indicated she was not.

"No!" Her sharp, quick breaths were easily discernible now, and I jerked to my feet.

"Are you running?" I hurried toward the house, planning to get my keys and drive to her place in my nightgown if necessary. "What's wrong? How can I help? Do you need Mason?"

Oh! I'd nearly forgotten I had a sheriff in my shower. That was better than me in my nightie. I jogged up the back porch steps with a new plan in mind.

"Bessie's missing," Mama said. "I've looked everywhere, and I'm scared to death something's happened to her."

I stopped short in my kitchen. "Bessie, the barn cat?"

Clyde leapt onto the counter and stared into my soul.

"Yes!" Mama cried. "I fed her last night, but now she's absolutely nowhere. What if someone took her? Or a hawk picked her up?"

I wrinkled my nose. "Bessie is an incredibly resourceful creature," I said. "I'm certain no one picked her up, hawk or human. She's probably just out hunting, or asleep somewhere. Maybe in the tall grass, or by the water in the sun."

Mama groaned. "I always see her around this time of day."

"Well, today you have a wedding to attend, and a reception to work, so you'll have to see her in about four or five hours instead. Cami said everything's on for the lantern launch." I bit my lip, hoping the change of subject worked as well as a distraction for Mama as it had for me when Mason used the tactic.

Long moments passed while I awaited her response.

"Fine," she said. "I'll get ready, but you have to promise to help me look for her later."

"I'll do you one better," I said. "I'll bring Clyde with me when I come over. You know he'll hunt her down in a blink."

"Deal."

I hung up with a smile, then locked eyes with my cat. "Sounds like you've got a job to do later."

"Meow!"

CHAPTER SIXTEEN

Three hours later, Mason and I arrived at the Clarke farm along with hundreds of other locals and guests. Mason shifted smoothly into cop mode, keen eyes scanning, stance loosening, and a normally tight expression going soft. *Blending*, I realized. Disappearing into the mesh of new and familiar faces. His smile brightened, and his voice grew congenial in the extreme. He asked probing questions of unsuspecting people, then moved onto chitchat about the weather, or how the fish were biting at the lake.

I smiled, mesmerized, as if I'd come to a play and been seated onstage.

This was my boyfriend. Yet it wasn't. He seamlessly matched the body language of everyone we encountered, leaning in when he spoke or laughed.

This, I realized, was Undercover Mason.

Suddenly, I felt less like part of some bizarre charade and more like I was in on something fabulous. Mason was allowing me into his world. Letting me take part in his investigation. Trusting me in new ways.

I squeezed his hand, then began playing along too.

"It must be so hard to say goodbye to a dear friend," I told George's bandmates.

And, "Can you believe one little date night led to all this?"

"A wedding and a move to Nashville!" I repeated during every conversation, eyes stretched comically wide. Waiting to catch each person's response.

I didn't notice much, beyond the occasional hint of jealousy, but I knew Mason missed nothing. Hopefully, there was something to see. Preferably something that would close this case before any other threats were made.

Meanwhile, Mr. Clarke darkened the periphery, moving silently, arms crossed, and wearing a serious frown until it was time for the ceremony to begin.

We took our seats, and the crowd fell silent when the music began. We were collectively whisked away from the vast patch of earth on Clarke's Dairy Farm and taken to a place where big white bows hugged chair backs and rose petals formed a silken path to carry Sadie to her groom.

A mini pergola waited at the front, wrapped in soft white tulle and flower garlands. George stood in front of a preacher with a row of groomsmen at his side.

Mason laced his fingers with mine, then raised our joined hands to his lips for a soft kiss. When Sadie made her grand appearance, raising all guests to their feet and turning them in her direction, Mason looked only at me.

"I love you," he whispered.

"I love you too."

Twenty minutes later, the crowd moved to a large white tent draped in boughs of greenery and flowers. We enjoyed a delicious lunch while three hundred people got day drunk and tried their best moves on a makeshift dance floor.

Safe from the sweltering Georgia sun, guests formed conga lines and got down to the funky chicken between trips to the open bar.

Mason and I steered clear of the alcohol, determined to keep our minds sharp, and hoping the free drinks would loosen someone's lips in our favor.

An hour later, no grand schemes had been uncovered, but nothing had gone wrong either.

It was a perfectly normal, excessively lovely day.

I spotted Mama and Gigi near the dessert table soon after the cake was cut, and I rose onto tiptoes at Mason's side. "I'm going to see if I can help," I whispered, pointing in the cake's direction. He squeezed my hand in understanding, and I hurried away.

Sadie hadn't been able to pick a favorite flavor from Gigi's samples, and who could blame her? So, Gigi baked a half-dozen smaller cakes instead of one, large, grandiose affair. Ivory squares of linen cardstock stood on silver stands behind each option, the flavors written in elegant script.

Lemon

Coconut

White Chocolate Raspberry

Almond with Strawberry filling

Dark Chocolate Decadence

Hummingbird

My mouth watered a little at the last option. The banana, pineapple, and spice cake with pecans was one of my all-time favorites. Composed of multiple layers, stacked on smooth cream cheese frosting, there was nothing more incredible in all the land.

I made a mental note to get a slice for Mason, who'd likely never had the pleasure. He'd missed out on too many of my favorite things while living up north all his life.

A shame all folks couldn't be southern.

I paused several feet from the dessert table, cut off by a

clueless crowd of groomsmen making their way from the bar to the tables near the back. Their heads and voices were bent low, and they carried fresh drinks in their hands. My irritation at their slow-moving blockade passed when I recognized the best man, James, from our introduction at my shop. The chatty lead was Tom, the grouch from the night of the rehearsal.

Tom patted James on the back, shoulders curved, as if he could carve out an inch of privacy in the packed party tent. "This is rough, man," he said. "Singing was always your thing. Even as the backup, you carried us. Now George gets the big deal? The limelight. The girl."

James tossed back the lot of amber liquid in his glass, then released a heavy sigh. "Yup."

I couldn't help being impressed with their ensembles. Like the bridesmaids, they wore western-style boots with their dress clothes, pale gray suits with white shirts, and hat bands coordinated with their ties and pocket squares.

Except James, I realized. The best man had already abandoned his hat and tie.

"I'm married now," the first guy continued. "Got a wife and baby at home, another little boy on the way. My time for making it in this industry has passed, but you could still do it. I can't help thinking this should've been you. I kind of hate that it wasn't."

"I'm sure a big country music career would've helped make ends meet for your family," James argued.

Tom frowned. "True, but I mean—"

James's eyes rose as his fellow groomsman rambled. He scanned the area, perhaps in search of George, or listening ears. His gaze met mine, and my mouth dropped open.

He grabbed Tom's sleeve and jerked him forward with a scowl. The handful of others in the group hurried along behind.

I beetled to the cake table, hoping I hadn't just irritated a killer by standing still, eyes open and mouth closed.

"There you are," Mama said. "I still haven't found Bessie. How soon are you coming with Clyde to help me look?"

"As soon as we leave here," I said, shaking off the discomfort of being caught in earshot of the groomsman's awkward declaration. "We'll run home, grab Clyde, and head over to the farm as soon as the reception ends," I promised.

Mama nodded, worry creasing her ivory brow. "Okay. Thank you."

Gigi passed a stack of dessert plates into my hands. "Help me, would ya?"

I lifted one plate at a time in her direction. She deposited a narrow slice of cake onto each, then set them before the corresponding flavor card.

"Lots of gossip flying around today," Gigi whispered. "Everyone's speculating about everything."

Mama crept closer and nodded. "Some are saying this was a shotgun wedding. Others are just calling folks out for miscellaneous suspected offenses and affairs."

Gigi shook her head, exasperated. "The financial status of the farm is a hot topic, too. You name it, and we've probably heard it said."

"It's as if no one even sees us here," Mama said. "Like we're invisible."

I nodded. That happened when you got enough people together. The help just became part of the woodwork. I'd spent my share of time on both sides of that truth. "Any chance you've seen the new talent manager?"

"Who?" Mama asked.

The sudden sensation of being watched raised goosebumps on my skin, and I turned away from Mama in search of the cause. A wave of guests headed to the dance floor, but none seemed especially interested in me.

Mason appeared in the crowd's absence, making his way to my side.

The easy smile I loved graced his face as he moved, and I knew this was my Mason. Not the undercover guy or even Sheriff Wright.

"Hey," Gigi called. "What about the cake?"

"I'll help," Mama said.

Mason extended a hand in my direction. "May I have this dance?"

He spun me in a slow circle, then held me in a tender embrace. One strong forearm across my back, he pulled me against his chest and held my opposite hand.

We swayed to our own music, miles away from the cake table, murder investigation, and boisterous crowd. I set my cheek against his chest and prayed for decades of more moments like this one.

I imagined the finished lake house and us with gray hair. We sat on rocking chairs outside, holding hands and laughing while children played on the shore. I dreamed of helping others with Mason by my side, of fostering kids, collecting food for schools, organizing clothing drives for families, and raising money for fundraisers. Making a big difference in a small community however we could.

Then I remembered the ugly red message spray-painted upon the floorboards, and I wondered again why someone had left a message for me in that location. I didn't live there. No one did.

But Mason's name was on the property deed.

CHAPTER SEVENTEEN

We arrived at my parents' place late that afternoon with Clyde in tow. Mama and Gigi had packed up and left the reception quickly while Mason and I lingered to say our goodbyes. It was nice to chat with so many locals, neighbors, and friends. Many I hadn't seen in decades. I especially enjoyed hearing their stories of meeting the new sheriff. My high school physics teacher said Mason helped her change a tire when she had a flat on her way to class. Cami's mama's neighbor, who plays bridge with Evelyn, said Mason once stopped traffic to return a waddling of her ducks that had gotten onto the road. When he realized they'd been out there circling a storm drain, they found seven little ducklings had fallen through a grate. Mason saved them too.

One guest described how Mason rescued their great-aunt's cat from a tree, something she only thought firemen did. Mason joked that he was a jack of all trades, but I knew it was in his nature to help anyone in need.

A young single mom said Mason filled in for on career

day at her son's elementary school after learning she couldn't get the time off work to attend.

Mason's compassion was one of my favorite things about him. My town clearly felt the same way, and that touched something in my soul.

Mason parked and opened my car door for me before lifting Clyde's crate from the backseat. He held my hand with one of his and toted Clyde with the other.

"How are you feeling?" he asked, likely noting my fatigue.

"Tired," I admitted. "I think the restless night and long day have officially caught up with me." And we still had several hours to go before I could collapse into bed again.

"I can get you a coffee," he offered, eyebrows furrowing. "Have you had enough water? It was pretty hot today."

I laughed. "I'm just tired," I promised. But he was right, I'd gone easy on the water, not wanting to miss anything at the wedding reception— or use the portable bathrooms.

He watched me closely for a long moment before releasing his concern. "Okay, but let me know when you've had enough. I'm sure your folks, Gigi, and Cami can handle things here."

"I know they can," I said. "And, yes, I'm beat, but I'm enjoying this day with you, and I'm not ready to see it end."

He grinned. "It has been a pretty great day."

"It really has."

We sauntered toward the cobblestone path at the edge of the gravel lot, now lined in shepherd's hooks. Faux candles flickered in mason jars at their bases and tiny floral arrangements swung in little baskets from the crooks above.

"Wow," I whispered, utterly enchanted. The hooks and candles stretched into the distance, past the barn and flower fields toward my parents' home and greenhouses beyond. "This had to take all day."

"Your dad probably set it up while we were at the wedding," Mason said.

"Do you think it goes all the way to the lake?"

"I wouldn't be surprised."

I smiled. My dad was a hard worker, and he loved his job almost as much as he loved this farm. He probably enjoyed his day far more than he would've enjoyed ours. "So true."

"I'm really glad things went well for George and Sadie today," I said. "I worried something might go wrong, like after the rehearsal dinner."

Mason squeezed my hand. "I'm glad too. They're good people and deserve every happiness."

Something shifted in me then. Maybe it was the thought of the newlyweds, or my need to be a better girlfriend to Mason, but suddenly I needed to air my grievances and concerns more than I needed sleep. Or air. I'd pretended to be unbothered for too long. I didn't have to hide things from Mason, and I shouldn't have.

I felt my big mouth opening before finalizing the decision. "I called Cat."

Mason stopped walking.

I waited, examining his expression and finding it blank. So, I carried on. "I believe you're covering up something," I said. "What is it?"

His eyes flickered away then back, jaw clenching. He looked frozen. Tense. Unhappy.

"You aren't surprised. Why?" I gasped, as the answer burst into my mind. "You knew I called her?" *How?*

Again, the answer registered before he said a word. "She told you!" Yet she hadn't called me back. So I must've been right about the other thing too. Mason was hiding something. "What is going on?" I demanded. "I want to know everything. Right now. I'm tired of pretending this doesn't bother me. I. Am. Bothered."

Mason released me, then set Clyde's carrier on the ground. He turned his palms to me in surrender.

"If your first words are I can explain, I'm leaving," I said. "Just say what you need to say. Be straight about it. I've worried myself to death these last two weeks. I'm half nauseous all the time. My appetite is gone. My nerves are completely shot."

Mason bunched his features. "I'm so sorry. I had no idea you were suffering. I thought you were just busy with the wedding and worried about the recent threats."

I shook my head. "I should've told you sooner."

"I should've known there was more," he said. "I should've at least asked. Instead, I've let myself get so caught up in protecting you, physically, I forgot to check in with you mentally and emotionally." He pulled me into a hug on a long groan. "Cat's in town because she followed one of The Investors' scouts as far as Atlanta. She worried they might've found me. When it turned out to be a false alarm, she headed this way to fill me in and spend a couple of days. As it turns out, she's a big fan of Cromwell."

I pulled back to gape at him. "Cromwell!"

He chuckled and ran a nervous hand through his hair. "Yeah. She's a bit of an outdoorswoman. She's thinking of buying a cabin on the mountain."

I hugged him, realizing how much must've been on his mind too. A local murder and an Investors scout all in the matter of a few days. "No wonder you bolted when she called."

His arms tightened around me. "All she said during that call was that she was in town and we needed to meet. I assumed the worst," he said. "I left on autopilot, terrified I'd brought a killer to your doorstep."

"Our doorstep," I corrected.

He set his chin atop my head and sighed. "I'm not

convinced the scout made it as close as Atlanta just to give up, so I've been on edge since her first call. I should've told you sooner, but I didn't want to worry you. Then Beau Mercer was killed, your dad was the initial suspect, your mom was a mess, you were being threatened— again." Mason groaned. "This hasn't been the best couple of weeks, and I am sorry."

"Don't be sorry for that," I said. "This level of stress puts us in survival mode, and it's all we can do to navigate the days. I will, however, accept your apology for not bringing me into the loop sooner about the scout. Just don't do it again."

He pulled back and smiled. "Sometimes it's hard to decide where the job ends and our relationship begins. I want to be open and honest with you, but I don't want to burden you."

"Excuse me? It's never a burden when you let me carry part of your load. I will not break. I thought you'd have seen the evidence of that by now. And frankly, not knowing what's going on with you is worse than having the facts. Even the scary ones. What if an Investor scout was in town, and no one told me? I wouldn't know to be on guard, and I might walk right over to his car with a big, helpful, smile when he pretends to need directions or something."

Mason winced.

"Exactly." I nodded, lips pursed. "If I know there's danger in town, I can be hypervigilant and let you know if I see anything that sets off my creep-o-meter. You're my best friend, Mason Wright. I don't want to be pushed out of any aspect of your life, barring legal necessity, of course."

Much as I hated it, Mason's job required secrets on occasion. Details in ongoing investigations and such. But that wasn't the kind of thing I meant, and he knew it.

His cheeks twitched, fighting a small smile. "All right, but be patient with me. It's going to be hard to break the habit of constantly protecting you."

"Protect me from spiders," I suggested. "And field mice. I hate both of those, especially when they get into the house. Heaven knows my cat won't help."

Mason's gentle laugh warmed my spirit. "Don't go shaming your cat, or he might put me out of work."

I stepped back and raised a hand between us. "Partners?"

Emotion flickered in the depths of his eyes as he accepted my handshake. "Partners. And I hope you know you're my best friend, too."

"I know."

He grinned. "Do you recall asking me what I was up to that morning on the patio, before Cat called?"

"I do."

Mason glanced around us. We were alone, save one black cat and endless fields of wildflowers swaying in the gentle breeze. "Bonnie—" He cupped my hands in his, and something solidified in his expression.

A rush of energy zigzagged through me, stealing my breath and anchoring my feet to the earth. "Yes?"

"There you are!" Mama called. "Finally!"

Mason's gaze darted over my shoulder, and I turned slowly to launch mental tomatoes at my mother.

How was this happening again?

Gigi hurried along the path behind her, and I sagged.

Dad stepped into view in the distance and waved. "Did you bring Clyde?"

Mason crouched and opened the cat carrier's little gate.

I sighed.

Clyde shot out like a sleek black bullet, moving full speed past Mama and Gigi in Dad's direction.

"We caught a glimpse of Bessie earlier," Mama said,

reaching our sides. "She wasn't much more than a flash of spots in the field, but we're sure it was her."

"Good," I said. "I'm glad. Clyde will be too."

Mama nodded. "Your dad is hoping Clyde will show him where she was hiding so we will know where to check if she goes off the radar again."

Gigi motioned us in her direction. "Well, come on. We've got a lot of work to do if we want all those lanterns set up before folks begin to arrive."

Mason and I worked with Mama, Dad, and Gigi, at Turtle Lake for hours, assembling hundreds of paper boats and lanterns, then testing an equal number of battery-operated votives to be certain they worked.

Dad repurposed several flower carts as supply stations for guests. One held instructions for floating the boats without sinking them, a collection of framed poems about the power of hope and love, and a plethora of markers to write well-wishes onto the lanterns before the send-off. The other carts were nearly buried in boats.

Mama set up tables with pitchers of iced water and sweet tea, then hid a few speakers in the greenery and initiated a playlist of love songs.

Gigi arranged the remaining cake slices from the reception on trays beside the drinks.

When everything was finished, I stood with Mason at the water's edge. Waning sunlight dappled the still surface, the reflections of historic trees and pussy willows on its face. At the center, a large rock held a stone turtle in remembrance of the pond's namesake.

Mama approached with an odd look in her eyes. She handed a lantern and marker to Mason. "Clyde will be here in a second," she said. "The setting sun is horribly romantic. Isn't it?"

I smiled at her. "It's a beautiful night," I agreed. "What's going on with Clyde?"

Dad approached and tugged her against his side.

"Ready," Mason said, pulling my attention back to him. He pocketed the marker as I stared at the lantern Mama brought him.

At the center of the delicate white paper, two little words were written neatly in his hand.

Marry me?

I gasped as he lowered onto one knee.

If his phone rang, or anyone interrupted this, they were going straight into the lake.

"Bonnie," he said, taking my hands in his once more. "I came to Bliss hoping to escape my past. I never dreamed I'd find my future here."

Behind me, Mama cooed.

"I should've returned to Cleveland by now," he continued. "But I never again want to be anywhere you aren't. I think some part of me knew from the very start. Hell, I was already half in love with you while hoping you hadn't killed that old lady."

I barked a laugh, and he grinned.

"I love you," Mason said. "I love your big heart and creative mind, your family and friends, your sweet little town, and your insatiable curiosity." He released my gaze, looking away from me and rising.

I followed his line of sight to Cami, Dale, Sutton, and an array of our closest friends. My eyes brimmed with tears, and a small sob fell from my lips. They'd all known. And they were here for us.

Gigi delivered lanterns and markers into everyone's hands.

Cat moved through the group carrying Clyde under one arm like a football. He looked dapper in a red silk bowtie and didn't seem to mind the awkward position.

When she handed him to Mason, I noticed the small ring box tied to his collar with a ribbon.

Mason removed the box, then the ring, and presented me with a beautiful sapphire and diamond band.

Clyde grabbed the little red ring box and wiggled free. He hit the ground lithely and cut out of sight like a bandit, causing everyone to laugh.

Except me.

I was transfixed by the kind, courageous, and loving man before me who was peering directly into my soul.

"Bonnie Balfour." He cleared his throat, eyes misted, and obviously as choked by emotion as I was. "Would you do me the incredible honor of being my wife?"

I nodded, wiping tears and laughing with utter joy when all words failed.

"I'm going to need to hear that out loud for the record," he teased.

I launched at him, feeling lighter, younger, and more bliss-filled than anyone had any right to be. "Yes!"

Mason caught me easily, as I wound my arms around his neck and kicked both feet off the ground. Cheers rose around us, and he carefully returned me to the ground.

Together with our loved ones, we sent the first batch of lanterns onto the lake. The little lights flickered over the water, ablaze with the setting sun and my hope for a beautiful future.

Adrenaline replaced my prior fatigue, and I knew nothing could ruin this perfect night.

CHAPTER EIGHTEEN

Hours passed, and my joy expanded as guests strolled contentedly around Turtle Lake. Sadie and George held hands, posed for photos, and smiled, while Evelyn accepted boatloads of praise for pulling off such an incredible day on such little notice. No one mentioned the recent murder, or that the crime had occurred on this property

It really was a perfect night.

I tried to stay in the moment and not to stare at my engagement ring, or the man who'd recently proposed, more than absolutely necessary. But that was an incredibly big ask.

Thankfully, the evening was quieter and more relaxed than the reception had been. The music was low and the crowd unhurried. There were enough floating lanterns for all of the wedding guests, but only about one hundred people had made the trip to the farm. The attendees seemed to be greatly composed of the bride and groom's extended families and closest friends. All appeared delighted for the extra time to chat with the newlyweds.

I alternated between mingling and checking on the refreshments.

Mason, Cat, and Dale were reliving a shared crime-fighting moment from their days together in Cleveland when Mama approached. Her tight expression told me something was amiss before she did.

"Have you seen Sadie and Evelyn?" she whispered. "Guests are starting to ask. They want to call it a night but need to say goodbye first."

"I haven't," I said. I'd been looking for Sadie, too, hoping to make a polite escape with Mason after I caught her. The night was beautiful, but my fiancé and I had some celebrating of our own to do.

Mama frowned, eyes scanning the night. "Maybe they went home to convince Mr. Clarke to join us?"

"Maybe," I said. Mr. Clarke's absence hadn't gone unnoticed, and it would probably mean a lot to Sadie if he'd come by for a few minutes. "Do you want me to give her a call?"

Mama bit her lip, then hesitantly nodded. "I'll take another look around and offer everyone more tea and cake."

I squeezed Mason's hand, then waited for the predictable dip of his chin in acknowledgement before stepping away with Mama. We split up at the edge of the crowd. She went hunting, and I made my call.

A flash of black and red whizzed through the darkness in my direction as I waited for the phone to ring.

I stooped to stop Clyde before he ran into the guests. "Whoa," I cooed. "Slow down. What do you have there?"

He stopped short and dropped a piece of fabric at my feet.

"A hat band?"

"Meow!"

My call went to voicemail, and I disconnected before leaving a message.

Instead, I stood with the fabric and turned in search of a groomsman.

James came into view several yards away, eyes scanning as mine had been.

"Hey!" I waved a hand overhead, then hurried in his direction. "Have you seen Sadie or Evelyn? People want to say goodbye before they leave. Or how about George?" I added belatedly. Surely the groom would know what had happened to his bride.

James frowned at the hat band in my grip. "George overdid it at the reception. He's sleeping in his truck."

I frowned. If James was right, then George wouldn't know where Sadie was, unless she'd gone looking for him and had success. "Is this yours?" I asked, raising the fabric. "Or would you mind returning it to whichever groomsman it belongs?"

James accepted the accessory.

"Thanks. My cat is a bit of a thief, and I—" Several long scratches on the back of James's hand and fingers stole the rest of my words.

My gaze bounced to the cat at my feet, then back. "Did Clyde do that to you?" I asked.

"No." James took the fabric and stuffed it into his pocket. He left his hand there as well. "I'll take care of this. No problem."

"Okay," I said, relieved. "I just thought—" Clyde was feisty, but the scratches weren't fresh. I scooped the furry little outlaw into my arms. "James, this is Clyde." I smiled. "Clyde, this is—"

"Meow!" Clyde wrestled free and hit the ground running.

"Whoa." I chuckled. "I guess he's really not in the mood for socializing." I couldn't blame him. I'd kill for a little downtime.

I cringed internally at the mental word choice.

James pulled a phone from his pocket as I rambled. He looked at the screen, then me. "I found the bride. She's having a problem with her dress. Apparently she and Evelyn are in your parents' bathroom trying to figure out a fix."

"Oh, shoot." I looked at the group behind me and waved when I caught Mason's eye.

He lifted his hand in acknowledgement, a wide smile still on his face from whatever had been said by his friends.

"I'm going to check on George again," James said. "Good luck with the dress."

"Thanks." I sent a text to Sadie letting her know I was on my way.

"Any luck?" Mama asked, approaching from the lake. "No one knows where George went either. You don't think they're together?" She worked her brows.

"Unfortunately, no." I told her about George, then filled her in on what was happening with Sadie.

Mama frowned and nodded. "I'll tell folks she'll be back around in a few minutes. I won't mention the groom."

I smiled. "Good idea. I'll hurry."

I jogged up the path toward the house, hoping I could fix whatever was wrong with Sadie's dress using only the thread kit Mama kept in her kitchen junk drawer.

"Wait up," James called.

I pressed a palm to my chest. "Oh, my stars and heavens! You nearly scared the tea out of me! How's George?"

He frowned. "Drunk. Sawing logs. I took his keys just in case."

"Good idea," I said.

I walked onward, dropping my hand to my side and ignoring the heavy thunder of my heart against my ribcage. I made a mental note to watch how much I drank on my wedding day. I didn't want to miss a single moment, and I wanted every memory to remain crystal clear.

My phone rang before I reached the porch steps. Mason's name centered the screen.

"Hi," I said, smiling at the thought of our wedding day. "I'm helping Sadie with her dress at the house."

A text message vibrated the device as I spoke, and I pulled back to check the sender. "Hang on," I told him. "She's texting now."

Sadie: On your way where?

I snorted, then typed a quick response.

Bonnie: To fix your dress

Her next message arrived before I could relay her response to Mason.

Sadie: What's wrong with my dress?

My gaze snapped to James, and he grabbed my arm. "Hey!"

"Bonnie?" Mason asked.

"Help!"

"Hang up the phone," James seethed as I struggled to break free from his grip. "You and I need to talk."

"Where are you?" Mason's voice roared across the line.

"The house!" I yelled. "With Ja—"

My cheek stung, and the phone flew from my grip. I'd barely registered the fact James had hit me before he pulled me into his arms.

"Help!" I screamed.

One big hand clamped hard against my mouth faster than my rattled brain could process. He clutched me against his chest with the other, seizing my arms and extinguishing my words.

Then he dragged me off the trail and into the shadows.

CHAPTER NINETEEN

I moved through the tall grasses and wildflowers with James at my back. Me bumbling along in the pitch darkness, and him prodding me forward with every awkward step.

It was too dark to see more than a few feet in front of me, and the densely grown plants made it impossible to watch my step. James kept one broad forearm tightly against my torso, effectively flattening my lungs and limiting my breaths. I couldn't scream. Could barely speak. And I feared I'd soon join Beau Mercer if I didn't come up with a plan.

"Hurry up," he seethed.

My stomach churned with terror and the relentless pressure across my middle.

In the distance, a bevy of frantic voices carried on the wind.

My rescue party.

I faked a stumble, and James heaved me upright with a curse.

"Move," he snapped. "Or I will carry you."

I straightened and trundled forward. He could easily

move faster with me over his shoulders. I couldn't let that option become my reality. I had to give Mason time to find me. "Where are we going?" I panted, working for oxygen and biting back the rising bile.

"To my truck," he said. "I told everyone goodbye and drove away from the parking lot, so some folks saw me leave. Now I'm parked on the other side of this field."

I raised my eyes to the horizon and spotted the silhouette of a pickup truck near Gigi's cottage. I hoped her new doorbell camera was installed. Better yet, that it caught him parking there and would see us approach.

A narrow pillar of hope rose in me. If Mason and the others didn't find me before we reached the truck, there might still be a record of who had taken me.

Something warm and soft brushed past my leg as I took another step through the grasses, and I yipped.

"Shh!" James hissed. "Shut up, or I'll finish you here and leave your body in the field."

"Like you did with Beau?" I asked. The words were out before I thought better of them, and James tightened his hold on my middle.

His hot, sticky breath clung to my cheek as he leaned close and whispered a grotesque and descriptive threat to my person.

My head lightened, and my peripheral vision blurred. I was losing too much oxygen under his grip.

A sudden, feral wail sounded nearby, and a moment later, fresh, cool air rushed into my lungs.

James cursed and Clyde became visible in the night, attached to my assailant's side by razor-sharp claws. He set me free in the next breath, and Bessie leaped into the mix as my knees collided with the earth.

In the next moment, I was in motion.

My body jerked into flight before I could make a plan to run.

"Stop!" James snarled.

But it was too late for that.

I sprinted through the field, propelled by adrenaline and desperation. Waist-high wildflowers and grasses whipped and beat against my legs, hips, and thighs. I'd dashed through these blooms a hundred times in my life. Chasing Clyde. Playing hide and go seek with friends. In search of the perfect shot for senior photos.

Never had I dreamed that one day I'd be running for my life here as well.

James's footfalls pounded against the earth behind me.

I imagined his long arms reaching. His fingers tangling in my hair and jerking me to a stop.

And I ran faster.

The ancient red barn my parents used for supplies and storage drew my focus away from Gigi's house. The barn was closer to me and farther from James's truck. I was ahead of him now, but my lead wouldn't last long.

I changed trajectory and thought of nothing but the barn doors until I reached them.

"Be unlocked," I whispered on repeat.

To my great delight, they swung easily under my command, and I dove inside. I raced to the back and unfastened the rear door, out of breath as I released them to rattle in the wind. Each rasping breath raked up my throat like wildfire, and a painful stitch began in my side.

I slid behind a wall of hay bales and reached for my phone.

Any sense of victory I'd felt vanished as I recalled my cell phone lying on the ground outside my parents' house.

And I prayed Clyde and Bessie were okay. I hadn't looked

back once I'd started running. Now, I wondered what their bravery had cost them.

Desperation burned my eyes as I crouched on the dusty floor, praying not to be found. I needed help. Needed to catch my breath. Needed a plan.

The cavernous structure was still and silent around me, making my frantic breaths and pounding heart seem louder than any marching band. I couldn't stay here, but I wasn't sure where else to go.

And I couldn't hear the search party anymore.

Silver moonlight shone through a lone window high above, illuminating a wide path across the ancient floorboards.

I sank lower into my crouch, making myself as small as possible as I searched my mind for a plan.

The door I'd used to enter swung open, then slammed shut, sending a burst of air pressure to the newly unfastened barrier at my side.

If James assumed I'd kept running, maybe he'd go look for me outside.

A set of slow, careful footfalls made their way in my direction. The distant shape of my attacker's head appeared above the stacked bales of hay.

"Thought you could hide, huh?" James asked. "Looks like you found us a little privacy instead."

Gooseflesh pebbled my skin as his low, menacing chuckle rose in the air. I scooted deeper into the corner, allowing the darkness to swallow me whole.

Sharp, biting pain lanced one palm, and I sucked in a quick, shallow breath. I'd set my hand on something I shouldn't have in the shadows. A piece of broken glass or flowerpot? I jerked my hand to my chest and felt the blood spill across my skin before hearing the distinct sound of a single nail bounce against the wooden floor.

James spun in my direction. "I knew you didn't leave," he said. "You can't hide now." He stopped on the other side of the hay bundles and scanned the area, then thankfully turned away. "All of this could've been avoided if you'd just stayed out of things that aren't your business."

I bit my tongue against the urge to say my dad's reputation, Mama's emotional stability, their farm's success, and their livelihood all depended upon clearing Dad as the killer.

"I hate small towns," he said, interrupting my thoughts. "Everyone acts as if they're friends until you turn your head for five seconds. The whole band hates George for what he did, cutting us all out of his new success the way he did. But we still stood up there and pretended to be happy for him today. Sadie's dad doesn't think George is good enough for her, because George comes from a family that struggles financially, but he still showed up and gave his little girl away." He looked around, turning in circles as he spoke. "It's all fake. Everyone and everything. And I'm tired of it. Why do I have to be nice all the time? Why can't I ask for what I want? For what I deserve?"

He punched a bale of hay, and dust motes floated into a beam of moonlight. "Why does George get all the breaks? What about the rest of us?"

Outside, I heard my name again. This time on Mason's tongue. I heard it rising from my parents' lips and on the voices of many others.

The search party was getting closer.

James cussed.

I peered up at him from my hiding spot and watched in horror as he kicked piles of empty plastic topsoil and fertilizer bags. His temper was getting the best of him. I couldn't let him get ahold of me again. Not if I wanted to survive.

"I hate this farm," he complained. "This place makes me feel so—" He dug his fingers into his hair and pulled it toward the sky. A guttural sound escaped his chest as he lowered his hands to his sides. "First, I drive all the way out here to try to talk to Beau privately about my talent. It was my one chance at catching him without the rest of the guys around, and I took it. That's supposed to be called initiative. Passion. Heart. But, oh no," he said, dragging out the final two words. "Beau went berserk, saying I was out of line for starting the conversation. It was so unprofessional." James switched to a mocking tone. tone. "Apparently, I was embarrassing myself and being completely inappropriate. I apologized, but he just kept going. He threatened to tell George and everyone else that I approached him." James looked to the ceiling, then stomped his foot hard enough to knock a flowerpot from the supply table.

"Dammit!" He cursed again, then kicked the fallen object hard enough to send it into outer space. The terracotta vessel collided with a wall above my head and crashed back to earth in a million pieces only a short distance away.

"I didn't mean to kill him," James muttered. "I just wanted him to hear me sing. Instead, we argued. I lost my temper and called him a few names. He swung at me." James hung his head and laced his hands against the back of his neck. "The whole thing would've been over, but he grabbed me on his way down that last time, and he wouldn't let go. I had to pry him off of me. I didn't even notice I'd lost my ring until I was at home."

I bit my lip. I knew evidence could've easily been missed at the crime scene. I hadn't even seen two cats approach tonight. Finding a single ring would take days.

I'd felt someone watching me when I came to look that day. I'd felt their gaze on my skin, then found the threat in the greenhouse.

It'd been James all along.

"Your damn cat attacked me while I looked for that ring.

Then he took the only evidence that could prove I was here and ran away," James said. "Then you showed up. Everyone said you were a colossal snoop. I just never had any reason to care until now."

And that, I realized, was how James had gotten those scratches on his hand.

The voices of the search party grew louder, and he walked to the barn door and peeked out. "Dammit."

I pressed my back to the wall and inched silently toward the rear doors. I couldn't stay here any longer. I had to run.

The next time he looked the other way, I would make my move. Even if he caught me outside, James couldn't kill me with his bare hands before someone heard my scream and came running.

As if he'd somehow heard my thoughts, James backed away from the front door and approached the workbench several feet away. He rifled through the stack of tools on the surface.

I listened intently for signs that the search party was headed this way.

"I have to finish this and get off the property, or duck outside to join the search party," James said. "Either way, I can't be found in here, and I can't let you leave."

Then he turned and raised a machete into the air.

CHAPTER TWENTY

I held my breath as I scooted along the floor, left hand throbbing. My senses heightened as I tuned in to the moment and waited for my opportunity to run.

James was near and armed, but there was always hope, and I had too many things to keep me motivated.

The faces of my loved ones, friends, and community passed through my heart and mind in a kaleidoscope of treasured memories.

I shifted into a ready crouch, balanced on the balls of my feet like a sprinter in cramped quarters, braced for whatever came next. Fight or flight. Either way, I wouldn't let a killer win without doing all I could to survive.

James moved fully into the moonlight, and my confidence wavered. His usually congenial expression had been replaced with one of resolve. His friendly blue eyes were flat with indifference.

Machete in one hand, he raised something small in his opposite palm, and a thin beam of light scattered the shadows along one wall. His cell phone's flashlight app was on the hunt.

For me.

"Where are you?" he called. "Because time is ticking."

I winced at the flatness of his tone, as if he simply wanted to get my death over with so he could move on to other things.

Something small and narrow nudged my fingertips, and I knew without seeing. This was the nail that had fallen from my injured palm. I curled it into my hand like a talisman. It wasn't much in the way of a weapon, but it might still save my life.

Two steadying breaths later, I tossed the tiny metal object toward the front of the barn.

James turned his head in the direction of the small sound as it connected with wood, and his flashlight beam followed.

I launched through the back doors.

Night wind rushed over me as I landed into the field behind the barn with a horror-movie-worthy scream. "Help!" I shrieked and ran on trembling, unsteady legs.

Dozens of distant flashlight beams bounced in my direction.

Vehicles had been arranged along the edge of the field, headlights on, assisting in the illumination of the land.

Tears of hope blurred my vision. My foot hit a clump of earth, and my ankle turned. I collided with a wall of hard muscle.

I wailed and pushed instinctually against the strong body.

"Hey," Mason whispered. "Sh-sh-sh. I've got you."

I paused to look into his eyes and let the truth of his words take hold. Relief hit me like a bullet. My head lightened. My limbs weakened. And darkness snatched me away.

I woke to the rhythmic bounce of my cheek against Mason's chest as he jogged with me in his arms. We moved swiftly toward the lineup of headlights, as if I were light as a feather. A baby. Or a bride carried over the threshold.

Emergency flashers carouseled through the distant inky sky.

I was safe, but my chest felt too tight, and the cool night air was slow to fill my lungs.

EMTs loaded me quickly into an ambulance and started an IV with fluids. They pried my eyelids open when I didn't realize they'd shut. And they cleaned my palm where the nail that saved me had first punctured my skin.

The emergency room was busy when we arrived. My injuries were non-life-threatening. A nurse suggested I'd suffered a panic attack induced by trauma and dehydration from a long day in the heat and sun. They ran several tests anyway. Due diligence, they assured us.

Mason and I stayed behind a privacy curtain for hours. I was instructed to rest while I waited for a doctor to sign my discharge papers.

I slept more than I was awake.

"We got James," Mason told me sometime around midnight. He set his phone on the little stand beside my bed with a smile.

I rolled to face him, curling onto my side on the narrow bed.

"Deputies picked him up on the highway outside of town."

James hadn't chased me, as I'd expected. Instead, he'd made a run for his truck, probably knowing the odds of finishing his mission were nil with a search party so near.

"He tried to say he'd left the farm before you went missing, but Gigi's new camera ruined that story. He's at the station now, asking for an attorney."

Tears welled in my eyes but didn't fall. A bone-deep numbness had settled over me hours before. I didn't like it, but I suspected it was my mind's way of protecting itself. I hoped it would pass in time.

Mason slid a comforting palm across my cheek, shoving my hair away from my eyes and caressing my skin lightly, as if I was made of glass. "I'm sorry this happened to you."

The grief in his voice was raw and palpable, but not enough to send the building tears over my cheeks.

I nodded when words failed me.

The privacy curtain wiggled, and Mom and Dad appeared at the end of the bed. Dad bounced his knuckles off the fabric. "Knock, knock."

I smiled.

Mason greeted them with hugs. "She's just waiting for discharge. She was dehydrated. They cleaned and bandaged the cut on her hand, then ran some tests to be sure nothing else was wrong. She hasn't been feeling well this week."

"How's Bessie?" I asked. I wasn't the only one seeing a doctor tonight.

Mom had found Bessie limping in the field before Mason found me. She and Dad took her to the emergency vet after I'd been deemed well enough to go home tonight.

"Did James hurt her?" I asked.

Mom's nose wrinkled a moment, and then her lips curled into a small, mischievous smile. "Maybe, but Bessie's going to be just fine. The vet found a fracture in her foot. It's possible she was stepped on in the tussle, but the paw is wrapped now and will heal in time."

"She and Clyde saved my life," I said, voice cracking.

Dad nodded. "They're fighters," he said. His eyes misted with emotion. "Just like our little girl."

Normally, being called a little girl at forty would've made me laugh. This time, I opened my arms and welcomed my parents into the tightest hug I could manage.

When we broke apart, Mom pulled tissues from the box

on the little table and dabbed at her eyes. "We also figured out where Bessie was hiding the other day when I couldn't find her," she said.

A smile bloomed on Dad's lips at her words. "Clyde showed us when we got home from the vet."

I rolled my eyes, imagining the treasure trove of things he and his partner in crime had likely stolen. "What were they hiding?"

Mama leaned against Dad's side. "Kittens!"

"What?" I straightened, feeling my chest puff with pride. "Clyde's a dad?"

"We think so," Mama said. "Those two are pretty tight, and we can't imagine who else could be the father. Plus, one of the kittens is jet black."

"You should've seen him with the little ones," Dad added. "He's a natural."

I swung my legs over the bed's edge. "I want to meet the kittens. Let's flag down a nurse and see if we can hurry things up a bit."

Mom lifted a palm, mouth open, likely planning to tell me to sit still.

But a young woman in blue scrubs appeared with a tablet, and we all hit pause. "Bonnie Balfour?" she asked.

"Yes," the four of us answered.

The woman grinned. She was small and narrow, with freckles across her cheeks and a button nose. "I'm Elyse, a medical resident here, working with Dr. Ambrose. You're all set to go home. We just need you to sign at the Xs on this page and the next two."

She passed me the tablet, and I marveled at how young doctors were these days.

I looked for the Xs, then signed the screen with my finger.

"Rest," she said. "Hydrate. Maintain a healthy, balanced

diet, and don't forget to move. Exercising now will be the key to your ability to continue as you progress."

I returned the tablet to her with a frown. "Progress?"

She scanned the screen, then pulled a small square of paper from her pocket. "Perfect." Elyse passed a written prescription to me. "Follow up with your obstetrician and get started with the prenatal vitamins as soon as possible. Our first three months are crucial for proper development. You can also call your general physician or Dr. Ambrose tomorrow with any non-emergency concerns. Any questions for me right now?"

The space inside the curtain fell silent as my parents, Mason, and I stared at the young doctor.

I dropped my eyes briefly to the prescription and read it. *Prenatal vitamins.*

Then I read it again.

"Best of luck and congratulations." Elyse turned on her sneakers and headed for the exit.

"Wait!" Mason whipped out a hand in her direction. "Bonnie's pregnant?"

Elyse frowned, then returned to us in a few slow steps. Her cheeks reddened, and she pulled her tablet back into view. She ran a fingertip over the screen, swiping through the signed documents. "When was the first day of your last cycle?"

"I don't know," I said. It was the same answer I'd given anytime anyone asked since puberty. "I'm not predictable, but that's normal for me. I explained all this to the intake nurse."

"Dr. Ambrose ordered a pregnancy test," Elyse said.

"And?" Mason demanded, still awaiting a direct answer to his question.

"I am so sorry." Elyse lowered her voice and moved to the edge of my bed.

My emotions ping-ponged from hope to disbelief. From joy to desperation. "Why are you sorry?" I asked carefully.

Elyse tipped slightly forward, speaking directly, only, to me. "I thought someone already told you. I just got here, and it's so busy tonight." Her gaze darted over her shoulder, toward the sounds of doctors rushing past. "I was told to go over the paperwork for discharge. That's all."

Mason's hand landed on my shoulder, and I reached for Elyse's wrist. "I'm pregnant?" I asked.

Her eyebrows rose. Then, she nodded. "Yes."

Mama squealed.

Those piling tears of mine began to fall. "I can't be pregnant," I argued. "I'm forty. And a lifelong sufferer of reproductive issues." Including severe endometriosis. I'd never had a "cycle"—it was more like a riotous roller coaster.

And I hadn't been able to get pregnant in my twenties when I'd diligently tried.

"I can't get pregnant," I said, repeating the words of numerous medical professionals over the years.

Elyse's gaze slid to Mason, then back. "If you're sexually acti—"

I raised a hand to stop her. I knew how babies were made, and I'd survived a killer's clutches tonight. I had no plans to die of embarrassment in front of my parents.

She nodded and regrouped. "Based on the hormone levels from your test, you're at least ten weeks pregnant," Elyse said, calmly reviewing her tablet. "That, or you're having twins."

Mama buried her face in Dad's chest, and he set his chin on her head. A broad smile curved his lips.

Mason sat in the chair at my bedside with a soft thump.

I suspected his knees gave out.

I was already seated but actively considering a roll onto the floor.

When I dragged my gaze to Mason, there were tears on his cheeks.

"Bonnie?" he asked.

"Any other questions?" Elyse pushed.

Mason's brow tented, but his attention remained fixed on me. "What do you think? How do you feel?"

He was giving me the space I needed to process this news. And he'd allow me to make the decisions about what happened next.

"We're having a baby," I said.

The hoot that burst from his lips made me jump, then laugh.

"We're having a baby!" he repeated.

And a round of applause rose outside our curtain.

"Congratulations," unfamiliar voices called.

I was on my feet in a moment, as was Mason, and he swept me off the ground in his arms.

Two weeks passed before my life returned to semi-normal. The exhaustion from my recent trauma, coupled with a forty-year-old body doing pregnancy was a lot to process, physically and emotionally. But Dr. Rosie, my obstetrician, assured me all was well.

James confessed to everything under the pressure of a proper interrogation, and he was in jail awaiting trial. He admitted to losing his temper and using a pair of my parents' shears to take Beau's life. Now, he'd likely spend the rest of his years behind bars.

I glanced at the time on my watch, then grabbed my purse from behind the counter at Bless Her Heart.

"Are you heading out?" Lexi asked.

I turned with a smile. "Lunch with my fiancé," I said,

wiggling my fingers to showcase my engagement ring. Something I did every chance I got.

She rolled her eyes. "Show-off."

I beamed. "I'll be back in an hour."

Clyde leaped onto the counter and ran to the corner as I passed.

"Not yet," I told him. "I'll take you to visit your family after work. Right now, I have a date."

I kissed his soft head and waved to Lexi, then hurried onto the sidewalk in search of Mason.

He was easy to spot at the café across the square. He'd already secured a table with an umbrella so we could enjoy the unseasonably cool day.

I smiled at the pleasant breeze on my skin as I headed in his direction.

Movement near the trees on the square pulled my attention to a dark figure as I stepped into the crosswalk.

The handsome, dark-haired man from weeks prior leaned against the wide trunk of an ancient oak. When we made eye contact, he tipped his hat to me.

Something in the simple move made my heart rate jump and my thoughts spiral.

I hadn't seen this man since before Sadie and George's wedding. If he was the new music talent manager, replacing Beau Mercer, why hadn't he returned to Nashville with George?

And if he wasn't the new talent manager, could he be—

HONK!

I yipped and darted forward at the blast of a car horn, hurriedly finishing my trip across the road.

Mason closed the distance between us before I could catch my breath. "You okay?"

I nodded, but my eyes searched the nearby trees.

The man I'd seen moments before was gone.

"Hey," Mason whispered. "What's happening?"

I swallowed past the sudden lump in my throat. "Is Cat still in town?"

His eyes narrowed. "Yes." He turned to look in the direction I'd been searching. "Why do you ask?"

"Because I think The Investors' scout might be here too."

Thank you so much for reading STABBED IN THE RACK! I hope you'll enjoy each new story in the Bonnie & Clyde Mysteries more than the last!

If you're new to the Bonnie & Clyde Mysteries, you can go back to the beginning and read them all, starting with BURDEN OF POOF!

Or get them in bulk with the newly available box sets 1 & 2! Each box set includes a special short story!

BOX SET 1 (Books 1-3 + a special prequel, When Bonnie Met Clyde!)

BOX SET 2 (Books 4-6 + a special, magical, short story from the local bookstore!)

ALSO BY JULIE HATCHER

Patience Price Mysteries

Murder by the Seaside (Book 1 of 3)

Sun, Sand and ... Murder?

Downsized from the FBI's human resources department on the Virginia mainland, Patience Price is setting up shop as a Counselor at Large in her quirky island town. And she's making the best of her reinvention, until a high school boyfriend is accused of murder, and his determined mama wants Patience to save his hide.

Local golden boy, Adrian Davis, once crushed Patience's teenage heart, and now he needed her help? She can't help offering a chef's kiss to Karma.

Not that Patience holds a grudge.

Reluctantly, she agrees to look into the case, with the help of a hunky former coworker, but what she finds will rock their coastal community to its core, and put Patience on a lurking killer's hitlist.

Geek Girl Mysteries

Hi! I'm Mia Connors. I'm the IT manager at the gated community where I live. I'm also the CIO of my family's holistic beauty products company, and I play Queen Guinevere at the local Ren Faire. I wear a lot of hats, and I stay in my lane. Or— I did.

Until a body dropped in my lap, and an infuriatingly handsome detective thought my family, or I, were behind the killing!

My family might be nuts, but they're MY nuts, and no one's accusing them of murder on my watch.

I just wish the real killers didn't take my good deeds so personally.

Thelma & Louisa Mysteries

No Farm No Fowl

It's out of the frying pan and into the fire for Thelma and Louisa in this new farm to fun cozy mystery series!

Polish chicken breeder Louisa Eggers and her beloved hen, Thelma, are enjoying life sunny side up in their earthy cottagecore community of Meadowbrook. Friends and neighbors can't get enough of Louisa's special breakfast recipes, and she has high hopes of feathering her nest with income from the budding egg enterprise.

But when a local naysayer, seemingly determined to bring bad press to Louisa's community, lifestyle, and café is found dead with a belly full of her quiche, and the coroner crows murder, all eyes turn to Louisa for an explanation.

To save their business and reputation, Thelma and Louisa lay a plan to find the killer. Can they crack this case before it's too late? Or will they find themselves in a heaping helping of trouble?

ABOUT THE AUTHOR

Julie Anne Hatcher is an award-winning and bestselling author of mystery and romantic suspense. She's published more than sixty novels since her debut in 2013 and currently writes series as herself, as well as under the pen names **Julie Anne Lindsey, Bree Baker, Jacqueline Frost, Julie Chase, and Julie Hatcher**.

When Julie's not creating new worlds or fostering the epic love of fictional characters, she can be found in Kent, Ohio, enjoying her blessed Midwestern life. And probably plotting murder with her shamelessly enabling friends. Today she hopes to make someone smile. One day she plans to change the world.

ROUGH HEM JUSTICE

JULIE ANNE LINDSEY

Copyright © 2022 by Julie Anne Lindsey

All rights reserved.

No part of this book may be reproduced in any form or by any electronic or mechanical means, including information storage and retrieval systems, without written permission from the author, except for the use of brief quotations in a book review.

The characters and events portrayed in this book are fictitious or are used fictitiously. Any similarities to persons, living or dead, is purely coincidental and not intended by the author.

ISBN-13: 978-1-954878-23-5

Published by Cozy Queen Publishing LLC

Dedicated to my Cozy Queens

A NOTE FROM THE AUTHOR

Hello Lovely Reader,

Thank you so much for joining me on Bonnie & Clyde's newest adventure! I hope you're having as much fun in Bliss as I am.

As you know, there will be eight novels in the Bonnie & Clyde Mysteries, along with additional, spin-off series, as secondary characters rise to the front and insist their stories be told. So, if you have a favorite, be sure to let me know!

You can keep in touch between the books via my Cozy Club newsletter.

And if you enjoy ROUGH HEM JUSTICE, don't forget to check out my other books here.

Now, let's go check in with your favorite furry little outlaw!
 -Julie Anne Lindsey

CHAPTER ONE

Modern-day Bliss, Georgia, was about as much like the Wild West as my grandmama, Gigi, was like a saloon girl. At least until a few hours ago, when the Pioneer Days traveling event and show had begun setting up shop on the town square. Now both Bliss and Gigi were undergoing dramatic transformations.

And I was loving both processes.

"What do you think?" I called through the dressing room curtain at Bless Her Heart, my second-chance shop on the square.

Gigi harrumphed but didn't answer.

I smiled, thankful I'd held onto the box of donated items from our local high school's presentation of *Annie Get Your Gun*. Making old and out-of-style things new and beautiful again was my specialty, and at the moment, all the former costumes were being refreshed and prepped for sale. I could think of at least a dozen locals who would want to dress the part while meandering the old-timey booths and games being erected in the square. Gigi and I were two of them.

"This corset's too tight," she complained, bumping into

the curtain as she flailed behind it. "Help me loosen the strings."

"If you don't wear it snugly, you might as well take it off."

The curtain swept back, and Gigi appeared with a grimace. "Let's try that."

I looked like Gigi. My mama looked like us too. Our wild red hair, warm hazel eyes, and hefty smattering of freckles over impossibly fair skin made it hard to mistake our shared DNA. Also, we loved to be involved. Whatever the cause.

This week Pioneer Days was calling.

My best friend, Cami, had found the group online and convinced them to make a stop in Bliss. She'd been working diligently to increase tourism and bring new engagement to the community. Usually by luring folks with events and promotions.

"Bonnie," Gigi said, tugging at the corset I'd fixed over a scarlet satin dress. Her black stockings and gloves matched the garment's corset and lace trim. She gripped the constricting device, pulling down on the ribbing until it pressed against her hips. "I don't have enough torso for this contraption. My girls are blocking the view."

I set my sewing needle and thread aside, placing them atop the dress I was currently altering. "Let me see."

"Why don't you have to wear a corset?" Gigi asked.

"I'm a shop keeper, not a saloon girl." My taupe gingham dress and simple white apron were cute and comfortable while staying on theme.

Gigi had wanted to turn heads, and her outfit would easily accomplish that goal. Not that she needed a certain outfit to generate attention.

She met me halfway between the set of chairs where I'd been working and the room she'd just exited. "Untie it."

I turned her back to me and plucked at the corset strings.

The accessory wasn't tight, but she had a point about her torso…. And her girls.

"Just give me an apron to wear over this, and no one will know I skipped the cincher."

I wiggled the binding loose, and she shoved it over her skirts until it hit the floor.

"That's better," she said.

Gigi owned the bakery next door and was in the process of giving Oh, My Goodies a makeover to match the Wild West theme. She thought customers would enjoy buying their morning pastries and coffee from a saloon. She'd even hired an old-timey piano player to entertain during the rush.

"I hung a few new apron options on those hooks," I said, pointing to the far wall.

She hustled toward the display. "A group of history enthusiasts came into the bakery yesterday and bought two of my hummingbird cakes. They liked the way my apron matched my shirt. I'm going to try to match more often. Can you make these look more western?"

"Sure. Set your favorites on the counter, and I'll take a look."

"You're a gem."

I carried the dress I'd been working on back to the large circular desk at the center of the shop and tucked it out of my cat's sight. Clyde was a sleek black thief with ongoing plans to steal my stuffed-tomato pin cushion and anything else he could run off with.

I'd met Clyde on a visit to Bliss while I was still married and living in Atlanta. He'd stolen a ribbon from my sleeve, and I'd given chase. I'd documented the whole thing in a story I called *When Bonnie Met Clyde*, but that was a secret between him and me. Writing wasn't my strong suit.

"I'll take these," Gigi said. "Do you still have that embroidery machine? Can you put my logo on them?"

"Absolutely." I folded her aprons neatly together.

She gave my shop a long look, seeming to notice recent changes for the first time. "I like what you did here."

"Thanks. It's a work in progress." I'd done what I could to add some Wild West appeal. The sales floor was filled with items I'd given new life. Racks of reimagined clothing, shoes and jewelry. Bookcases lined one wall, heavy with beautifully covered tomes as well as vases and knickknacks. A few select chairs and furniture items doubled as displays for throw blankets, pillows and decorative rugs.

Typically I dressed the place in as many colors and hues as possible, but I'd spent several hours preparing for Pioneer Days. Now the color palette was muted by tans and browns. I'd borrowed a number of potted cacti in various sizes from Gigi's friend Sutton, our local succulent lady, and I'd dragged everything I could find with fringe, leather or a horse-related print from the storage room. Cowboy hats and faux-fur pelts covered a table beside a display of boots. I'd added branding irons to the collection of fire pokers and a lot of turquoise jewelry to the racks.

Gigi moseyed back toward the fitting room and stopped in front of the full-length mirror. "I think this looks better without the corset. Don't you?"

The bell over my front door dinged, saving me from answering the question.

Sutton walked in dressed like Gigi. "How do I look?"

I grinned. "Fabulous."

Sutton was tall and thin, with gray hair and blue eyes. Her sage-green satin saloon-girl ensemble was definitely a new aesthetic for her, given that she normally wore a muumuu. She'd even opted for cowgirl boots. And she was rocking the corset.

She curtsied, and I whistled.

"I need one of those hats," Gigi said, crossing the space to greet her friend with a hug. "You look great. I like the little feather in it," she said, reaching up to run a fingertip across Sutton's sage plume. "Do you have any more of those?" she asked, swinging her gaze to meet mine.

"That's not mine, but I can probably make one like it."

Sutton's smile drooped a bit, and she moved closer to my counter, tugging Gigi along with her. "I bought it from a clothing stand by the gazebo. Tish's Threads. The lady, Tish, said she was the show's seamstress and the event's premier outfitter. She wanted to know where I got my dress, so I told her a friend made it, and she didn't seem very happy. She wanted to know who made it and when. I wasn't sure what to say, so I bought a hat to change the subject, but I think she watched me come in here."

My gaze flipped to the door and back, glad to see another seamstress wasn't on her way inside, proverbial guns blazing. "Jeez," I said. "How were we supposed to know there wasn't room for another seamstress? This whole event kind of popped up overnight. Cami barely had time to announce it."

Cami had pulled everything together on the fly. Finding the group and booking them had come together quickly, and they'd arrived within a few days. It was hard to believe they weren't already en route when the invitation was extended.

"That Cami's one smart cookie," Gigi said. "Putting her in charge of town events was the best decision our mayor's made since he stopped wearing that toupee. And that Tish is a pill. I met her this morning when she came for coffee and scoffed at my cut-out cookies. She didn't say anything, but she looked like she'd sooner stomp on them than taste them."

I grimaced. "What shapes did you choose?"

"Boots and sheriff stars."

Sutton rubbed Gigi's arms. "I liked those cookies. They were adorable."

"I know it!" Gigi said. "They're delicious. Not that she'll ever know."

I considered the two ladies' stories, and a memory flashed into mind. "Now that you mentioned it, I think Cami said something similar about her. The producer she spoke to was very friendly during their initial conversation, then she had an attitude during the call to finalize details. The woman's name might've been Tish. Cami definitely said something about costumes. Would one of the producers also be the costumer? Selling her wares from a booth?"

Gigi shrugged. "Seems possible. Folks in a traveling show like this must have to wear a lot of hats."

Sutton wrinkled her nose. "Is it wrong if I hope it's the same woman? Because at least then there aren't two of them?"

I peered through the shop's glass door, examining the hustle and bustle of our overcrowded square.

The large oval-shaped swath of grass was outlined by roads, shops and cafes, polka-dotted with massive ancient oaks and more recently adorned with an octagonal white gazebo. A town-wide landscaping bonanza had resulted in several new flagstone paths and a plethora of gorgeous flower beds and baskets.

This morning the normally peaceful setting was overrun with locals and members of the Pioneer Days staff in costumes and period clothing. Wooden booths had been erected to sell everything from funnel cakes and turkey legs to ears of corn and baked beans. Banjo music echoed from speakers on telephone poles holding banners to announce the event. And a kaleidoscope of square dancers spun and swung to the beat.

It definitely looked like a good time, and there wasn't an open parking space in sight.

"So long as she isn't invited to tonight's hatchet throwing," Sutton said. "I have a feeling the line to take a toss at her would be long."

Gigi snorted and dug her elbow into her friend's side with a giggle.

"Are they really throwing hatchets?" I asked. It didn't seem like a great idea to throw anything with so many people in one place. Especially not something sharp.

"I don't think so," Sutton said. "But tonight's the big opening ceremonies, and I read that Tish has a major role." She dug into her purse and unearthed a folded piece of paper. "You can keep that one. I picked up a few to hand out."

"Thanks." I opened the Pioneer Days program and smiled. "'Four Days of Rootin' Tootin' Wild West Fun,'" I read. "This is perfect. Now I won't miss a thing."

A black streak of fur and mischief darted out from beneath a rack of gowns and around my friends' feet.

Gigi tracked the cat with her eyes. "I wondered where he was hiding."

Clyde dove onto my counter and slid to a stop near my plants. He wore a black bandana in place of his usual collar. I'd embroidered the word OUTLAW across the fabric in white thread.

"Look at you," Sutton cooed. "You like playing the bad boy, don't you?" She nodded. "I'll bet you're wanted for robbery."

I stroked a hand over his head and down his back, sending his bottom into the air. "It's his favorite crime."

Clyde began to purr, and Sutton joined me in fussing over him.

She scratched behind his ears and under his chin, taking a moment to admire the bandana. "I bet you could sell a lot of these this week, and it wouldn't even upset Tish, because she didn't have anything for pets at her stand."

That was a good idea. I had plenty of bandanas and a

machine that made the process simple. "I might do that if I get a little extra time. First I have to spruce up a few costumes from the high school donation. I hate to ruffle Tish's feathers, but I've already promised Mama, Liz and Gretchen I'd get those ready." I hooked a thumb over my shoulder, indicating the rack standing behind my checkout counter.

Sutton's eyes widened. "Well, at least put those out of sight."

Not a bad idea, though, hopefully, Tish wasn't as frightening as Sutton thought. Maybe she'd just caught the woman at a bad time.

Gigi floated in the rack's direction, mouth open in appreciation of the shiny, sequined and feathered gowns. "I should've been a dance hall girl."

I'd added the extreme flair and bling to a few older gowns, then adjusted the hems and necklines to suit my mama and friends. The results were admittedly impressive, and the new owners were sure to be tickled.

"Do you want to try one on?" I asked, joining Gigi at the rack.

The bells above my front door jingled, and Sutton made a soft strangled sound.

"Welcome to Bless Her Heart," I said, turning to greet the newcomer.

A pair of women stood inside the threshold, gazes darting from Sutton to Gigi, then to my gown rack and me.

The older, taller woman stood a step in front of the other, her long brown hair draped over one shoulder in a hundred perfect narrow ringlets. She narrowed her stormy blue eyes on mine. "Hattie."

The young woman snapped forward and placed a stack of half-page flyers near the register. "We're delivering coupons for Tish's Threads. This is Tish." She lifted a hand to the first woman, as if she were a prize on a game show. "She's the premier stop for Pioneer Days dress and fashion. You can get everything you need from daily cowboy attire to evening finery for women." She paused to swallow, then cleared her throat and began again. "Tish is one of our producers and also plays the role of an heiress who rides into town and kicks off the event at each location. You won't want to miss the horse-and-carriage parade tonight at seven." She glanced at her companion, who continued to appraise my shop and the period gowns my friends and I were wearing.

"Thank you," I said, offering as warm a smile as I could muster under the other woman's hard stare. "It's lovely to meet you both. I'm Bonnie Balfour. This is my shop, and this is my grandma Gigi. Our friend Sutton, and my cat, Clyde."

"Nice to meet you as well," Hattie said softly.

All eyes turned to Tish as her protégé apparently awaited instructions.

The rest of us waited to see if we got to keep our heads.

Slowly, Tish's eyes grew hooded, her cheeks red. "I never should've agreed to come here."

She turned on her toes without another word and pressed back through the door with a growl.

My jaw dropped, and my feathers ruffled.

"See?" Gigi asked. "A pill. Just like I said."

"Apparently," I agreed. But I couldn't help wondering if Tish had been speaking about my town or my store. Either way, the event wasn't off to a promising start.

CHAPTER TWO

I closed up shop a few minutes before seven and left Clyde in the window display, lounging on a faux cowhide rug.

The southern Georgian sun was hot despite the hour as I cut through the throngs of people in search of my best friend. In August, things never truly cooled, not even in the dead of night. Cami stood at the center of the chaos with a clipboard and glowing smile. She'd worn that goofy grin for several weeks straight, following a surprise proposal from her fiancé. She wore white jeans and a tan Pioneer Days t-shirt with platform wedges.

"Hey!" she said, taking notice as I tied a grand white bonnet over my humidity-swollen curls. "You look adorable. Very *Little House on the Prairie*." She pulled me into a quick hug, her brown eyes twinkling in amusement as she shook her head at my ensemble. "This is fabulous."

I curtsied.

She snorted a laugh. "Are you responsible for Gigi's and Sutton's getups too?"

"All but the hat," I admitted. "That was from Tish's collection."

Her smile drooped. "I forgot to tell you something."

"One of the Pioneer Days producers is a bit of a bully and doesn't want anyone else selling western attire?"

"I wouldn't say she's a bully, exactly," Cami offered in her most diplomatic tone. "But she did claim all rights to any period costumes and related fashions while the show's in town."

I rolled my eyes.

"I'm so sorry. I've been swamped, pulling this together so fast. I confirmed with everyone applying for a booth, but I wasn't thinking about what was sold in local shops. Not that you should stop selling western clothes. You're a private business and can do what you want."

"It's no big deal. I'm the only one on the square who does this sort of thing, and I won't make more as soon as I finish the dresses I promised Mama, Liz and Gretchen. But how wild is this?"

I waved a hand at the scene around us. "You pulled it all together in a matter of days. I'm guessing most towns take months to put something like this into action."

Clearing the roads around the square for the big horse-and-carriage kickoff parade was a huge job all by itself. Never mind the rest.

Applause drew my attention to a cowboy in jeans, chaps and a fringed leather vest as he moseyed through the crowd. He spun a rope before him and tipped his hat to passersby.

Kids carried caramel-covered apples and played chase near a small petting zoo with sheep, goats and a llama.

Ladies in fine silk costumes carried parasols and made loud chatter about the arrival of an heiress. "I hear she wants to buy the town and put a railroad through it!" one woman said.

Another gasped, drawing more attention and quieting the folks nearby. "I heard she'll build hotels and a train station."

"And dress shops and a milliner!" the first lady added.

The third of the group pressed one gloved hand to her collar. "The stagecoach should arrive any minute."

Cami lowered her clipboard. "That's my cue to be sure the parade starts on time. Catch up with you in a bit?"

I smiled and waved her off, then scanned the crowd once more. Chickens wandered loose among the people, and I was sure Clyde the Outlaw would have had a field day, given the chance. He strangely enjoyed chickens, and counted a hen named Thelma as one of his dear friends.

A sharp wolf whistle drew a smile across my lips. My favorite human popped into view a heartbeat later.

Sheriff Mason Wright, AKA my boyfriend, strode confidently through the masses in his usual uniform of jeans, boots and a t-shirt. A blue-and-gray plaid button-up hung open at the front, partially concealing the badge and sidearm on his belt. Having spent the better part of his career as a homicide detective in Cleveland, Ohio, before moving south a couple of years back, Mason wasn't a fan of crowds. He thought people were reckless when they gathered in groups, causing trouble and behaving badly. Which meant he usually was on edge in places like this.

"Well, look at you," he said, dragging me against his chest the moment he was close enough to reach me. "You look like a Laura Ingalls Wilder impersonator."

"Why thank you, kind sir." I rose onto my toes and craned my neck for a peck on his perfect lips, no easy task given he stood a foot taller than me.

Thankfully, he always met me in the middle.

"Ow." He pulled back to rub his forehead, where my bonnet's brim had poked him. "Let's try that again." Mason bent his knees and tilted his head one way, then another, attempting to work his face beneath my curved ivory brim. "This is how they kept ladies from being ruined by stolen kisses," he said, backing up with a frown.

I puckered up again and waited.

Being the tenacious man he was, Mason met my lips a moment later and looked extremely self-satisfied for the win.

"The bonnet didn't work on you," I said.

"Because I'm a man on a mission. And you're highly incorrigible."

I feigned offense. "If that's how you talk to a lady, it's no wonder you wound up with such a scandalous one."

Mason winked. "I'm willing to keep your secret. Especially since you look so darn cute in that goofy outfit."

"Where's your costume?" I'd encouraged him to wear a black shirt, boots and jeans today. Maybe even a bandana like Clyde's.

"I decided to leave the outlawing to your cat. Besides, I ran into the Pioneer Days sheriff around lunchtime. Looked like he had things covered."

I laughed. "You had lunch with that guy?" I pointed to a man arriving across the square. He seemed slightly out of breath, and it was impossible to miss his golden star-shaped badge. "Is that a lawman-to-lawman courtesy or something?"

Mason frowned. "He's not a real lawman. So, no. I ran into him at the campgrounds where the cast and crew set up their temporary digs. Someone called the emergency line to report an argument out of control, so I went to take a look. Dispatch didn't get any details beyond location, and by the time I got there it was nothing but crickets. I talked to everyone I saw, including the sheriff, but no one claimed to know what happened."

"Weird."

"Yeah." He gripped the back of his neck. "I'm not sure they were telling me the truth, but what could I do? People that travel together like this put me on edge. Do they all share the itch to wander, see the country, meet new people? Or are they on the run? And if so, from what?"

"That's your inner cop talking."

He nodded, his keen blue eyes raking the crowd. "True. I'll be glad when they leave. The hoopla's fun and all, but you get this many people in one place and there's always trouble."

"Pretty sure I'm the only trouble you're getting into tonight," I said, leaning against his side as the music volume increased around us.

Everyone quieted collectively, and actors made their ways to the sidewalk as horses' hooves beat a peppy rhythm against the road.

An MC's voice joined the music as it quieted a moment later, regaling the crowd with his tale. "A wealthy heiress dreamed of settling a town and bringing commerce to its people by way of the new railroad system."

The stagecoach parade came into view on cue.

Slowly the dark carriages and rows of horses encircled the square.

"She arrived with hope for a better future," he said with renewed dramatic flair. "And she opened her door and her heart to possibility."

The stagecoach doors opened in unison, and couples in finery stepped out. They looked into the air and made a show of turning in circles, admiring the new land.

Mason tipped his head toward mine. "Overacting a little, aren't they?"

"Big motions and expressions work best when the crowd is large," I told him. "It helps people in the back know what's going on."

He grunted. Unimpressed.

Soon silence fell over the square.

I turned for a look at the MC, looking confused in the gazebo, microphone in hand.

The actors began to titter and whisper outside their carriages, either waiting for something or having collectively forgotten what came next.

The MC cleared his throat, and a thread of feedback screeched through the speakers. "Then she opened her heart and door to possibility," he repeated, adding comically excessive enthusiasm to the line.

I returned my focus to the confused actors, then followed several sets of eyes to a single carriage with no one standing outside. "Uh oh."

"Don't say that," Mason whispered. "It goes too well with what I'm thinking, and I don't like what I'm thinking."

"Were you thinking the person who belongs in that carriage was part of whatever argument went on at the campground this morning, and they were so mad about it, they refused to show up for the performance? And the carriage is definitely empty?" I asked, my voice rising hopefully on the final word.

"No."

"Me either," I admitted, and we fell into stride, making our way to the carriage that now held the crowd's attention.

Mason flashed his badge at the driver.

He hopped down and gave the horses a pat. "Everything okay?"

"I hope so," Mason said. "May I?" He reached for the carriage door without protest from the driver.

The click and grind of hinges seemed amplified in the silence. Then Tish's body rolled gracelessly out, landing in a heap at Mason's toes.

Blood pooled over her neck and shoulders, where a pair of fabric shears had been jammed into her throat.

CHAPTER THREE

An hour later, the crowd had been largely dispersed. The roads were closed around the square, and the deputies had done their best to shield and protect the crime scene.

I stayed to support Mason.

The square was a surreal hodgepodge of the Old West and modern Georgia. An ambulance and coroner's van stood beside a line of abandoned carriages, their horses already ferried away.

I inched closer to Mason as he evaluated the crime scene. Guilt and frustration twisted his handsome features, and I knew he was blaming himself for Tish's death. He'd received a call about a fight at the campgrounds this morning, and he'd let it go without a full-scale, door-to-door search for the problem. Now, he clearly thought he could've stopped her death, assuming she wasn't already dead when he'd arrived.

"Hey." I ran a hand down his arm, drawing his troubled eyes to mine. "This isn't your fault. There's nothing you could've done to prevent it. But I know you'll get her justice, and that's something."

He pressed his lips together and dipped his chin.

"I mean, it won't be easy," I said. "All the people who knew her best aren't going to want to talk to you anymore now than they did this morning. And they'll likely be hesitant to talk about one another, since they have to travel together. Plus no one wants to provoke a killer. Also, they're leaving town in a few days, so you'll be limited on time."

His expression went flat and impossibly bland.

"And let's be honest, I don't think she was very popular to start with, so there's bound to be a lot of hard feelings to sort through."

Mason's brow furrowed. "What do you mean no one liked her? What do you know about her?"

I shrugged. "We met earlier." I recapped my run-in with Tish and Hattie, then relayed the stories Gigi and Sutton had offered.

The coroner raised a hand several yards away. "Sheriff?"

Mason scrubbed a hand over his face and shook his head. "I guess I need to talk to Sutton and Gigi when I finish here."

My phone rang, and Gigi's name appeared on screen.

"Oh, this is her now," I said.

He nodded before crossing the grass to join the gray-haired man beside the body.

I accepted the call. "Hello?"

"Bonnie?" Gigi whispered.

"Yeah?"

"Come to the bakery. Don't tell Mason. And hurry."

The call disconnected, and I raised my eyes to Oh, My Goodies.

Gigi waved frantically in the window.

I gave Mason a glance to be sure he wasn't watching, then darted across the road as Gigi had asked.

The door opened when I arrived, and she pulled me quickly inside.

Sutton locked up behind me, then I followed the ladies into the bakery's kitchen, where a group of women dressed as saloon girls grazed on sweets and sipped coffee.

"Bonnie, these are the girls," Gigi said. "Girls, this is Bonnie."

I lifted a hand hip-high in greeting and smiled. I recognized a few of the faces from town. Others were less familiar, but still local, I suspected. "What's going on?"

"We're getting a jump on this one," Gigi said. "We've all heard about what a pain Tish was. Some of us even saw her in action."

The ladies nodded.

"I don't understand."

Gigi brought me a cup of coffee, then patted my arm. "Someone died on the square. We all saw the body. You like to solve these things. And we want to help."

I opened my mouth to protest, but she interrupted.

"Why don't you start, Olivia?"

A brunette pushed away from the counter, where she'd been leaning and sipping a drink. "I'm Olivia."

"Hi," I said, dragging my attention from her to Gigi, then back.

"I saw Tish on the phone today," Olivia said. "She seemed upset."

"How so?" I asked, the words popping out before I had time to think better of it.

"She was pacing and pinching her bottom lip between her thumb and first finger." Olivia began to impersonate Tish while pretending to hold a phone to her ear. "I only caught the end of the exchange, but she agreed to meet someone somewhere later. The whole thing seemed pretty dire."

It didn't seem dire to me, but maybe I had to be there for the full effect. Still, my curious mind had questions. Who had Tish been meeting and why had she been nervous? More importantly, was the person on the other end of the line her killer?

A petite woman with black hair and freckled skin spoke next. "When I picked up my costume from her booth this morning, she wasn't there. The lady who handed me the garment bag apologized for Tish's absence and admitted she was under a lot of pressure. She said she wasn't herself lately, but she'd love to see me in her creation if I had time to stop back later."

I scanned the dress and nodded. "It's a beautiful gown." Royal-blue silk with black lace and a corset to emphasize her tiny waist. "She certainly had talent. I'll bet you spoke with her assistant, Hattie."

"She bit my head off for accidentally getting in her way," a third woman announced. "Then another Pioneer Days cast member told me to ignore her because she was like that all the time lately."

"Lately," I repeated. "So she wasn't always like that."

Gigi nodded. "That's what we thought too."

"So what was going on?" I wondered aloud.

Gigi swept an arm out, indicating the little crowd in her kitchen. "That's what we're going to find out."

A petite woman with a pixie cut and glasses raised her hand. "I saw something too."

"What was it?" I asked, once again unable to help myself.

"I saw her slap the sheriff."

My jaw dropped. "Tish hit Mason?"

"No, the Pioneer Days sheriff," she said. "Short, portly little man with a bald spot and handlebar mustache."

I frowned. "He does look a little like Yosemite Sam, doesn't he?"

"A little," she admitted. "The cartoon's better looking."

It wasn't a lie.

"Any idea why she slapped him?"

The woman shook her head. "No. I was just passing by the campgrounds on my way to the square. My family has a farm out that way."

Olivia frowned at the other woman. "I'll bet he got handsy with her. He looks like the kind of guy who gets handsy."

I grimaced. "I hope not."

"Wait a minute." The second woman who testified took the floor again. "I thought she was seeing the cowboy. I bet the sheriff wouldn't mess with the cowboy's lady."

"Who's the cowboy?" I asked.

The group gave me a collective look of disapproval that said I needed to catch up.

Gigi sighed dramatically. "He does all the rope tricks."

"Of course," I said, trying to appear less lost and making a plan to read the Pioneer Days website tonight. If I wanted to look into Tish's death, I'd have to study up on my suspects. "Someone called the sheriff's department about an out-of-control argument this morning, but when Sheriff Wright showed up, everyone was tight lipped. I wonder if the call had anything to do with that slap?"

Sutton raised a star-shaped cutout to her lips. "Groups like these aren't big on outsiders. I'm surprised anyone reached out at all."

"Do you think that means the caller is new?" I asked, planning to make note of all the newcomers in the cast and crew. "Or could a local have seen what she saw"—I nodded to the woman with the pixie cut—"and called it in?"

"I'm Lane," Pixie Cut said.

I smiled, glad to have a name to go with the face. "Wait." Something else came to mind. "If someone from town called the police, they would've probably given their name."

"Unless they were doing something they shouldn't have been doing," Gigi said.

I sighed. Investigations were exhausting, and I'd been working with my therapist to leave things like these alone. But all the unanswered questions really were intriguing.

"I traveled with the circus one summer," Gigi said. "They handled all their drama internally. Those folks had to live and work together all year round, so they tended to keep things in house and work them out internally as often as possible."

Lane crossed her arms. "I can try to find out about the rift at the campgrounds," she said. "One of the actors was flirting with me on the square. I can pay him a visit tomorrow and ask about the argument, kill two birds with one stone." She cringed at her word choice. "You know what I mean."

"Be careful," I said. "He could be the killer. Until we have some suspects, everyone's a suspect."

"But mostly the fake sheriff right now," Gigi said helpfully. "I think his name is McCoy."

I smiled. "Right. But don't push the matter if you feel uncomfortable or unsafe at any point, Lane."

She nodded.

My smile grew. "And good luck with the actor. Is he cute?"

She arched one perfect brow. "He's a hottie with a body."

The other saloon girls laughed.

I looked at Gigi, wondering if it was a good idea to get so many people involved in an investigation, especially considering I often ended up facing off with a killer. I liked the idea of added eyes and ears around town but hated the thought of anything going wrong for one of them.

Gigi rubbed my back. "They came to me."

"Who?"

Gigi pointed to the women in similar saloon-girl dresses. "Them."

The ladies looked at one another, then me.

"You always get justice for the people who die in this town," Lane said. "We read the paper and keep up as much as we can. As soon as we saw Tish roll out of that carriage, we wanted to help."

Olivia offered a shy, lopsided grin. "We asked Gigi what she thought."

Gigi lifted her palms. "I called you as soon as the coffee was ready. You should probably get back to Mason though," she instructed. "We'll fan out, stay on alert and stay in contact."

"Sounds good," I said, heading for the door with a cautious thumbs up. "Just be careful out there," I repeated the words from earlier. "Watch and listen. Nothing else. And stay in communication with Gigi or me, so no one goes missing."

Their faces paled a little, but they nodded in agreement.

I slipped onto the sidewalk, unsure how I felt about working with a team of eavesdroppers but enjoying the fact I already had two leads. A cowboy and a sheriff.

CHAPTER FOUR

Mason and I shared breakfast on the patio the next morning, enjoying the peace and sunshine while admiring the lake. It was the sort of predictable, reliable routine that made having a significant other all the more appealing to me. As if we'd made a silent pact to begin all our days this way, tuning in to one another before parting to take care of business until dinner.

"Have you had time to look at my proposed color palette for the house?" I asked, forking another piece of pancake. Mason's former home, a houseboat, had unfortunately been sunk, leaving him in need of a new permanent residence, so he was building one on the land he owned near his dock.

"Not yet." Mason wiped his mouth on a napkin and grinned. "Because you never sent it. I meant to ask about it yesterday, then that lady rolled out of the carriage and our date took a turn for the worse."

I frowned, both about Tish's death and my mistake. "I must've forgotten. I had so many dresses and costumes on order for this weekend, I barely slept. I've read studies showing driving while fatigued is like driving while intoxicated, and based on those, I haven't been completely sober in weeks."

Mason leaned across the small glass top table and kissed my head. "Send the link to the color palette when you have time. I think it's nice you include me in the plans. As if I have a clue about interior design."

"Building a house takes a team. And you're the only one who can tell me what you like. I'm just trying to be useful."

"I think you know what I like," he said, a mischievous grin curving his lips.

"Me?" I guessed, pulling him close to kiss his lips. "Thank you for letting me help with the house. I love working on a big project like this. All the possibilities and choices." I shivered for effect. "It's so exciting."

Mason stilled, looking more closely at me. "Bonnie. I want it to be your home too." His phone buzzed, and he lifted it for a look at the screen.

My heart bounced and jolted in my chest. Because when he said things like that—and he'd been saying them more frequently—I thought he might be thinking of marrying me.

I bit my lip, fighting a smile. Until recently, I'd been married to the absolute worst sort of man for all of my adult life, and for that reason, I shouldn't want to remarry ever again. I should know better. That some people hide their true, awful, vicious selves. And men can go from doting on to wholly ignoring a woman, or turn from her protector into her tormentor the moment the vows are said.

But my traitorous heart could only imagine one kind of future with Mason. One where we grew old together, sharing breakfast on the patio and teasing one another mercilessly in good fun. A lifetime of holding one another through the heartbreaks and cheering together through the victories.

Mason set the phone aside. "I've got to get to work as

soon as we finish here. What?" He caught my eye and stilled. "What did I do?"

"Nothing. I'm just thinking I'm a lucky lady, that's all."

He shook his head, as if I was being silly, then went back to his meal. "What do you think of the pancakes?"

"They're good." As was evidenced by my utterly empty plate.

Mason had dragged me to the farmers' market in Cromwell, a neighboring town and long-time rival of Bliss. Coincidentally, and unfortunately, also the same town where Mason was building his home.

"Excellent. And what do you think about adding an extra bedroom to the plans when we meet with the architect this week?"

I set my hands in my lap. "Another one?" We'd planned for three already. One master and two guest rooms. A pretty standard number for local homes, and two more than we needed. "Why?"

Mason leaned forward and frowned. "How do you feel about kids?"

My heart clenched, and my stomach churned. I couldn't have children, and Mason knew it. Something was wrong with me, or maybe a bunch of things were wrong with me, but I'd tried when I was married and still young enough to make a healthy go of it. I'd tried, and my body had failed. Repeatedly. Now, I was forty and uninterested in revisiting that pain.

"Mason," I whispered, heartbreak returning with a slap. The years of negative pregnancy tests. Month after month. The trials. The medicines. The overwhelming disappointment from my miserable ex who couldn't believe he'd chosen a spouse who couldn't provide him the most basic things. The familiar guilt and shame spiral began to coil inside me. "You know I can't."

"I'm not asking for biological children," he said, reaching for my hand to anchor me. "I'm asking how you feel about children, and there's no wrong answer. I'm just curious about your feelings on having a family with me," he said. "Where do you stand on fostering kids who need stability and love? Maybe even adopting siblings who want to stick together when other families only want to take on one kid at a time. Or just adding the extra room in case we ever hear of someone who needs a place to stay. If their house sinks, for example."

He winked, and I laughed. Mason's houseboat was still sitting at the bottom of Cromwell Lake, waiting for a tow to the junkyard, which had been rescheduled roughly a million times.

"Are you crying?" he asked, expression suddenly horrified. "I didn't mean to upset you. I just thought— Hey. Shh. I'm sorry. We don't have to talk about this now. Or ever. I just wanted to put it out there." He stroked a broad thumb across my cheek, drying a tear I hadn't noticed fall.

"Mason." I grabbed his wrist and pulled him closer, then nearly fell off my chair wrapping myself around him. "I would love to foster or adopt with you. And I think I might love you even more for thinking ahead about people who might one day be in need."

His lips twisted into a small smile. "I guess you're softening my edges."

"I think you've always had a big heart. You just try to hide it under all that snark and muscle sometimes."

Mason stroked my hair and held me tight. "Well, don't tell anyone. I've got an image to uphold."

"It'll be our secret."

Mason finished his meal, then carried our plates into the kitchen and rinsed them in the sink.

We dressed and prepped for our days and met at the front door.

"Have fun at work," he said, bending to kiss me goodbye.

"You too. Make sure you shake down the Pioneer Days cast and crew until someone tells you about the fight at the campgrounds yesterday. They might not have wanted to talk then, but with Tish dead, someone might've changed their tune."

Mason's eyes narrowed. "What are you up to?"

"Nothing." I unlatched the door on Clyde's carrier and scanned the area. "Kitty, kitty, kitty."

"Bonnie." Mason's tone went flat and hard. "Please don't get involved in this investigation. I'm already pinched for time with the whole show moving out of town in a couple days. I can't afford to divide my attention so I can keep an eye on you too. The killer will literally get away with murder."

I pushed my lips out in a pout. "Not if we find him first."

Mason straightened to his full height and pressed big palms against narrow hips. "I'm serious."

"So am I. Go do your sheriffing and leave the gossip collection to me. The event is down a seamstress, so my shop's bound to get a lot of traffic."

His phone beeped and he swiped the screen to dismiss an alarm.

"What was that?"

"An appointment reminder. I've got to go." He kissed my cheek. "Please be careful."

"Back at ya."

Clyde arrived a moment later, and I rushed him into his carrier, suddenly dangerously curious about where Mason had gone.

He'd been oddly coy for months, and my patience was losing the fight against my curiosity.

I took a roundabout route to work, desperate for a distraction that would stop me from following him. Interestingly, the new route took me past the campgrounds.

Rows of black RVs, horse trailers and vans with the Pioneer Days logo filled the spots along the road and extended into the tree-lined grounds. A small memorial had been erected near the gravel lane connecting camping spots. Tish's photo hung from a makeshift cross.

I slowed my white convertible to a crawl. "What do you think, Clyde? Ever met a cowboy or a pretend sheriff?"

He blinked lazily from the shaft of sunlight stretching into his carrier.

"Me neither," I said. "We should change that right away."

I made the next turn into the campgrounds, crunching over gravel and taking in the beauty of the area. Mature oaks offered shade on one side, their reaching limbs draped in wispy moss. Wildflowers poked through tall grass along the lane. And in the distance, horses trotted, their riders dressed in jeans and t-shirts.

A woman with a long red braid came into view, reading a book outside a camper.

"Hello!" I called waving as I slid my car's shifter into park. "I'm Bonnie Balfour. I run a shop in town. Bless Her Heart," I clarified.

"Whose?"

"What?"

We stared at one another for a long beat, before her question suddenly made sense. "Oh. No. Bless Her Heart is the name of my shop."

"Oh," she said. "Okay. Well, nice to meet you." She returned to her book.

I climbed out of the car. "Are you with the Pioneer Days cast or crew by chance?"

She raised impatient eyes in my direction, as I often did when interrupted while reading.

"Sorry," I said sheepishly. "I don't want to keep you from your book, but I wondered if you knew Tish..." I couldn't remember her last name. I cringed. "And if you knew her well?"

"No one knew her well," the woman said. "She kept to herself, except for meeting with her assistant and the other producer. And, of course, Case."

I nodded. "Thank you. One more thing?"

She sighed. "Yes?"

"Who's Case?"

The woman pointed a finger toward the distant horses.

"Thank you." I slid back behind the wheel of my car without another look from the red-headed reader. I gave her a long look before shifting into gear. "I didn't get your n—"

She rose fluidly and walked away.

"Never mind." I sighed. "Let's go see about that cowboy," I told Clyde.

CHAPTER FIVE

I drove as far as the gravel road would take me, then parked beside a massive pickup truck with an extended cab and too many wheels. I grabbed my purse and cat and started through the grassy field toward the cowboys, hoping at least one of them was the man I wanted to find.

The walk was longer than I'd anticipated and slightly uphill. Also, Clyde was heavier than I'd remembered, and the southern Georgia sun, hotter. A sheen of sweat broke across my chest and brow, collecting into droplets before skating down my temples and my back, or gathering in my bra.

I sorely regretted the white linen dress I'd chosen this morning. More than that, I regretted the shoes. Open-toed sandals weren't great for walking distances or through a field where horses played.

A thunderous round of stomping hooves drew my attention to an approaching horse. The rider steered his stallion around a set of poles with empty water jugs on top, then guided him over several low obstacles.

When the pair finished, I applauded, and they took notice.

A bright smile split the young man's face, and he pointed the steed in my direction.

I held Clyde's carrier to my chest, unsure what he'd think of horses.

The stallion stopped before us with a puff of air from its massive nose, and Clyde hissed, causing the stallion to backpedal.

"Sorry," I said. "It's my cat. I hate to leave him in the car when it's so hot. I'm Bonnie Balfour."

The cowboy dismounted with ease, gracefully airborne a moment before landing at his mount's side. "Whoa," he cooed, stroking the beast's powerful neck before turning his eyes back on me. His tan skin and solid physique spoke of long days in the sun and plenty of hard labor. "Bonnie Balfour." His playful gaze traveled my body and lingered on my smile. "I'm Rune Dupree. How can I help you?"

I smiled in return, unable to help myself and realizing this was the charm of a man perfectly executing his role. "I'm looking for a cowboy," I began, and his smile grew.

I cleared my throat. "I'm looking for a cowboy who was particularly close with the Pioneers Days producer named Tish."

Rune's expression sobered, and he removed his hat to place it over his heart. A mass of sandy hair sprang loose, sweaty curls looped against his neck and around his ears. "I believe you're looking for Case." He tipped his head in the direction of a man dressed in black, practicing rope tricks alone at the opposite end of the field.

"Thank you," I said, wishing I'd left Clyde in the car and could ask for a lift.

Then, I began to walk.

And walk.

And walk.

I groaned and grunted in the blazing heat, certain my painfully fair skin would soon catch fire. Until finally, the roping cowboy turned and headed my way.

His pace stalled a moment before he regained his stride, probably stunned to see a strange woman with a bejeweled cat carrier and flames rolling off her skin.

Since he was moving in my direction, I stopped to wait.

"Case?" I asked, when I thought he was near enough to hear.

He removed his hat and ran the back of one arm over his forehead. "Yeah?"

"I'm Bonnie Balfour. I own a shop on the square. Can I ask you a couple of questions about Tish?"

His pace faltered again, but he kept moving until he stood before me, grim-faced, sweaty and tall. His long lean body looked natural in the leather boots, jeans and vest. A wide-brimmed black Stetson shaded his eyes from the sun. "How did you know Tish?"

"I met her at my shop yesterday morning." I hoped that was enough to get him talking. When it wasn't, I pressed on. "I hate what happened to her, and I understand the two of you were close. I wanted to pay my condolences and ask if you have any idea who would've wanted to hurt her."

I raised a hand to shield my eyes as I looked up at him, the relentless sun at his back.

He glanced over his shoulder before taking a step to his right, fully blocking the blinding light.

I nearly sagged in relief. "Thank you."

He nodded. "I'm not surprised Tish made a friend in town so quickly. She was beloved everywhere we went. She just had that kind of personality. You know?"

I tried and failed to match the person he described with

the woman I'd met. One of us apparently had the wrong impression about her. "Absolutely."

He turned his hat over in his hands, then returned it to his head. "No one would want to hurt her."

I bit my tongue against the obvious retort. Someone had.

"Were you two close?" I asked instead.

"We were getting there." He sent a shy look my way. His features were angular, his jaw square. Even the bit of scruff across his cheeks played into his role. The strong, desirable cowboy.

"More than friends?" I guessed.

His lips twitched into a sad smile. "Maybe. I'd hoped as much. I still think we could've been something great, but I guess that wasn't meant to be," he said, shoulders slumping.

"Did something go wrong in the relationship?" I asked. "Or do you mean it wasn't meant to be because …." She'd been murdered in a stagecoach.

Case exhaled long and slow. "Before," he clarified. "And I don't know what exactly happened. We took this gig, and she seemed to get more tense by the day. Then we got here, and she just pulled away. No explanation. Just…needed space, I guess." He scanned the distance where Rune and the other cowboys rode their horses.

"So," I pressed gently, "She didn't give any indication of what caused the change?"

"No. She told me to lay off when I pushed. I wanted to help her through whatever had upset her, but she wasn't interested."

I waited, but he didn't go on. "So you…" I prompted.

"I did the only thing I could do. I left her alone. I'm under enough pressure to keep my place in this show, and I needed to concentrate. Stress activates wrinkles. I'm already fighting the age limit for this role. No one wants to watch an old cowboy."

I squinted at him, fighting the urge to demand his age, which couldn't have been a day over thirty-five. "Do you think the sudden change in Tish had anything to do with Sheriff McCoy?" I asked, recalling Gigi's friend's claim there was a romance between Tish and the Pioneer Days lawman.

Case's features bunched, and he blew out a bellowing laugh. "The sheriff? Heck no." He rubbed his forehead, then the back of his neck. "Not a chance."

I considered the possibility he was lying through his teeth in an attempt to cover his own jealousy. Especially since he'd just made it clear he was at least a little concerned with his age and appearance. I couldn't help wondering if the man playing the sheriff was younger than Case. "If not Sheriff McCoy, something else?" I asked.

"Money, maybe," he said, frowning as he seemed to weigh the possibility. "Tish had been upset about her finances more than usual. She didn't offer details, just cut back on things like eating out and shopping. She missed both, I think."

"Would the other producer know about her financial situation?" Her business partner would have some additional insight on the matter. Wouldn't he?

Also, was the whole show in trouble? Or just her?

Maybe the two partners had a conflict over finances that got out of control.

"I can't be sure," Case said. "David posts his office hours on the trailer to help us catch up with him. He tries to see all our shows or at least parts of them. So, he's usually on the move."

"Good to know," I said. "Can you point me to his trailer so I can check the hours?"

"Sure." He outstretched a hand in the direction of Clyde's carrier. "It's a long walk back, and it's hot. Would you like me to carry your cat for you?"

I looked down at the weight secured in my arms. Then I passed it his way. "Thank you."

We walked back to my car together, and I got directions to the producer's trailer.

"What's David's last name?" I asked.

"Smith." He set Clyde's carrier on the passenger seat of my convertible. "If you don't catch him at the trailer, you can always try the B&B on Maple."

I frowned. "He doesn't camp out here with the rest of you?"

Case's expression turned bemused. "No, ma'am. Never."

I slid behind the wheel and donned my sunglasses, then fired up the engine and blasted my air conditioning. "One more thing," I called as he began to walk away. "Were you here yesterday morning? I heard a pretty big argument went on. Someone called emergency services to help break it up, but when police arrived, no one claimed to know anything about it."

Case shook his head. "I start my days early. Tend the horses. Practice my shows. I'm usually not here from sunrise until after lunch."

"And you didn't hear about a scuffle after the fact?"

"No, ma'am."

I suspected he was lying, but this time, I let him walk away.

CHAPTER SIX

David the producer wasn't at his trailer for office hours, and the bed and breakfast on Maple was nowhere near the square, so I made a mental note to check there later. Meanwhile, I needed coffee and to open my shop on time.

I texted the highlights of what I'd learned from Case to Gigi, then I took the most direct path possible to the square from the campgrounds. I spotted Mason striding over the sidewalk at the edge of town, and I turned my radio down so I could concentrate while I waited for the light to change.

He moved swiftly around the corner between two buildings.

His Jeep was nowhere in sight.

The traffic light turned green, and I rolled forward, craning my neck to stare between each set of buildings. Wondering where my boyfriend had gone.

How had he become vapor in the ninety seconds it had taken for the light to turn green?

I made a mental note to mention it to him later, then focused on getting to the square.

I snagged the last spot at the end of the block and dashed across the street to Gigi's bakery. Several horses were tied up out front, and Clyde hissed as I hurried past.

"Sorry," I cooed to Clyde and the horses as I let myself inside.

A collection of townsfolk in modern clothing and others in Wild West attire filled the bakery's dining area. When I reached the counter, I told Gigi to make mine a double.

She grinned. "That kind of morning, huh?"

"You have no idea. I'm looking forward to our next group chat." I winked to convey my full meaning.

Interviewing actors was going to be much more difficult than interviewing regular people. This time our suspects were all professional pretenders. If the killer was pretending to be innocent, how would I know?

I was deeply thankful for Gigi's posse of saloon girls and their willingness to help collect information.

Gigi set my coffee on the counter, her happy eyes crinkling at the corners. "You decided to pursue this?"

I nodded, humbled by my apparent inability to let these things go. "Yeah."

"I'll text you about that meeting."

"Thanks." I sidestepped an incoming crowd on my way out, then squawked when the sound of firecrackers exploded on the street nearby.

The anxious horses reared and whinnied, creating a domino effect among them. Each time one panicked, the others followed suit, and the blusters and bucking grew.

Clyde fuzzed out to twice his size, hissing menacingly as the massive beasts from inside his carrier.

"You're not helping," I whispered, dodging the horses as they huffed and panicked.

I bumbled onto the street, barely escaping being trampled, and just in time to hear a car horn blast. I yelped and spun, catapulting back onto the sidewalk.

The horses went berserk at the sound of the horn and at my lurching return.

Costumed people flooded from the bakery and surrounding shops, hands up and working to settle the horses.

I caught Gigi's wide eyes through the bakery window, and knew she'd seen the entire kerfuffle. "I'm okay," I mouthed, raising one hand in a pledge.

Then I fumbled toward Bless Her Heart, afraid the timing of those fireworks wasn't an accident.

Lexi, my teenage shop keep, arrived around lunchtime, wearing jeans and a Pioneer Days t-shirt. Her long, dark hair was swept back in a ponytail and tied with a tan scrunchie to match the shirt. "Hey," she called, waving to me and smiling at shoppers. "I love all this Wild West stuff. I'm having so much fun."

The handful of folks in earshot nodded and murmured their agreement.

Somehow despite a murder and the body's public appearance, the show had gone on. I wasn't sure if that made these actors true professionals or just cold, but I was leaning toward the latter. I was also trying hard not to think about what my town's continued enthusiasm said about them.

Clyde jumped onto the counter to greet Lexi.

She tucked her bag and keys away, then scratched Clyde behind the ears and looked me over with a frown. "I don't think I've ever seen you wear shorts to work."

I glanced at the outfit I'd pulled off the rack when I'd arrived. My white linen dress was stained with sweat, so I'd changed into navy blue walking shorts and a cream silk tank top before opening the shop. I'd been hoping for a casual chic vibe, but given Lexi's reaction, I'd missed the mark. "I changed when I got here. The dress I was wearing needed a drycleaner."

She bobbed her head in understanding, probably assuming I'd spilled coffee on it, which was slightly better than the truth.

I hooked my purse over one shoulder and pocketed my phone and keys. "I don't mean to run off when you just walked through the door, but would you mind holding down the fort for a bit?"

Her brown eyes twinkled. "Don't worry about me. Everyone knows there was a murder in town. I'm honestly surprised you're still here."

I thanked her and headed for the door, hoping the smattering of shoppers hadn't overheard our exchange.

Outside, I slid sunglasses over my eyes and hopped back into my car, careful to avoid all horses. I headed for the historic theatre, where according to the schedule Sutton had given me, a series of skits featuring Sheriff McCoy would begin shortly. With a little luck, I could get him to tell me more about Tish. And maybe a little about Case the cowboy.

The road outside the theatre was blocked with wooden barricades, and people clogged the street, carrying snacks and mingling with Pioneer Days cast members. I parked and started walking, then tried the theatre's front doors.

Locked. A sign on the glass instructed folks to hang around and enjoy the music, because Sheriff McCoy would be outside soon.

I huffed and scanned the crowd, thoroughly discontent. Then I hurried around back and tried the stage entrance.

The battered old door swung open with a groan, and I

slipped into the chaos of a performance about to begin. People in various states of undress hurried in every direction.

"Excuse me," I said, catching a man with a headset and t-shirt identifying him as STAFF. "I'm looking for Sheriff McCoy."

He scanned the clipboard in his hand. "Harlot?"

"What?"

"This way." He tipped his head, then ducked swiftly through the crowd.

I followed, bumping into everyone and everything in the process. Also wondering if he'd called me Harold. Maybe that was the sheriff's first name? Why hadn't I thought to ask?

"There," the man said, pointing a finger toward Yosemite Sam and several women dressed like...harlots, apparently having a meeting on the otherwise empty stage.

Really? He looked at me and immediately thought *harlot*? Before I could ask my guide any further questions, he dissolved into the chaos behind us.

I refreshed my smile and headed for the man I'd come to see. "Sheriff?"

The women dispersed, and he heaved a sigh at the sight of me. "Finally. Where's your costume?"

"I don't—" I began, then realized his error. He also assumed I was part of the show. "Actually I just have a few questions if you don't mind."

"Talk and walk," he said, pressing a hot hand to the small of my back and steering me toward stage left. "What's on your mind, honey?"

I blinked, hating the pet name immediately. "My name is Bonnie Balfour—"

"Darling, don't take this the wrong way, but I don't care

what your name is. Can you perform a basic box step and lip sync with any believability?"

I frowned up at him. "I think so. But I was hoping you'd tell me why Tish slapped you."

He halted, cheeks reddening under red-hot stage lights. "Who told you that?"

"I spoke with her yesterday," I hedged, both avoiding the question and implying she'd confided the news.

"She told you she hit me but didn't say why?" he queried, clearly seeing through my thinly veiled lie.

"We were interrupted."

He pressed his lips into a thin line, and they practically disappeared beneath his thick red beard. "We were acting. Going over lines from a play. I've been trying to get a bigger role, and she was helping."

I considered the words, reminding myself he was an actor, and possibly a killer, then nodded. "Not an argument then? Or a lovers' quarrel?"

"No."

"Any idea who'd want to hurt her?"

If she'd been a close-enough ally to help him try out for another job, they must've talked about their lives at least a little.

Assuming he wasn't lying.

"Everyone liked Tish." He furrowed his neatly groomed brows. "Why are you so interested? Why were you talking to her yesterday?"

I scrambled for an acceptable answer to his question, in no hurry to end our conversation when I had so much more to ask. "I was auditioning," I said, taking the lead from him and recalling his questions when I'd arrived. "She needed another box stepper."

He looked me over more closely, possibly realizing for the

first time I was nearly twenty years older than all the other dancers and dressed in a blouse and walking shorts.

"She was agitated when we spoke," I said, recalling the words of one of Gigi's researchers. "Any idea why?"

"She gets that way at every new town. It takes her a while to acclimate and settle. That's all."

I nodded. "What do you know about her relationship with Case the cowboy?"

He frowned. "Nothing, but Case is a showboat and not my kind of people. Now if you'll excuse me." He pushed against my back again and waved overhead to a woman with a headset and armload of costumes. "Get her ready for the dancehall number. She's a harlot."

"A what?" I pasted my hands on my hips.

The woman turned curious eyes on me, then nodded and hauled me into a crowded dressing area. "Put these on. You've got about two minutes to get outside." She shoved a bagged dress into my arms. "Cinch the back as much as you can and try to show some cleavage. Boots are lined near the wall."

I glanced at my chest, feeling suddenly less than adequate. Then the rest of her instructions caught up with me. "Outside?" The sign had said Sheriff McCoy would be out soon. Wasn't anything happening inside the theatre? And if not, how was I supposed to get away?

Her brows rose. "You're kicking off the show. Harlots dance while Sheriff McCoy sharpshoots, then you lead the crowd inside. Tell me you've read the script and know the music?"

Her utter disapproval caused me to squirm. I checked the exits, both fully blocked with scrambling people, now mostly in costumes.

"I can box step," I said, repeating the sheriff's words,

though I'd accidentally made them sound more like a question.

She pinched the bridge of her nose. "Get dressed." She turned and walked away.

I gave the bagged ensemble a curious look. I really did enjoy a good costume. And I could box step when I was younger, so why not?

"What are you doing?" a frantic voice snapped.

I spun to find an older woman in a full gold skirt and black lace corset top that revealed cleavage for days. "We're on in less than two minutes. Get dressed! Get dressed! Get dressed!" She pulled the bag up and over the gown, setting the fabric free over my arms. "Do you need help?" She reached for my waist, and I jumped back.

"No. I've got it. Thanks." I held the gown up, telling myself I'd already taken the ruse too far.

Tish's assistant, Hattie, came into view, quietly speaking with other women in costumes. She moved from lady to lady, setting a hand on their shoulder or arm, giving final instructions or maybe words of encouragement.

Her eyes landed on me, and she frowned.

I pulled the dress on over my head. Then I worked my arms out of my silk blouse and pulled it off through the neck hole of my costume, baring miles of freshly sunburnt skin along my collarbone and shoulders.

The neckline was too low. The hem dangerously high in front, while hanging to my knees in back. I suddenly couldn't remember if I'd shaved my legs.

The older woman watched with amused eyes. "I don't know how you've spent any time in the theatre and maintained that level of modesty."

"I'm new," I said, reaching behind me to tug on the strings of the lacy corset.

She motioned for me to turn, then she laced me up until

it hurt to breathe. "I didn't think we ever brought on a new dancer."

"I met Tish yesterday, and she mentioned she could use an extra. I wasn't going to do it," I fibbed, "then, after what happened, I felt as if I should."

The woman finished, and I turned to face her. "I'm Darla," she said, lifting a fallen set of black and gold plumes from the ground. She pinned them into my hair. Then passed me a pair of heeled black boots. "Put these on. You look like a size eight."

"I am." I quickly kicked off my flats and slid my feet into the boots, careful not to lose my feathers or spill the contents of my bra in the process.

"Follow me. It'll be fine."

Hattie's gaze trailed us as Darla led me toward the back of the building.

I fought the urge to explain myself further, certain she recognized me from the morning we'd met at my store.

"Have you been with the show long?" I asked Darla, forcing my attention back to her.

"About three years," she said. "I was ready to retire from corporate America but wanted to see the country. This seemed a good compromise."

We stepped through the theatre's backdoor and onto the sidewalk outside. Heat smacked me in the face and stole my breath. The humidity level seemed to have reached suffocation levels while I'd been inside.

"Did you think Tish was acting strangely after you arrived in Bliss?" I asked, eager to get more information before someone really made me lip sync and box step. "Because I spoke with Case earlier, and he thought she was unusually uptight. As if something was bothering her."

Darla moved along the building to the corner, where eager theatre patrons waited to get in. "I suppose. But you can't put a lot of weight into anything Case says. He's a know it all who doesn't always know it all, if you know what I mean."

A hearty whoop shattered the air, and Sheriff McCoy appeared on the street.

"Howdy ho!" he called, and the crowd cheered.

I inched closer to Darla hoping to be heard over the eruption of applause and enthusiasm. "Did you hear anything about a rift at the campgrounds on the morning she died?"

Darla frowned. "No."

"Are you sure?"

She gave the sheriff a pointed stare, then turned to me, brows furrowed. "Talk to Hattie. That's Tish's assistant. She'll know the whole story, but I heard Tish slapped him."

"He said it was Tish. They were running lines for a potential new role," I said, still trying to be heard without drawing unnecessary attention.

She shook her head. "I don't think that's true, but you didn't hear it from me."

The crowd roared with fresh applause.

Sheriff McCoy gave a deep bow.

"He's not in any hurry to leave Pioneer Days," she said. "Look at him."

I could certainly see where she was coming from. He had an entire street full of people hanging on his every word. "What do you think really happened?" I asked, leaning closer and hoping she'd hazard a guess.

A long beat of silence stretched between us while the spectators continued to marvel over the sheriff. Darla bit her lip, and fresh color flooded her cheeks. "I think they might've been involved. Romantically," she clarified. "Or at least physically, and she might've wanted to call it off."

"He didn't?" I guessed.

She nodded. "That's just my speculation."

Slowly, the roar of applause became a steady, rhythmic clapping, and a row of women in dresses like mine formed a line before us. Then they began to box step. A merry tuned pumped through hidden speakers, and the dancers gripped the fronts of their already too short gowns and hiked them a little higher.

Sheriff McCoy gave a long and appreciative yee-haw.

Darla locked her arm with mine and pulled me into a line behind the other dancers.

I tried to spin away, zip back into the building to find my shirt and shoes, but Darla held tight.

"Time to dance, doll," she said, falling into step with the ladies before us.

The other row moved on to a Rockette-style kick line I was sure revealed their ruffled pantaloons. A wardrobe piece that had not come in my costume bag. Thankfully, I still had my walking shorts on.

I stumbled into a terrible box step, too rattled to think and move my feet at the same time.

Then the kick line broke apart and moved to the back, pushing us forward.

An old wooden bench came into view on the street, and the sheriff pulled a pistol from his holster several yards away. He spun the gun on his finger, making a show of his handling skills. Then he took aim at a cluster of old green bottles.

I jumped with every pull of his trigger, hyper aware of his proximity and the resulting consequences if he made a significant error. But he shot them down one-by-one without a single miss.

Darla released me to clap along with the crowd, and I nearly toppled over, tripped by my own two feet.

I took advantage of the freedom and box stepped my way backward, through the line of dancers behind us and onto the sidewalk. I high stepped and clapped myself right back around the building and into the theatre's side door.

The cool air and relief hit like a bat, and I broke into anxious laughter. I definitely could not box step, but at least no one had seen me in the harlot costume, high-kicking off-rhythm with the bulk of my bosoms on display.

Then I noticed Mason with the stage crew, sharp blue eyes on me and standing less than ten feet away.

CHAPTER SEVEN

Mason moved in my direction, broad hands hooked onto his hips. Eyebrows high. His gaze trailed over my exposed sun-reddened skin until I burned for new reasons.

"Hello," I said, attempting to be cool and hoping he hadn't seen me dancing.

"Got a new gig?" he asked, amusement playing at the corners of his mouth. "What sort of costume is this? And what happened to the other one with the apron and the kiss-thwarting hat?"

"I'd like to say I'm dressed as a show girl, but I think this is definitely meant for a trollop." I glanced down at myself and grimaced.

He covered his mouth with one hand, the smile evident behind his fingers. "And why are you dressed as a trollop?"

"For fun," I said, but the words came out like a question.

"Uh huh."

"What are you doing here?" I asked. "Got a hot lead?"

Mason pulled the hand from his lips and turned his palm toward me like a traffic cop. "Wait a minute. I have more questions. Like, why are you outside in that outfit, callously blinding a hundred people with the glint of sun off your legs." His teasing smile lightened my heart a little.

I feigned offense. "It's not my fault I don't tan."

"Is it your fault you're in a chorus line?"

I fought the urge to laugh again. "A little."

"Care to elaborate?" he asked, leaning casually against the nearest wall. His expression suggested this was more interrogation than friendly conversation. And he knew exactly what I was up to. He'd likely followed the same leads I had right to the sheriff.

I walked forward and rested my cheek against his chest in surrender. His arms came around me instantly.

"You still have to answer the question," he said.

"Ugh." I stepped back and fessed up, explaining about my chats with Darla, Rune and Cowboy Case, then the weird exchange with Sheriff McCoy. For my grand finale, I shared the fib that landed me on the street in a kick line.

He sighed, and it sounded a little judgmental.

"What's important here," I said, "Is that we now know Tish had something going on with Case, and there is definite friction between him and Sheriff McCoy. Also, Case thought Tish had money problems, which is why someone should talk to the other producer, David Smith. If he and Tish were business partners, he probably knew about her financial issues."

The idea Mr. Smith was Tish's killer wiggled in the back of my mind. Her business partner would've had private access to her. Maybe the show had been sinking, and that was why Pioneer Days had been available without notice. An argument about their failing enterprise seemed like as good of a reason as any for murder.

"I'll be sure to keep all that in mind," Mason said. "Are you about done here? Or do you have an encore performance?"

I rolled my eyes. Apparently he wasn't going to discuss my theories or let me in on his. "Give me a minute to get my shoes and blouse."

I redressed for work and Mason walked me back to my car.

"Have time for a late lunch?" he asked.

I checked my watch. "I really shouldn't. I barely spoke to Lexi when she arrived for her shift. I'd better go help out at the shop."

He nodded. "Guess I'll grab a burger from the pub and take it to the station with me. I've got some leads to follow and a few phone calls to make."

"Sounds like my kind of afternoon."

Mason's mischievous grin returned. "You'll never catch me dressed as a trollop to get information."

"Never say never," I said, allowing myself a long beat to imagine Mason in my shoes, high-kicking in a ruffled dress. An ugly snort of laughter erupted. Then I remembered something else. "Hey, I saw you walking at the edge of downtown this morning, but you disappeared between buildings before I could honk or say hi. What were you up to?"

His face pinched. "Let's talk tonight. Over dinner?"

"Dinner sounds good. Seven-thirty?"

"I'll pick something up on my way home," he promised.

I wanted to press the issue, but I bit my tongue instead and told my brain to put a pin in it. I'd get answers soon enough.

My phone buzzed and I tugged it from my pocket for a quick peek.

Gigi's name graced the screen.

Gigi: DS @ BNB!

I pondered the jumbled letters a moment, wondering what she might mean. Then, it hit me.

David Smith was at the B&B. My gaze jerked to Mason,

and I forced a tight smile. "I guess I'll leave you to your burger. I'm going to see Gigi, then get back to work."

He scrutinized me a moment, probably knowing something had changed. "No more pretending to be part of Pioneer Days today," he said. "Promise me."

"No more today," I repeated.

Mason kissed my cheek. "Call me if you need anything."

"Back at ya," I said.

"I need more antacids."

I smiled. "I'll pick them up on the way home."

I pulled up to the bed and breakfast on Maple ten minutes later and hurried over the sidewalk to a massive oak tree where Gigi and her friend Olivia waited in corresponding western gear.

"Finally. I was starting to think you weren't coming," Gigi said.

I frowned. "I was with Mason when I got your message, but I drove straight here."

She motioned to the home beside us. "David Smith is staying here, and we heard he didn't come down for breakfast or leave to start his day yet. So, we're watching to be sure he wouldn't get away before you had a chance to talk to him."

A little jolt of adrenaline shot through my chest and limbs. Part of me realized that wasn't a healthy response for a resale shop owner. The rest of me embraced the thrill. "He's at the top of my suspect list," I said. And best of all, he was unlikely to kill, attack or abduct me at a B&B with other guests and the innkeeper nearby. "This is perfect."

The Whispering Willows B&B was a grand estate from nearly two centuries past. What had begun as a private home had later played the roles of boarding house, Bliss History

Museum and our town hall. Eventually, we didn't need a boarding house and both the history museum and town hall moved to newer buildings closer to the square. A couple in love with the charm and architecture had restored the home and made it a bed and breakfast. If I recalled correctly, the husband had passed away, but the wife was still living the dream.

"Have you seen him?" I asked, looking from Gigi to Olivia and back.

They shook their heads.

Olivia's barrel curls danced against her cheeks on the wind. "I pretended to be from the show this morning and stopped in before breakfast. I heard he was staying here, and figured his schedule was busy, being the last producer and all. So, I tried to get here before he left. I was going to follow him when he did, but the owner said he hadn't come for breakfast. I called Gigi to see what I should do next, since you told us we should only watch and listen."

"I came right over," Gigi said. "Sutton's at the bakery."

"And I need to get to work now." Olivia stepped forward to hug Gigi goodbye, then hurried away.

"Thank you!" I called after her, still processing what I'd been told and considering how best to open the conversation with David Smith. I supposed I'd follow my usual format, which was to dive right in.

"Olivia does my coloring at the Flip N Snip hair salon," Gigi explained. "She's really good. If you ever think about covering your grays, you should see her."

I frowned, one hand instinctively smoothing my hair. "I thought the white ones blended with the others," I said a little self-consciously. My red hair had always leaned toward strawberry blond, which I'd thought was incredibly forgiving when the grays began to appear.

Gigi blinked but didn't respond.

"I guess I'll give her a call then."

"Atta girl," Gigi said. "Meanwhile you should talk to Mr. Smith before he heads out and tells you he's too busy to chat. I'm sure he's underwater with paperwork now that his partner is dead. Or grieving."

"Or hiding out and lying low," I suggested.

I gave the gorgeous, but massive, old home another look, wondering how far inside I could get without being spotted or removed by the innkeeper. "Any chance you know which room is his?"

"No. But the innkeeper told Olivia he hadn't come down to breakfast. I think that means his room is upstairs." Gigi's phone buzzed. She fished her reading glasses from her handbag and slid them on. "Oh, hang on. This is Mary Margaret. Hello?"

I dragged my gaze over each upstairs window, wondering how to explain myself if I was caught wandering. And what I'd say when I knocked on each door, searching for Mr. Smith.

"Okay," Gigi said, lowering her phone. "Mary Margaret just heard it was Tish's assistant, Hattie, arguing with Sheriff McCoy at the campground. Apparently she's the one who slapped him. Not Tish."

"That's interesting," I said, picturing the small blond woman and bald, portly sheriff. "I just confronted the sheriff, and he let me believe it was Tish."

Gigi frowned.

"Did Mary Margaret know what they fought about?" I asked.

"Didn't say."

"Did she hear anything specific? Something that could clue us in on the general direction the spat had taken?" Whatever it was, it had to be salacious, or untrue, to prompt the sheriff to go along with my assumption.

"Afraid not," Gigi said. "She heard about it from one of the cowboys who do the horse tricks. She said he's quite a looker."

Overall, the new intel wasn't very helpful, but Rune immediately came to mind as the cowboy. "Okay. I'll chew on that later." And maybe pay the cowboys another visit. "I'd better get in there."

Gigi patted my shoulder, and I lifted my chin.

"Here goes nothing."

Shoulders back and a faux shield of confidence in place, I moved down the walkway toward Whispering Willows. Past perfectly mulched flower beds and decorative trees. Up wide cement steps lined in colorful pots and blooms.

When I'd been nervous on campus in Atlanta my freshman year of college, someone had advised me to put my chin up and pretend I belonged wherever I was. Because no one knew any differently. I said a prayer that those rules also applied to historic B&Bs.

I raised my finger to ring the bell, then reached for the doorknob instead.

The door opened smoothly, and I slid inside.

The magnificent two-story foyer nearly stole my breath. Miles of polished hardwood floors rolled out before me, and a sweeping mahogany staircase climbed one wall. The baseboards and crown molding were wide and intricately carved. The sculptures and oil paintings were perfectly placed and chosen. I felt a little as if I'd stepped back in time.

Tinkling sounds of flatware on plates and the rush of running water floated to my ears from somewhere deep inside the home, underscored by the soft melody of classical music.

I tiptoed across the soft carpet runner, then dashed up the creaky steps, wincing at each wooden groan.

On the second floor large tapestries hung on bold floral

wall paper. Doorways lined the hall in both directions, some open, others not.

I wasn't sure where to start, so I reached for the closest door and knocked. No one answered. "Mr. Smith?" I took a deep breathe, then turned the knob, prepared to humble and excuse myself if I found someone else inside.

A pile of splayed papers shifted across the floorboards and rug, nudged by the swinging door. My limbs went rigid as I took in the visible sliver of a room in upheaval, as if someone had thrown a tantrum or dropped a case of receipts and invoices from the ceiling, then attacked the mess with a leaf blower. I stiffened and began to back out, before whoever had made the mess took out their rage on me.

Then I saw the bottom of a large man's dress shoe, a wide puddle of blood sprawling out from the body attached.

CHAPTER EIGHT

An hour later, Mason approached me on the sidewalk, tossing chalky tablets into his mouth. He watched me carefully while he chewed.

"How's it going?" I asked, sliding my gaze to the historic B&B, now awash in emergency flashers.

A row of first responders lined the driveway and curb. Ambulances. Deputy sheriffs' cruisers. A coroner's van. A firetruck.

He continued to chew, stress radiating off him.

"Mrs. Pennel called 911," I explained. "I told her that wasn't necessary. The non-emergency number would do. Mr. Smith was clearly dead, but she insisted."

Mason closed his eyes and pressed the pads of his fingers against the lids.

I glanced nervously around, hating the role I'd played in the discovery of another body. It always upset Mason, and I was sure to have nightmares for a few weeks at minimum.

Knots and clusters of neighbors had gathered on every nearby corner. Others walked their dogs back and forth, feigning disinterest, while stealing repeated curious looks.

Teens had appeared on bikes and skateboards, then filled the lawn across the street, taking photos and selfies with their phones.

Gigi made her way across the expansive historic porch, offering tortes and coffee from her shop as a means of comfort and chatting up the unnecessary firemen.

"I'm surprised Mirabelle isn't here," I said, suddenly recognizing her absence. The octogenarian reporter typically covered local crimes with her elderly, overweight Pekingese.

"Mr. Dinky had a vet appointment," Mason said. "She called to let me know she'd need a statement later."

"Oh. I hope everything's okay." I made a mental note to check in on her when the mess of the week had cleared a bit. She'd be lost without that old guy.

Mason dropped his hand to his side, blue eyes flickering with frustration. "You found another dead body."

I lifted both shoulders, holding the exaggerated shrug for a long beat. "I didn't mean to."

I rolled my head to one side, gripping the sore and tightened muscles along my neck. What could I say? "I just wanted to talk to him. I never dreamed he'd be dead."

Mason's brows lifted, and I knew I'd misstepped. "Why would you want to talk to the co-producer of a traveling Wild West show?"

"To pay my condolences," I said, because that was partly true. "His partner just died, tragically," I added. "It seemed the right thing to do, and I thought it might be nice to let him know the town cares."

Mason's expression grew mocking. "You're here representing the town?"

I pursed my lips. "Mmhmm."

"And you came to pay your condolences without any sort of cake or casserole?"

I stared. He had me there.

"You're investigating," he said. "Just like you were when you wound up in that ridiculous dance routine two hours ago. When, I want to add, you told me you were done doing this for the day."

The tension in my shoulders increased. "I didn't mean to. And I think my promise was to stop pretending to be part of Pioneer Days. Then this came up."

"What came up?"

I glanced at Gigi, then quickly away, hoping Mason hadn't noticed. "I just think it would be awful to lose your partner. Don't you? You're always worried about me, and I live in fear of something from your past coming back for you."

"Smith and Tish were business partners," Mason said. "They weren't in love. And as far as I can see, their relationship was strictly business."

"You can't be sure. No one can. Except for them, and now they're both gone. They must've spent plenty of time together that the cast and crew didn't know about."

Mason shifted, his thinning patience and increasing irritation evident. "I know because I spoke to Mr. Smith at length yesterday following Tish's death."

"You did?" My mouth opened in awe. "What did he say?"

"That they were business partners, not lovers."

I crossed my arms, not appreciating the undertone of sarcasm. "Well, we know Tish had financial concerns before her death, and now Mr. Smith was murdered too. That can't be a coincidence."

Mason's hand came up, halting my momentum. "How do you know it was murder? He might've fallen and hit his head."

I narrowed my eyes. "I saw his head wound when I checked his vitals. The only way he sustained that kind of damage without a little help was if he fell from the sky and landed in his room headfirst."

Mason and I engaged in a staring contest.

As usual, I cracked first. "What do you think the killer was looking for?"

He looked away, refusing to engage.

"Someone scattered every paper in the room all over the floor. They had to be looking for something." I considered the problem. "Is there a way to know what's missing?"

"Maybe nothing's missing," Mason suggested.

"What do you mean? Do you think the killer left something instead? Made it look like something was taken, when really they added something to point the finger away from them?"

Mason appeared to be counting silently to ten or contemplating another handful of antacids.

My mind continued to reel. "I suppose they might've just snapped a photo of the information they needed. Or created the mess to make it appear as if the deaths were about something in the paperwork, when in reality this has nothing to do with that at all."

The group of lookie-loos on the corner began to break apart, and a pair of familiar faces came into view. Cowboys Case and Rune moved swiftly in our direction, then broke into a jog as they reached the center of the street a few yards away.

Mason bent down to press a kiss to my head. "I've been waiting for these guys. Dinner later?"

I nodded. We could pick up our chat then. Meanwhile, Mason had a couple cowboys to interview, and I spotted a familiar blonde moving in the opposite direction.

Tish's assistant. The one who'd slapped the sheriff, according to Gigi's friend Mary Margaret, who'd heard it from an unnamed cowboy.

I hurried across the street, racking my brain for the assistant's name. The only thought that came to mind was that this woman knew more than she was letting on. And I needed to talk to her.

She glanced at a clipboard on one arm, then into the distance and moved impossibly faster, as if she was running late for something important.

"Excuse me!" I called between pants and puffs. Quickly losing all hope of catching her.

Banjo music twanged merrily as I crossed the next block. A crowd had gathered in the community park beside a popular Little League baseball field. A local jug band was performing, and members from the Pioneer Days cast were leading a crowd in line dancing. According to the schedule Sutton had given me, there would be square dancing later tonight.

Tables were spread with red-and-white checkered cloths and covered in casserole dishes and desserts. Folding chairs lined the space around a makeshift stage, where the band and caller stood. Dancers skipped and spun for the crowd.

I pushed myself into the mix, having completely lost sight of the woman I'd been chasing.

Strategy was my only chance at finding one small person in a crowd of dozens. So I moved in a broad arch along the periphery, using a row of loosely piled hay bales as my guide. Distance provided a better view of the big picture, and I felt the tickle of hope rise again.

I paused in front of a large arrangement of hay, straining to concentrate despite the intensity of combined sounds. Speakers on nearby poles seemed to pipe the music directly into my ears while locals clapped to the beat. Children screamed and laughed, mimicking the moves on stage, and fifty random conversations created an undercurrent that tensed my nerves to spring.

A farmer caught my eye near a big red barn across a large pasture running parallel to the park. I turned my full attention in that direction, suspecting he might've seen something I hadn't, specifically the petite blonde wielding a clipboard.

Enthusiasm renewed, I took two quick steps toward the barn before my toe caught on something unseen.

I bumbled forward, arms outstretched to brace my fall, and I landed with an oof.

Then the pyramid of hay bales crashed over me.

CHAPTER NINE

I dragged myself back to work, dirty and sore from the tumble. Also mildly horrified by the number of people who saw me dig my way out from beneath the hay. No one, on the other hand, had actually seen what caused the bales to fall. And no one had any suggestions on how a pile of heavy, stable bales could simply tip over. Precisely when I'd walked by.

I imagined the culprit had also recently spooked a line of horses outside Gigi's bakery as I'd passed.

Both were incidents I needed to tell Mason about soon.

"Whoa." Lexi strode in my direction, eyes wide and hands flapping uselessly in front of her. "What happened to you?"

"I fell."

She grimaced. "There's hay in your hair."

"A few bales fell on top of me."

She plucked a long piece of the evidence from my bangs. "Were you inside a barn? Oh, your knees are muddy. I guess you were in a field?" She groaned before I could get a word in. "Your shoes are so cute but completely ruined."

"Thank you," I said slowly, hoping not to sound nearly as curt and hostile as I felt. "I'm aware."

Clyde darted to my side and sniffed my legs.

"Hi, sweetie." I bent forward to scoop him into my arms, but he wrestled free and escaped under a rack of dresses.

So much for getting a little cuddle comfort.

I headed for the small hallway leading to the restroom and my office.

"Have you seen Sheriff Wright?" Lexi asked. "Does he know you…fell?"

"No. He's still at the B&B. There was another murder." I peeled the bathroom door open and jammed the stopper into place.

My reflection in the mirror was worse than I'd imagined. A blade of grass clung to my right ear. I gathered a handful of paper towels and wet them, then began to clean the mud and grass from my cheek, knees, shins and shoes.

Lexi crossed her arms and leaned against the open doorway. "I should've guessed you were there. So, how'd you wind up in a field?"

I grabbed a clean wad of paper towels and tried to spot clean my shorts and blouse.

I gave Lexi a quick rundown on my day, then managed to salvage my sandals, which cleaned up easier than the rest of me. "I need to borrow another outfit."

She followed me back to the sales floor, where I picked through the racks. "I saw your boyfriend on my way in today," she said. "He had his hat pulled low and he popped onto the sidewalk between two buildings. I was going to honk at him for fun, but he got into his Jeep pretty quickly."

I selected a pair of capri jeans and checked the size, rushing to get out of the ruined clothes before anyone came into the shop and saw me. "Mason?"

"Unless you have another boyfriend I don't know about." She grinned. "Hang on. I have the perfect top for those."

I went to the nearest dressing room and shimmied out of my dirty clothes, then into the jeans. My short legs made them look more like ankle pants than capris, but I was currently a beggar and therefore could not be a chooser.

"Here." Lexi poked a hanger past the curtain, and I grabbed it.

"Thank you." I tugged the petal-pink tank top over my head, appreciating the butter-soft material, broad straps, and forgiving A-line cut. The fabric fell in ripples over my chest, creating an impression of generosity while hanging loosely at my equally ample waist. "This is really cute."

"Right?" Lexi responded from the sales floor.

I removed the tags from the garments and exited the little nook, my mind spinning over what she'd said earlier. "I saw Mason near Udder Delights this morning. Where was he when you saw him?"

"Same."

An uncomfortable thread of panic tugged at me. My counselor worked upstairs from the popular ice cream shop, and the idea he might somehow gain access to my private records was horrifying. Not that he'd ever do anything like that or that she would part with my secrets. But it was a personal fear nonetheless.

The bell over the front door dinged.

"Welcome to Bless Her Heart," Lexi and I sang.

Mason smiled. "Hey. How are you, Lexi?" He passed her a disposable cup on his way to my side. "I saw a stand with strawberry cheesecake shakes on my way over and knew better than to pass it up."

She beamed at him, taking an immediate drink. "Bless you," she said a moment later, eyes closed in reverence.

"Anytime." He pressed a kiss to my temple and looked me over. "Is this the fourth outfit I've seen you in today?"

I did a mental tally. White linen dress, walking shorts and blouse, trollop costume, and this. "Yep."

His brows furrowed, and I forced a tight smile.

"How do you feel about a spin around the square?" he asked. "You've had a rough day, and I could use the fresh air."

"Everything okay?"

He pulled me closer. "We didn't get to talk about how you're feeling earlier. I was focused on the crime scene, when I should've been focused on you."

My heart thudded over his compassion, reminding me I'd really found a good one, no matter what he'd been up to near Udder Delights. "It's your job to handle the crime scene. I can hardly blame you for your distraction."

"Well, I was cranky too," he said. "You didn't deserve that. And David Smith is going to be dead forever. I should've supported you when you needed it. I'd blame too many years stuck in cop mode without someone special in my life, but since I'd like to keep you, I figured I'd better get over here and apologize."

I hugged him. "Thank you."

Having someone to care about me the way Mason did was something I was still getting used to, and it never stopped filling me with joy.

"Aww," Lexi cooed.

My cheeks heated, and I stepped back, taking Mason's hand in mine. "How about that walk?"

Outside, the day was scorching, and the square brimmed with locals enjoying the booths and music.

We got in line at a booth serving Tex Mex and took a minute to review the menu.

"What do you think Pioneer Days will do now that both their producers are dead?" I asked. "Will they finish their scheduled time here before moving on? How will they move forward without a leader? Will they have to cancel whatever was on the calendar?"

Mason looked around. "I don't see any of the cast or crew. Cami might have a better idea since she scheduled the event, but I suppose they'll have to figure the future out for themselves. Hopefully they aren't in a hurry to leave town."

The woman at the front of the line stepped aside, carrying her meal with her. She stopped abruptly as her blue eyes met mine.

I smiled despite myself. I'd never spotted my therapist running loose in the wild before. In fact, I'd spent an unhealthy amount of time wondering where she lived and why I never saw her outside her office.

Her stunned gaze swept from me to Mason, then back.

"Miranda!" I said, far too brightly. "How are you?"

"Good." Her gaze trailed down my arm to the place where my fingers joined Mason's.

I stiffened as an unfortunate little white lie returned to my mind. I'd told Miranda I was seeing a man named Clint. Or Cliff? Originally I'd intended to protect our new sheriff from unnecessary scrutiny, and once I'd learned to trust Miranda, it'd seemed too late to admit I'd lied. So I left the fake name in place. I could only imagine what she was thinking now.

"Miranda," Mason said, extending his free hand for a shake.

"Bonnie, Mason," she said. "Lovely to see you. Enjoy your evening."

She bustled off, and I turned narrowed eyes on my date. "Mason?"

"Hmm?"

"That was my therapist, Miranda."

He nodded, attention back on the menu board. "I figured."

"I didn't have a chance to introduce you."

He slid his pale-blue eyes my way. "It's fine."

"She called you Mason," I said, tapping the badge on his belt. "Not Sheriff Wright. Or even just Sheriff."

He turned to face me with a sigh. "I have a story for you."

I waited.

"You know how this is an unreasonably small town?"

"I wouldn't say unreasonably."

"And there aren't many mental-health professionals in the area," he continued.

"Yeah." In fact, there had only been one who wasn't specializing in children or marriages or trauma when I'd begun looking. Miranda had been the only general counselor. She was highly educated and trained to advise but specialized in listening and leading productive discussions. She'd guided me toward healing without telling me how to heal. And my time with her had worked wonders.

My mouth opened as I imagined sitting in her office. Above Udder Delights.

Mason inhaled slowly, then released the breath with resolve. "I've been seeing her off and on for about nine months, seriously for the past six. When I saw how much better you were feeling after seeing someone, I looked for someone too. Turns out we found the same person."

"Next!" the man at the counter called.

We placed our orders, then stared at one another.

"I didn't mean to choose your therapist," he said. "I didn't realize I had until I'd already been to two sessions with her. Then you called her by name at dinner for the first time, and I realized the problem. I didn't want to start over with someone else, and I hadn't mentioned your name in our sessions, so I kept what I knew to myself. Which was kind of shady on my part." He grimaced.

I rolled my eyes. "I just can't believe you didn't tell me you were seeing someone. I would've been happy for you."

"And you would've asked me her name."

I bit my lip, knowing he was right. "You didn't even give me a name?"

"I couldn't."

"I told her your name was Cliff."

A bark of laughter broke from Mason's lips. "That makes me sound like a mailman."

"I was protecting you. You're the sheriff, and she must live somewhere around here. I didn't want to influence her thoughts about you."

He snaked an arm around my shoulders and kissed my head. "So this run-in must've been really awkward for her."

I started to giggle and didn't think I'd ever stop.

Mason paid for our meals, and we carried them to an empty bench beneath an old oak tree. We ate in companionable silence, smiling and people-watching, soaking in the perfect southern summer day.

Recent murders aside.

"What are you thinking?" Mason asked, wiping his hands on a napkin.

"I'm really happy," I said. "And I knew you were up to something. I'm glad it wasn't anything scary. I like it when you're safe."

Mason set his paper taco boat aside. "I hate finding you at murder sites."

"I know. I'm sorry."

"It's worse when I get calls saying you were threatened or injured. I don't always say a lot about it when that happens, but the things I think aren't pretty. I've seen the ugliest parts of humanity in this job, back when I worked homicide, especially when I worked undercover. I want to keep you away from all of it, and I can't. Miranda's going to make a mint helping me unpack all my issues, but I'm okay with that. Maybe the process will make me a better man."

"You're the best man," I said.

"You're biased," he said. "But you make me think it's possible and worth the trouble. So, I appreciate it when you let me be grumpy from time to time."

I frowned. "I'm sorry I worry you."

"To be fair, I knew all about your bad habits when I fell in love with you."

"Solving murders is hardly a bad habit," I argued. "Not brushing my teeth regularly and spending all my money on tchotchkes are bad habits."

Mason feigned gagging. "Please never stop brushing your teeth. I don't really care about the tchotchkes." He pulled his phone from his pocket and turned the screen to face us.

The builder's name centered the screen, followed by a text reminder of our morning meeting.

Mason tucked the device away. "It's a good thing they send these texts, because I'd already forgotten we were building a house. It's been a day and a half since breakfast. And it's still afternoon."

"I put all the details and special requests in a spreadsheet," I said. "There's nothing left to do but show up."

"Special requests?"

"Sure. I can add anything you want, but I made a thorough list of necessities and a secondary list of wishes and whatnots."

"Gun safe?" he asked.

"Check."

"Large stamped concrete patio overlooking the lake. Natural gas grill and firepit. Outdoor seating. One of those massive showers with multiple heads in the primary bedroom?"

I grinned. "All of that. Yes."

He stretched to his feet and pulled me up with him. "What would I do without you?"

"Probably build a single room hut and spend less on therapy."

He laughed. "I have to meet a group of Pioneer Days actors in a few minutes. Are we still on for dinner? We can go over the details before tomorrow's meeting."

"Deal."

And then he kissed me.

CHAPTER TEN

*D*inner with Mason went exceptionally well, even if he opted for antacids over Gigi's seven-layer cake for dessert. I suspected the decision had a lot to do with my hay-bale debacle, which I told him about immediately after my spooked-horse suspicions.

He agreed the two events were likely related, given the timing and recent deaths, then insisted I start at the beginning and give him an hour-by-hour account of my last two days.

The exercise was eye opening. I really was a busy person.

Mason took special issue with Gigi and her friends acting as my eyes and ears. Thankfully he'd received a call during that part and relocated to the living room.

Now, he sat on the couch, hunched over his laptop on the coffee table, cell phone pressed to his ear.

And I rinsed the dishes with as little water pressure as possible, because I was attempting to eavesdrop.

Eventually I gave up my ruse and went to sit beside him on the couch.

He patted my knee when I arrived. "I can be there in ten minutes," he said.

His gaze traveled to mine and he winced. "Make that forty-five."

I folded my hands in my lap, holding back a rush of questions while Mason disconnected.

He tapped the phone against his thigh, examining me with narrowed eyes. "How do you feel about square dancing?"

"I'm not a huge fan at the moment," I admitted. "But I've had quite a day."

He frowned, probably recalling my earlier calamity.

"Wait," I said, recalling something my mama had called about earlier. "Gigi and my folks are going square dancing at the park tonight. Were you thinking of going?"

Mason visibly relaxed. "Right now I need to meet my deputy at the station, and I don't want you to stay here alone. I think you'll be safer in a crowd and with your family. I can drop you off there, hit the station, then meet you afterward."

"Why do you need to go to the station?"

"Because my deputy has Hattie Wills in an interrogation room, and I want to talk to her. I'm hoping she cracks under pressure." He smiled. "Then I can make an arrest for two murders and wrap this mess up tonight."

My brows rose. "I knew it. She's been everywhere. At the theatre. Outside the B&B. At the square-dancing thing earlier." I paused to rub my palms against my arms, then fluff my hair, still feeling the itchy hay there. "She had access to Tish," I continued. "Probably David Smith by proxy. And according to a cowboy, who told Gigi's friend Mary Margaret, Hattie was the one fighting with Sheriff McCoy at the campgrounds. Not Tish."

Mason watched me.

I scrutinized him.

"You'll have more fun square dancing than at the sheriff's department," he said. "And I'll be less stressed knowing you're with your family. I'll provide a full report when I finish."

I wasn't convinced I'd have less fun at the sheriff's department, but Mason looked like he needed the win. "You'll answer all my questions after the arrest?"

"Yes, and you can dress up again for the square dancing," he said, dangling the proverbial but delicious carrot.

"Would you believe I have a square-dance costume in my closet?"

"I never doubted."

I grinned. I'd been dying for an opportunity to wear the teal, black and white number with all the poofy layers of tulle. I'd brought it home from work on a whim and not been able to part with it. Strangely, I hadn't thought about it until now. I even had matching cowgirl boots. "Give me ten minutes."

Thirty minutes later, Mason kissed me goodbye at the park where I'd been crushed by hay. He waited until I made my way into the mix and waved from the safety of the crowd before pulling away. I'd let my family know I was coming, and they'd promised to keep an eye out for me.

My parents were already dancing when I arrived, and Mason promised to join me for a song or two when he returned.

I lifted my chin and tugged my braided ponytails over my shoulders, then scanned the space for signs of Gigi.

Like before, the music was loud and the crowd was thick, but it was dark now, and there were alcohol sales along with snacks and dessert concessions. A set of spotlights illuminated the caller and band, while multi-colored lights followed dancers around an enormous patch of grass turned dance floor.

My parents waved as they promenaded past, smiling, as usual, like a pair of lovestruck teens. I stuck my fingers into my mouth and whistled.

The music was lively and the energy contagious. I bought a cup of punch and took a seat on a folding chair to enjoy the moment. Friendly faces and happy couples, sleeping toddlers on fathers' shoulders. I absorbed it all and let it warm me to the core.

I tried not to focus on the sadness I felt for Tish and David. Two adults who'd chosen a life on the road over making roots like mine. I supposed the Pioneer Days cast and crew had become their families, which would've been nice if someone from their traveling family hadn't murdered them.

My phone buzzed with a text from Gigi, and I twisted at the waist in search of her smiling face before checking the message.

Gigi: Running late. Bringing a hummingbird cake

Gigi: Find your folks. They're probably on the dance floor

Me: They are. Be safe. CU soon

I slid my phone into my pocket and looked up in time to see Hattie arriving. I watched with confused interest as she crossed the grass into the chaos.

Had Mason lied to me about interviewing Hattie? Or had she gotten away?

My phone buzzed again, and I shifted to free it from my pocket. This time, it was Mason's number on the text notification.

Mason: Hang tight. Something came up. STAY PUT.

I frowned, then sent a response.

Me: Hattie's here

I waited for several long beats. Mason didn't respond, but my message was eventually marked as read.

I rose from my seat and inched closer to the dancers, searching for Hattie in the crowd.

"Bonnie!" My mama tugged me onto the dance floor, and Dad took my hand. They attempted to make the three of us into a couple, which was silly and confusing, and likely got on the nerves of nearby dancers, but it was also kind of wonderful.

I bounced and spun with them, smiles splitting our faces and laughter making stitches in our sides. Until the caller changed our orders, and I was released into the hands of a nearby dancer. "Bye y'all," I called, accepting the new partner with a smile and a bow.

The man took my hands and eagerly followed a few more calls, before releasing me into the next set of arms with a hearty yee-haw!

The couples blurred into one colorful mass of music and laughter as I twirled around the dance floor, carried by the caller and multiple partners.

My heart and head were light as I made another do-si-do.

Then Hattie reappeared, and I excused myself, politely.

I ducked around a swinging couple, only to be grabbed on the next enthusiastic promenade.

"Sorry," I said, visually tracking Hattie as the gentleman led me out of line. "I was on my way to—"

Something that felt distinctly like the barrel of a gun pressed into my ribs, and I slowly dared a look at my new partner.

Sheriff McCoy glowered back. "Come now," he whispered into my ear, hot breath curling over my cheek. "Smile and walk. Do not make a scene."

A little cuss slid off my tongue as I recalled his sharp-shooting skills. Not that anyone could fail to kill me at this range. So I clamped my mouth shut and looked desperately for someone to notice my distress.

Hattie spoke with Gigi at the refreshments table, where she'd arrived and begun to cut her cake.

Were Hattie and Sheriff McCoy working together? Would my poor parents lose half their family in one fell swoop?

I said a prayer Gigi wasn't about to be abducted too.

My abductor forced me forward, away from the crowd and toward the big red barn I'd noticed on my last trip to this location. This time, a pen filled with horses stood outside it.

"Just a little farther," he said. "We're going to let the horses finish what they started near the bakery. A single shot should get them going, and we're far enough from the townies, dancers and musicians for me to be gone before any would-be rescuers arrive."

I dragged my feet, mind boggled by his gruesome plan. "Why are you doing this?" I asked. "Why are you on a killing spree?"

He ignored me.

The massive grassy field shrank rapidly beneath our strides. The pen of horses grew closer with every racing heartbeat.

"I heard it was Hattie who slapped you," I said, trying to push one of his buttons. "Not Tish. Why'd you lie to me about that? Wouldn't it have made more sense to tell me it was Hattie? Instead of connecting yourself to Tish?"

He made an ugly noise. "Hattie is as nosy as you are. The two of you would probably make great friends if tonight wasn't your last night—and she wasn't the next one to go."

"I wouldn't be so sure about her," I warned. "She's at the sheriff's department right now. You probably know I date Sheriff Wright. He was on his way to meet her when he brought me here, and he's coming back when he's done. Whatever you fear she might tell him, it's already been said. So, instead of wasting your time trying to get me trampled, why not go back to the campgrounds, pack your things and get out of here before you're arrested on two counts of murder?"

"Three," he corrected, shoving me ahead of him, toward the horse pen. "This will only take a minute." Standing just a couple feet away, he pointed the gun at my chest. "Climb in."

I scanned the world around us, praying for an escape.

The music and lights from the square dance were dim and muted by darkness and distance.

It was just me, a pack of anxious horses and a killer with a gun.

"At least tell me why you killed your producers," I said, lifting my palms in surrender. "Case said Tish had money problems. Are you the reason? Did she and her partner find out you were stealing from the show?"

Sheriff McCoy moved his thumb across the top of the revolver and there was an audible click as the hammer fell into place, ready to fire.

My raised my hands higher, and I swallowed painfully past the emotion clogging my throat. Then I slowly climbed to the top and lowered my backside onto the center rung of the pen. "At least I figured it out," I said as I swung one leg inside, careful not to flash him in my short, tulle-enhanced skirt. "It would be worse if I hadn't solved the case."

He bristled. "You think you're such a great detective because you asked a few people some questions. Anyone can do that. I doubt anyone could do what I did."

"Murder people?"

"Find the truth about Sophia Star."

"Who?" I racked my brain for a connection to the name, but nothing registered. I wrinkled my nose at the sheriff. "I don't know what you're talking about."

He gave a dramatic huff. "Sophia Star," he repeated.

"Broadway's one-time starlet. The phenomenon they still talk about, but no one knows where she went?"

I shrugged. "Sorry. I don't know her."

"I did. I recognized her." He tapped the gun to his temple before pointing at me once more. "I knew it was her the moment we met. She denied it, but I proved it was her. And no one helped me. That is true detective work. Now get in the pen before I take my chances with the dancers hearing a gunshot."

"Who is Sophia Star?" I snapped, agitation cutting through the remains of my calm.

"Tish!" he snapped. "Keep up! Tish was Sophia Star, and she'd been hiding in this awful traveling sideshow for years. And I found her!"

"If you're so proud of yourself for finding her, why'd you kill her?" I asked, sincerely baffled and feeling the heat of a half-dozen horses at my back.

A series of dark silhouettes moving steadily in our direction drew my attention into the night. People? Couples from the party seeking privacy? Sheriff McCoy's accomplices?

"Hurry up!" he growled. "Or do I have to shoot you?"

I leaned away from his gun, weighing my limited options. I supposed I had a better chance dodging horses than a bullet, so I resolved to obey.

"Terrance Small," Mason's hard-edged voice cracked like thunder through the night, and my frantic heart skipped anew. "Put down your weapon and get your hands where I can see them."

"Mason!" I called, thrilled to tears by his presence and timing.

The silhouettes swiftly became my beloved and two deputies. Hattie trailed behind.

Mason pointed his sidearm at Sheriff McCoy—er Terrance Small, I guess, and raised a brow in challenge. "You are under arrest for the murder and extortion of Tish Thompson, the murder of David Smith, and the kidnapping and attempted murder of Bonnie Balfour."

I sighed in relief as my captor lowered his gun.

I swung my leg back over the fence and gripped the bar with a hand on each side of my hips. I had no idea where Mason had come from, or how he knew to find me, but my limbs were trembling with relief.

Terrance froze, his gaze shifted, sliding over the inky scene, probably evaluating his choices as I had been moments before. Then his arm snaked out and shoved me.

"AH!" I toppled backward, landing inside the pen with a thud as breath rushed from my lungs.

And a gun went off.

The horses startled, rearing and panicking. Their powerful hooves beat against the ground at my sides. Dust clogged my nose and stung my eyes.

Mason's voice boomed through the night as I flipped onto my hands and knees.

"Help," I squeaked, speed-crawling back to the fence, then started squeezing through the rails.

A fresh scream cut through the ringing in my ears, and Terrance Small landed on the ground where I'd just been, courtesy of Mason.

Mason grabbed my hands and pulled me through, then scooped me into his arms and moved us to safety.

The other deputies advanced on the pen, cooing at the horses and reading the Pioneer Days sheriff his rights.

"I've got you," Mason whispered. "An ambulance is coming. Are you hurt?"

"No," I cried, overcome with emotion and no longer able to manage or process. "He was going to kill me."

Mason stroked my hair and back.

Hattie inched into the space beside us, looking as small and cautious as always. "Are you okay?"

I wiped my eyes, failing miserably at my attempt to pull myself together.

"I'm sorry," she said. "I should've told the sheriff everything I knew as soon as Tish was killed, but I was scared. I thought I could prove Terrance killed her, but all I could manage was speculation."

"He was blackmailing Tish," I said, looking back to Mason.

Hattie nodded, wiping a few tears of her own. "I don't know what it was, but he knew something about her, and he held it over her head. I confronted him, and he was ruthless. I lost my temper and slapped him. Everything unraveled from there. Tish was mad I'd overstepped, and he assumed she'd told me the whole story, but she hadn't."

Her shoulders began to shake, then Hattie began to sob.

I stepped away from Mason and offered her my hand. "I'm sorry you're hurting."

She squeezed my fingers and tried in vain to dry her tears. "Tish was my friend, and she's gone."

"Why don't we go to the sheriff's department and help the lawmen sort this out?" I suggested. "My grandma will bring cake. Everything is a tiny bit better when there's cake."

Hattie laughed awkwardly and formed a heartbroken smile. "Okay."

"Okay," I agreed.

And Mason followed us back across the field to his waiting Jeep.

CHAPTER ELEVEN

Ten days later, life had fallen back into its normal, easy rhythm. My family had stopped fussing over my most recent near-death experience, Mason had stopped clinging to me as if I might vanish at any minute, and the Pioneer Days cast and crew had packed up and left town.

My horrendous evening with Terrance Small, AKA Sheriff McCoy, hadn't been fundamentally worse than some of my other run-ins with killers, but my enthusiasm for murder investigations was significantly dented nonetheless. In the bizarre way that moving to Bliss and leaving my awful ex-husband had incited me to chase killers, open a shop and make a new and exciting life for myself, I suspected all of those things, plus the love of Mason Wright, had finally taken the edge off my need to prove something all the time. Like the fact I was a clever, or at least a persistent, detective.

I smiled at the thought while I sipped coffee and watched the morning sunlight dance across Lake Cromwell.

Clyde crept through the slightly overgrown grass, head down and backside wiggling, in hot pursuit of a winged insect.

"Sorry about that," Mason said, returning to our breakfast, cell phone in hand.

He set the device atop the blueprints for our new home and smiled, then kissed me before taking his seat.

"What was the kiss for?" I asked. "I need to know so I can make sure it happens again."

He rose and kissed me again.

"Careful. I can get very used to this," I warned.

"I already am," he said. "And I have no plans of making a change. How were your pancakes?"

"Delicious, but yours are cold."

Our routine of sharing breakfast on the patio had grown more robust and also more specific. Clyde joined us now, having proven we could count on him to come back when the meal ended. And Mason always made pancakes. As it turned out, he was a bit of a fruit-and-produce snob thanks to the farmers' market in Cromwell. And he'd diligently created every imaginable combination of fruit-flavored pancakes he could think of, with more occurring to him every day.

He kicked back, a bit triumphantly. "Taking that call was worth the trouble. Terrance Small was officially charged with everything I suggested. Two counts of murder, two counts of attempted murder, plus extortion and kidnapping. He's going to jail and not getting out again in this lifetime. As it turned out, Hattie and a few of the other Pioneer Days cast and crew members knew more than they wanted to say about him before he took you by gunpoint. Whether that was the final straw, or the fact he was in custody is what pushed them to talk, I can't be sure, but I'm grateful anyhow. I guess two dead producers helped. Whatever tight-lipped code the group had operated by, it's moot now that the show is officially defunct."

A rush of fear had raised goosebumps on my arms at the

sound of Terrance's name. "Did we ever get the whole story on Tish?" I asked, "or Sophia Star, or whoever she really was?"

Mason gave a sobering grunt. "Yeah, and she had it rough. Apparently she was a rising star on Broadway a couple decades back. Young, talented, beautiful, and making her way alone in the business. She was exploited by a slimy director, manipulated into making some choices that would've ruined her reputation. Then he used that to bend her to his will for a while. She eventually took her story to the press, but so did he, and you can probably guess how that went."

"Poor Tish."

"Yeah. His reputation was untarnished, and he retired rich and happy. She was blacklisted, and her career was over before it started. But she was strong, and she reinvented herself as the co-founder of Pioneer Days, got an investor and traveled the country under a new name and persona. She dropped the stage name and returned to Tish, then continued to do what she loved without scrutiny from all the ugliness she'd been through. At least for a while."

"I can't believe she had to deal with all that, only for another creep to show up in her happy place and start the blackmail all over again."

"Some people are the worst," Mason said. "Terrance wound up with Pioneer Days because no one else wanted to work with him. According to the cast and crew, it was the only acting gig he could find, and he spent most of his time scheming."

I made a deep, throaty sound of disgust.

"Tish paid to keep him quiet until she couldn't anymore. Then she went to David for help."

David had gone to Mason on the day she died and relayed his suspicions. Mason had known who was behind the murder all along. He'd just needed time to prove it. Unfortunately, I'd wound up in Terrance's grasp the next day.

"Terrance went to the B&B that night and killed David too. He wanted to keep the story from getting out, but I'd already heard. I just had to build a case too strong for him to weasel out of."

I set my hand on Mason's. "And you did it."

We watched Clyde for several quiet moments, enjoying the company, the sun, and the gentle breeze sending ripples over the water.

"Are you still free to meet with the builder today?" Mason asked.

"Absolutely."

We'd had to reschedule after my abduction. It'd taken me several days to find the emotional stamina I needed to spend a full day at the shop, let alone accomplish anything else. Thankfully, Mason had my back. He cooked. He cleaned. He shopped. He comforted. And day by day, I'd returned to myself. If ever he needed me to do the same for him, I'd be by his side each step of the way.

I tapped the blueprints with one finger. "I added that fourth bedroom to our list of requests, by the way."

"Yeah?"

I nodded. "Once the house is done, I think we should talk to Family and Children Services about applying to foster or adopt."

Mason's expression softened, and his smile grew. His soulful blue eyes instantly misty. "You looked into it?"

"I did."

I wet my lips and steeled myself for the next few words. "There are a lot of children in need of love and stability in Georgia. Everywhere, really. Any of them would be lucky to have you, but the system gives preference to applicants who are married." I raised a palm and a smile. "I'm not suggesting we get married so we can foster or adopt a child. I don't know how much you've looked into it, and since I have, I wanted to put the facts out there. Another fact is that there are many other organizations and opportunities for adults to get involved and make a difference for kids—without fostering or adopting."

Mason turned my hand in his, stroking his thumb against my knuckles. "To be clear, when I ask you to marry me," he began.

A small unintentional gasp broke across my lips.

"It will be because I adore you in every possible way," he continued, voice thick and low. "Because you make me a better human. And I can't imagine—don't want to imagine—spending my days—or nights," he said and winked, "with anyone else. You are the end game for me, Bonnie Balfour. You and your sneaky cat, your quirky friends and your loving family. Even your weird little town."

My throat tightened and my eyes glossed with unshed tears. Mason Wright had plans to marry me. "I love you too," I whispered, willing my cheering heart and shaky limbs to be cool. "Very. Very much."

And I knew without a sliver of doubt that when the day came, and he proposed, my answer would be unequivocally yes.

"Good." Mason slid from his seat and took a knee before me. "Because I've got something I've been meaning to ask you."

Thank you so much for reading ROUGH HEM JUSTICE! I hope you'll enjoy each new story in the Bonnie & Clyde Mysteries more than the last!

And if you want to see where it all began, you can grab

WHEN BONNIE MET CLYDE, the free prequel to the series at my website

—AND—

Join Bonnie and Clyde on their first adventure in **BURDEN OF POOF,** their series debut!

ABOUT THE AUTHOR

Julie Anne Hatcher is an award-winning and bestselling author of mystery and romantic suspense. She's published more than fifty novels since her debut in 2013 and currently writes series as herself, as well as under the pen names **Julie Anne Lindsey**, **Bree Baker**, **Jacqueline Frost**, and **Julie Chase**.

When Julie's not creating new worlds or fostering the epic love of fictional characters, she can be found in Kent, Ohio, enjoying her blessed Midwestern life. And probably plotting murder with her shamelessly enabling friends. Today she hopes to make someone smile. One day she plans to change the world.

ALSO BY JULIE ANNE LINDSEY

Bonnie & Clyde Mysteries

Stabbed in the Rack (Book 7 of 8)

COMING SOON!

Patience Price Mysteries

Murder by the Seaside (Book 1 of 3)

Sun, Sand and ... Murder?

Downsized from the FBI's human resources department on the Virginia mainland, Patience Price is setting up shop as a Counselor at Large in her quirky island town. And she's making the best of her reinvention, until a high school boyfriend is accused of murder, and his determined mama wants Patience to save his hide.

Local golden boy, Adrian Davis, once crushed Patience's teenage heart, and now he needed her help? She can't help offering a chef's kiss to Karma.

Not that Patience holds a grudge.

Reluctantly, she agrees to look into the case, with the help of a hunky former coworker, but what she finds will rock their coastal community to its core, and put Patience on a lurking killer's hitlist.

Geek Girl Mysteries

A Geek Girl's Guide to Murder (Book 1 of 3)

COMING SOON!

ADDITIONAL SERIES:

Seaside Cafe Mysteries

Live & Let Chai (Book 1 of 7)

Cider Shop Mysteries

Apple Cider Slaying (Book 1 of 3)

Christmas Tree Farm Mysteries

Twelve Slays of Christmas (Book 1 of 3)

Kitty Couture Mysteries

Cat Got Your Diamonds (Book 1 of 4)

Made in the USA
Columbia, SC
11 January 2026